FAKING IT

PORTIA MACINTOSH

B
Boldwood

First published in Great Britain in 2021 by Boldwood Books Ltd.

Cover Design by Debbie Clement Design

Cover Photography: Shutterstock

A CIP catalogue record for this book is available from the British Library.

Paperback ISBN 978-1-80048-109-1

Large Print ISBN 978-1-80048-845-8

Hardback ISBN 978-1-80162-565-4

Ebook ISBN 978-1-80048-110-7

Kindle ISBN 978-1-80048-111-4

Audio CD ISBN 978-1-80048-104-6

MP3 CD ISBN 978-1-80048-105-3

Digital audio download ISBN 978-1-80048-107-7

Boldwood Books Ltd
23 Bowerdean Street
London SW6 3TN
www.boldwoodbooks.com

For my husband, Joe

'I love a man in uniform,' I tell the man standing in front of me

Is it obvious, from that terrible clichéd line, that I've always been crap at flirting? Everyone is bad at it when they're a teenager, trying to get the attention of whichever horrible teenage boy they have a crush on, only for him to break their hearts because he prefers his PlayStation and pretends he doesn't care. But when you get into real adulthood, the power is supposed to shift. Men have to grind to get the attention of women. Flirting as a grown woman should be as simple as existing, surely?

Unless, of course, you believe the old binary bullshit perpetuated by romcom movies that all women are either a Beyoncé or a Bridget Jones. A total goddess or completely hopeless. To be honest, I never really understood what was supposedly so unattractive about Bridget, to make her so solidly single for so long, which made me think the spinster trope was probably a figment of fiction too. But anyone looking at me now, attempting to flirt while this poor chap cringes in front of me, would almost certainly file me under: Bridget.

'Erm, thanks,' he says awkwardly. I'm surprised he doesn't

hear this more often – don't all women love a fireman? – Then again, I suppose people don't say it out loud, do they? They just buy the sexy calendar and hide it in a drawer.

This clearly isn't working. And it's reminding me why I'm single. But to be honest, I hadn't been all that worried about it until the events of today.

I often wonder who decided that two's company and three's a crowd because, for some reason, they completely overlooked one. It's not as though I need validation for my life choices, it just would have been nice to be included, that's all.

It's not all bad, being a 'one'. I get to decide what I want to do and when I want to do it. I – and I alone – always get to choose what's for dinner, what I want to watch on TV, whether I want the radiator on full blast or the window wide open. I am my own person, free to do whatever I want, accountable to no one apart from yours truly...

I grew up being told by everyone I knew, and every bit of media I consumed, that I had two options. I was supposed find myself a fella, asap, settle down, get married, have kids – you know the drill – or I could take the more modern, feminist-y route of shunning all of that in favour of being a ball-busting career woman who doesn't need a man, or kids, who battles her way up the career ladder to smash the glass ceiling, and lives her best self-sufficient life.

There's a third route no one talks about though, and it's not so much the route I have chosen, more the road I wandered down, and now I think I'm probably too far along to turn back.

I know I'm not alone, as one of these third-routers, being in my thirties, unmarried, with no kids, not owning my own home, bouncing from job to job. There are plenty of us out there but many are too embarrassed to admit it. Well, of course they are; it's the pitying looks that follow the prying questions. 'Oh, has it not happened for you yet?' – as though I've lived my every waking moment on this planet just searching for a man, any man, with enough sperm to keep me popping out babies on the regular, and for what? Sometimes people say, 'But it's your job, to keep the human race going.' Well, guess what, I didn't apply for that job (and I'd probably suck at that job as much as I do my actual job anyway).

I just wish people would stop making women feel like failures for taking the third route. You never know a person's personal circumstances. You don't know why they don't have kids, or why they haven't met the right person yet. And, I promise you, the further you wander aimlessly down the third route, the harder it is to turn around.

I'm just me, alone, with a low-paying job, a crippling rent-paying addiction, and no one or nothing to fall back on. And sometimes, when you are just you, alone, things can go wrong, and there's no one around to have your back. That's when you end up in big messes, like I am right now, with no option but to try and – as a last resort – flirt your way out of sticky situations.

'I used to stay up late to watch *London's Burning* when I was a kid, even though I was far too young,' I say, because of course I do. What else am I going to do, when my flirtatious advances don't work, other than double down?

'*Soldier, Soldier* too – loved that,' I continue, but double-doubling down doesn't help my case either. 'Did you watch that?'

'I'm twenty-five,' he tells me, without a flicker of emotion. I'm not even sure he knows what I'm talking about.

Oh my God, this practical baby standing in front of me is nine years younger than me. It always blows my mind, when I meet people who are so much younger than I am, but seem so much more mature – like a real adult. I'm thirty-effing-four and I certainly don't feel like one of those.

'Sorry, when I asked you to tell me everything, I meant about your flat, not about your childhood,' the fireman explains. I think he thinks I'm stupid – stupid is preferable to arsonist though, right?

That's another thing pop culture has misled me with – I thought women were supposed to be able to use their sexuality to get them out of any bind? But, nope, more bullshit.

The fireman is tall, broad and handsome – exactly like the firemen in the calendars, but he's the only one here who makes the cut. The rest of the team, all rushing around me, doing their jobs, are a mixture of older men, and a couple of women. I'm not fetishising this man's job, I'm just saying, the calendar must be a really small sample from all over the country, rather than representative of firefighters everywhere.

And now I see where I'm going wrong. You know how they say, that if you wind up in prison, you find the biggest person and you punch them in the face? Well, what I've done here is try to flirt with the hottest fireman – and failed. But give me a break, it must only be 6 a.m. – it's not even light out yet.

'Ohhhh,' I say, as though I've just had some big epiphany. I cough to clear my lungs before I continue. The icy cold January air hurts my insides. 'Right, yeah. Well, I guess it set on fire.'

'Yes,' he says, ever so slowly, as though he were talking to an idiot. 'We're up to speed on that part.'

I rent an absolutely tiny flat above an Italian takeaway, run by a man called Antonio, whose cuisine is about as Italian as he is (which is not at all, he's Welsh, but he seems to think pretending to be Italian is good for business). Antonio is my landlord, and kind of a sleaze, so he's always either ticking me off for something I'm doing wrong or flirting with me for something I suppose I'm doing right. The only thing *my* sexuality gets me is free pizza – and the only thing free pizza gets me is an arse that jiggles when I run – I imagine. I definitely don't run. Even just now, from a burning building, I'd probably call it more of a jog.

'Just talk me through what happened with the fire,' he suggests. 'Before, during and after.'

Oh, God, where to begin?

'Well, it was the smoke billowing... billowying? Billowing?'

'Billowing,' the fireman insists. He's starting to get frustrated with me now. Looks like I've burned my bridges as well as my flat.

'Right, billowing. It was the smoke billowing into my bedroom that woke me up, so I grabbed my phone, ran outside, called you...'

'OK, so before you went to sleep?'

'Before I went to sleep...' I say slowly, stalling when I have one big realisation that gives this whole saga a new and horrifying spin.

I went out with some work colleagues last night and things got a little messy. The night out was in honour of Greg, the new guy, to welcome him to the team. I'm a receptionist at a digital agency – not that I'm all that sure what they do, but it doesn't matter too much to me, I just answer the phone. Not everyone likes to stay out late. But I do, and Greg clearly does, so when I finally called it a night at 3 a.m. he ran after me, asked if I lived locally and, when I said I did, he asked if he could crash on my sofa, because he had missed his last train home.

At first, I thought this might have been a chat-up line but he really did just come back to my place and make himself at home on my sofa, which was perfect, because even I know you don't sleep with the new guy on his first day. So, I left him there, sound asleep. I went to bed and then the next thing...

'Just a quick question,' I say, casually. 'If someone had been, say, fast asleep on the living room sofa, while it was on fire, would you be able to tell?'

The fireman's eyebrows shoot up into his helmet.

'If someone died in the fire would we be able to tell?' he asks in disbelief. He doesn't wait for a reply. 'Yes, yes, we would be able to tell if someone died in the fire.'

I try my hardest to mask my relief that Greg didn't burn with the sofa, but I exhale so hard I probably blow away the last of the smoke. To be honest I'd forgotten about him, and, with my bedroom door being nearer the front door than the living room is, I just charged straight out as soon as I realised the place was on fire. Thank God he'd already left.

'If someone was in there, do you think they could have started the fire before they left?' he presses on.

I wonder, only for a few seconds, what the new guy could possibly stand to gain from trying to burn my flat to the ground.

I notice the fireman glance over my shoulder. I follow his gaze to a firewoman who has something blackened and smoky in her hands. I'm no expert but it looks like what used to be the wastepaper bin from my living room.

'We've found what started the fire,' the firewoman says. 'Looks like a butt caused it.'

I bite my finger, to try not to laugh at something that is undeniably funny, but it tastes like charcoal so I quickly remove it. I know this isn't funny, this is awful, everything I had (even though it wasn't much) was in that flat, but if you don't laugh, you just cry and cry and cry. Thankfully most of my stuff was in the bedroom (like my clothes and my laptop).

'Do you smoke?' the fireman asks me.

'I don't, but the man who was sleeping on my sofa does... I did tell him, if he wanted to smoke, he needed to stick his head out of the skylight...'

'Well, it looks like he's discarded his cigarette end in your bin before he left,' he says.

'*Figlio di puttana!*' a not-all-that-Italian accent interrupts us.

Antonio appears from behind the fireman, seemingly popping up out of nowhere. He's on the short side with hair so black it had to come out of a bottle. He's obviously rushed over here but still found time to slick back his hair before he left the house. I swear, he must style himself exclusively on clichéd characters from mob movies, which is way off the mark for what he's trying to achieve.

'Antonio, *buongiorno*,' I say cheerily, as though that's going to get him onside.

'Don't you *buongiorno* me, Ella,' he replies. He sticks a stereotypical 'a' sound on the end of several of his words, which, frankly, even I find offensive. 'You set fire to my bloody flat?'

'We think it might have been her house guest,' the fireman tells him, helpfully, which is surprising given how unhelpful I've been to him.

'And what did I bloody tell you about house guests?' Antonio starts, getting angrier by the second. He's definitely got the stereotypical fiery Italian temper down to a fine art. 'After your last party, I tell you, no more house bloody guests, and here you are – burning my bloody business to the bloody ground.'

'We were actually able to contain the fire to the living room. Ella raised the alarm almost immediately,' the fireman tells him, but Antonio is having none of it.

'I don't give a damn, this one is nothing but trouble,' Antonio replies.

'I'll leave you two to talk for a moment,' the fireman says. I don't blame him for removing himself from the situation. I know you have to be pretty brave to do this sort of job, but you'd have to have a death wish to be standing between me and Antonio right now.

'Look, Antonio, I really am sorry,' I say sincerely. 'I had no idea. It was a friend from work who missed his last train. I was just trying to help him out. Obviously, I can't pay you back for the damage straight away, but I can over time – I'll even work shifts in the pizza place on an evening. Just... please don't kick me out... I have nowhere else to go.'

'*Bella, bella, bella,*' Antonio says. He softens as he wraps an arm around me. Oh, God, he always calls me Bella, instead of Ella, when he's about to say something sleazy.

'I'm sure we can come up with some way for you to pay me back,' he says as he begins to rub my shoulder.

'Ergh,' I can't help but blurt as I shake him off me. 'Forget it, I'd rather be homeless.'

Antonio snaps back to angry mode.

'Then pack up your shit and get out of my flat,' he shouts.

I sigh. I don't really have much choice then, do I? You see, this is what you get for trying to do someone a favour. It literally blows up in your face. I saved Greg from a night on the street – or a ridiculously expensive taxi – and this is what happens. I wish I'd left him to fend for himself now.

As soon as the fireman tells me it's safe to go back inside, I head upstairs to gather my things.

It's funny, the place always had a smell that I really didn't like, a sort of greasy kitchen smell that drifted up from the takeaway below. Now that the entire flat stinks of smoke it's hard to remember why I hated the original smell so much.

The living room isn't as bad as I thought it was going to be. I imagined a big black hole, with everything inside it burnt to a crisp. I must have raised the alarm pretty quickly because the damage is mostly concentrated around the sofa and the table. Thank God I did raise the alarm. Thank God I woke up. This is why I'm starting to think that maybe I do need someone to share my life with – if only to decrease my chances of dying in a fire.

I make my way to the tiny, pea-green bathroom to gather up my things. I quickly wash my face and try to brush my teeth, except my toothbrush tastes like smoke, so it's probably more hygienic to forgo brushing my teeth right now.

I blast my long blonde hair with half a can of dry shampoo, drag a brush through the knots, and cake on some make-up before moving on to the bedroom. I sniff out my least stinky work outfit and, through a combination of spraying it with deodorant and whipping it against the bed, try to get the smell of smoke out. I am the most presentable – and the least smelly – I can humanly be right now. I'm also weirdly fortunate enough that all of my belongings fit into three bags for life – they're big ones, at least, but it's not much to show for thirty-four years on this earth, is it?

Back outside the fireman takes my details, in case they have any more questions for me. I think he feels a bit sorry for me now. He gives my shoulder a squeeze as he reassures me that it wasn't my fault, and that Antonio's insurance should see him right, but I still feel bad.

'Antonio,' I call out cautiously as I head towards him outside the takeaway, which he's opened up for firefighters to go inside and check.

'Ella, if you are even thinking about asking me for your deposit back, no, forget about it, piss off,' he rants in an accent that would make Super Mario proud.

I just nod thoughtfully for a second before heading for my car. I load my bags into the back, sit in the driver's seat and cross everything I have that it will start today. Sometimes it does, sometimes it doesn't. My car, like my life, is riddled with problems. The battery runs flat for almost no reason, and it's leaking some kind of liquid.

'Come on,' I say as I go to turn the key. It makes a sound as if it's in physical pain every time I try to start it. I'll just have to get the bus to work – at least I can store my stuff in my car.

I have some cash. Not much, but enough for a couple of nights in a hotel while I figure out what my next move is. But right now, I have to get to work. I absolutely can't be late today – I already have a few late marks on my record, courtesy of my car. Now that I'm homeless, I need my crappy job more than ever.

Some start to the new year this has turned out to be. We're only days into January and already things are going so wrong. See, this is why I never go for that 'New Year, new me' rubbish, because getting pissed and singing Auld Lang Syne isn't the magic recipe for a new beginning people seem to think it is. New Year, same me. I just hope things get better as the year goes on, but I can't quite shake the feeling that it might be all downhill from here...

2

After a completely mortifying conversation with my usual mechanic – in which I innocently suggested he 'pull out and see if it's wet underneath' and he told me I should probably think about getting a new car now, because he's patched it up so many times – I managed to catch the two buses it takes me to get to work. But I'm very late.

I slink through the door at Agency XXL, where I've been working for the past six months, and as I sit down at my desk, I notice a note from Sylvie, the HR lady, asking me to go and see her asap. This means heading through to the other side of the office, which will be hard to do unnoticed.

We're oh-so impossibly modern here at Agency XXL. The office is practically a caricature of a millennial open-plan workspace. You know the type – there are more beanbags than there are chairs and every other room is for 'headspace'. We have four different machines for making drinks, but you can never just get a coffee-coffee, it's all macchiatos and lungos, and no, I don't know the difference. I don't mean to sound so cynical about it all, it just doesn't feel authentic, especially given how this company is owned by rich, severely out of touch old men.

Nipping at the heels of rich, old and out of touch is Declan, our Head of Digital, which means he's our first boss in a long line of bosses. He runs the show on the office floor but all that usually seems to entail is floating around the room like an over-caffeinated butterfly. His favourite job of all seems to be breathing down my neck. Apparently, a good receptionist is the heart of any office, and he thinks I'm a bad receptionist, so he's always on my case about it. I won't tell you what part of the body I think he is.

Declan spots me from his wall-less office in the centre of the room. Our gazes meet for a couple of seconds as I hurry through the room. I notice him leaning forward in his chair, as though he's weighing up if he needs to come over and speak to me immediately, but I don't look at him for long enough to see what he does. If I can just make it to the sanctuary of HR... It's actually one of the few rooms here with a door on it.

'Morning, Sylvie,' I say, brightly.

Sylvie is probably the eldest regular 'lowly' employee here, but she's cooler than the rest of them put together. She must be in her early sixties, but you wouldn't guess by looking at her bright purple hair and her kooky clothing. I knew she and I were going to get on well on my first day, when she sat me down to give me 'the talk' about workplace relationships, but instead she just stuck the DVD of *Fatal Attraction* on. This might seem lazy but have you seen *Fatal Attraction*? It worked a charm. Even if there was someone here who I fancied, I'm pretty sure that film would put me right off.

'Oh ho, don't you "morning, Sylvie" me,' she says in her deep Yorkshire accent. My favourite thing about the Yorkshire accent is just how warm and friendly it sounds – until it doesn't.

I'm originally from Cheshire but over the past decade I've

travelled around a lot, working all over the country. Not because I have a fancy job that requires travelling or anything like that, just because I've never really settled anywhere for long. Nowhere really feels like home – even home didn't feel like home, that's why I couldn't wait to leave.

I'm pretty sure Sylvie is going to tell me off right now but it's hard to worry too much when her accent feels like a double dose of Yorkshire charm.

'You're fucked,' she tells me.

OK, it just got easier to worry.

'What do you mean?' I ask with a faux innocence.

'They're letting you go this morning,' she tells me. 'You were on your final warning.'

'I take it this is because I let Greg stay at my place last night,' I start, a little annoyed, because that was me stupidly trying to do a nice thing for someone that blew up in my face. 'Honestly, he missed his last train, so I said he could stay on my sofa. You laid on the "no workplace relationships" thing pretty thick with *Fatal Attraction* when I started. But Greg... he didn't boil my bunny, he burnt my flat to a crisp.'

Sylvie just blinks for a few seconds.

'Are those sex things?' she asks me, ever so calmly.

'What? No,' I reply quickly. 'I let him sleep on my sofa, he literally set my flat on fire. That's all.'

'Well, you're getting the sack because you're late – again,' she tells me, glossing over the whole fire thing.

'I'm late because of the fire,' I insist.

'Oh, Ella, you really are the biggest pain in my arse,' Sylvie tells me. 'Come on, let's go speak to Declan.'

'Oh, yeah, that'll help,' I say under my breath.

Declan has wanted me gone for weeks and now he's got his excuse, I guess. The reason he doesn't think I fit in well here is because I don't subscribe to the 'office culture'. When we finish early on Fridays, I don't want to stay as late as I would if I'd worked a full day, just hanging out in the work bar, drinking trendy beers and playing table football. I'd rather just go home but apparently that makes me 'not a team player'. I don't know, I'm just the receptionist. I do a grindy job for no thanks, and even less money, and I just want to go home when I can go home, y'know?

Sylvie walks me from her office to find Declan. He's at one of the chill stations, next to Greg's desk, chatting with him and two female employees. The two men are throwing brightly coloured juggling balls between them. Greg seems as though he doesn't have a care in the world.

'Declan, I've had a chat with Ella, and there are indeed extenuating circumstances this morning,' Sylvie explains.

I squirm awkwardly on the spot behind her, like a kid who has sent her mum into school to yell at her teacher for being mean to her. I also feel weirdly self-conscious that we're not doing this in private but I've heard Sylvie say before that it's always better to air things in front of other employees, because it makes for a fairer outcome if the bosses think the other workers are listening.

'Oh?' Declan says. 'This should be good...'

'Is she the one who is always late?' I hear Greg ask the girl next to him. I frown at him. Acting as if he has no idea who I am is not the move of a gentleman.

Greg, and the two female employees either side of him, are giggling to themselves as they listen in. In fact, now that I'm looking around, it seems as though everyone has gathered for a floorshow.

'Yes – she says it's this one's fault, actually,' Sylvie explains, gesturing towards Greg.

Oh, God, we're really doing this here...

'Wh-what?' Greg says, changing his tune. He's not laughing now.

Oh, Greg. Poor Greg. Look at him, with his cool guy haircut and ironic moustache. He's wearing a plaid shirt, which, well, don't they all at digital agencies?

I am somehow too cool to be uncool enough to be cool here – even saying that gives me a headache. Greg is the type though. They probably gave him the job the second they laid eyes on him. And I'll bet he thought he was going to swagger in to work every day, drink flat whites, play table tennis, and sit around on a beanbag talking about the latest episode of whatever it is everyone is watching. I was so glad when *Game of Thrones* ended because wherever I worked it was all they talked about and, let me tell you, to someone who didn't watch it, the conversations about it were too nonsensical to follow. But there's always another show for me to be out of the loop on. Don't get me wrong, it's not that I'm against watching TV, but it turns out you need about ten different TV subscriptions. I guess most people here can either afford all the streaming services to keep up to date on the latest watercooler TV, or they're savvy enough to stream it illegally. I tried to stream *The Handmaid's Tale* once, a few years ago, but instead I saw so much weird porn I've never dared try again since. Plus, knowing my luck, someone would pop up from behind my sofa and slap some handcuffs on me. If I still had a sofa, that is...

Greg is blinking at me, at a frankly rather alarming rate – it's as if he's glitching. I do feel kind of sorry for him, this being his first week and all, but, you know, if you're that worried about making a good impression *don't burn people's flats down*.

'What did Greg do?' Declan asks. 'He's my nephew, so I'm highly surprised to hear this...'

Ah, good old nepotism. Always nice to see it's still alive and well.

'Ella says he set fire to her flat,' Sylvie blurts out, casual as you like.

'He did what?' one of the girls next to him says. I think her name is June or April – something monthy.

'Wh-wh-wh-wh...'

Greg sounds like a steam train.

'I think he might have started a fire in my flat, when he stayed over last night,' I offer, kind of weakly. Well, I feel seriously outnumbered, and I don't think being my often ballsy self is going to get me anywhere in a situation like this, and I know better than to flirt with anyone here, don't worry...

'No, he didn't,' the girl next to him informs me, very matter-of-factly.

'He definitely did,' I say a little more firmly. I turn to Declan. 'Smell my hair. It stinks of smoke.'

Declan pulls a disgusted face at the thought of smelling my hair.

'He really didn't,' the girl insists. 'Greg is my boyfriend – he slept at my place last night.'

I look at Greg and narrow my eyes thoughtfully. I was so sure that it was him who asked if he could crash on my sofa. But... now that I think about it... Oh, God. I know I'm terrible with names and faces but this has to be my grandest faux pas to date.

'Oh my God, Greg, I'm *so* sorry, I guess I mixed you up with someone else. I was so sure it was you...'

'Ella, seriously?' Declan says. 'You come in here, stinking of smoke, accusing my nephew of burning your house down. That's it, you're fired, effective immediately. You'll still get paid, but we don't want you to work your notice.'

It's finally happened. He's snapped. Sacking me right here, on the spot, in front of everyone.

'Declan, please, it was just one little mistake,' I insist.

'But it isn't just one little mistake, is it? Was it one little mistake when you ate a piece of Alex's birthday cake before we'd sung happy birthday to him?' he asks.

'Oh, come on, it was a cake with a piece already missing – how was I supposed to know that was part of the design?' I protest.

'Is it one little mistake when you constantly mix up Kerry and Sara?' he continues.

I don't think that one is fair either.

'It's not that I don't know who is who, they just look so alike...' I turn to the woman standing next to me. 'Don't you think Kerry and Sara look really similar?'

'*I'm* Sara,' she tells me, completely straight-faced.

'Oh,' is about all I can say. 'Right, OK. So, you want me to...'

'Yes, please leave,' Declan says. 'And don't forget to take that awful mug with you.'

I had guessed that my 'fucking Mondays' mug – like me, I suppose – didn't gel with the 'office culture'. The truth is that I haven't ever felt as if I fit in here, and I definitely don't feel as if I've made any friends, but I didn't think that mattered because it's just a job, right? It's just the thing that keeps a roof over my head – or it was, at least. Losing my flat, my car and my job in the same day is a new low, even for me.

I feel my phone vibrating in my pocket.

Isn't it always the case that, when you think things can't get any worse, that's when things really, really get kicked up a notch, to be the absolute worst they can be? It's my sister, Emma, calling. Fantastic. That's just what I need.

We've barely spoken in years so I doubt she's calling to talk about what happened on *Emmerdale* last night. Usually when she calls it's with bad news, but I don't think we have any relatives left who could have died – perhaps she's calling me to tell me she's having another baby, which may as well be bad news because, as wonderful as that is for her, having a twin sister who is super succeeding at life when you're doing so terribly just serves as a big fat reminder of what a failure you are as an adult. The fact that Emma has such a wonderful life just goes to show what a genuine mess I've made of my own. We're twins, we had the same start in life, the same upbringing – and I can pinpoint the exact moment where we diverted so spectacularly, and it's the reason we're not all that close any more. Still, if she's calling me, it must be something at least kind of important, but I can't exactly answer right now.

I grab a small cardboard box from the post room and do the walk of shame back across the office, with all eyes on me, to my desk so that I can pack up my things. Of course, I don't really have any things, so I plonk my mug, my notebook, and a handful of random office supplies in the box and head for the exit.

Well, I'll just have to find something else, it's as simple as that. Sure, I could worry about being jobless and homeless, but what good would that do me? Now isn't the time to worry, it's the time to be proactive.

Who knows, maybe, just maybe, I'll land on my feet this time?

3

Emma Cooper is my identical twin sister – but the similarities between us start and stop at our appearance.

We really do look alike – well, we did. I'm not sure if she's changed since the last time we saw each other a decade ago. When we were kids our own mum would struggle to tell us apart, although that changed as we got older, when she insisted that, despite us still looking so alike with our long blonde hair, our bright green eyes, and our dimpled cheeks, she could tell us apart because I had something in my eyes that my sister didn't – she never said what, exactly, but she never made it sound like something good.

Mum said that Emma and I were like Jekyll and Hyde, as though we had one personality between us that split in two. Emma was the good kid and I was the bad one. I suppose I did act up quite a bit as a kid, and I definitely rebelled as a teen, but I don't think you could blame me, given the way we were brought up.

Emma and I never met our dad. He passed away in a car accident a matter of weeks before we were born and, credit to my mum, she found a way through a terribly tough time – suddenly without a husband and with two screaming babies she'd never bargained on raising alone.

I don't remember at what age I realised what my mum did for a living, but I don't really remember a time before I felt as if I couldn't get away from it.

My mum was Auntie Angela – yep, *that* one – the famous agony aunt and life coach. She wrote books, hosted a radio show, and was a regular on daytime TV. Her speciality was parenting advice. You think you had embarrassing moments as a kid? Try having your mum talking publicly and honestly about the mortifying experience that was your first period, on national television. Growing up in a small village meant that everyone knew Mum and everyone knew me. So, when she would tell stories about her own kids, she was talking about me or Emma, and, given that we have pretty much the same face, it almost didn't matter which one of us she was talking about, it would always be embarrassing for both of us.

Sure, we had an amazing life growing up, as far as living in a massive house and having lots of money goes... except Mum never lavished us with everything we wanted, and because she was always working, I think it's pretty safe to say a series of nannies technically raised us. But while I felt mortified and suffo- cated and kind of unloved, Emma found it much easier to roll with it. She loved her life. Then again, Emma was the most popular girl at school, and she had the hottest, richest boyfriend.

In the kind of village where I grew up, money talks. Everyone is living in massive houses, sending their kids to private school. In fact, everyone there is so well off that it's almost an equaliser. Everyone is loaded, so the only way to truly rise to the top is to have the biggest house, the nicest car, go on the swankiest holi- days, and have the sexiest spouse. I absolutely hated growing up in that world, I couldn't wait to move away. Emma, on the other hand, she just let it absorb her. Now she's the rich mummy with the big house and the flash car and her rich boyfriend is now her rich husband. She seems happy with it, so good for her, but I could never have amounted to that, at least not without the financial leg-up she had. I don't want to think about that before I speak to her though – it will only rub me up the wrong way.

It's only the second week of January and I'm sick of winter already. I hate the cold, and the dark; I find it so depressing.

I'm sitting outside, on a bench, after stupidly forking out £4 for a caramel latte that I thought might cheer me up, and glaring at my phone as I try to talk myself into calling Emma back. She's so hard to talk to sometimes. Instead I decide to look up the cheapest nice hotel – or maybe the nicest cheap hotel – in the area, but as I type on my phone Emma calls again and I accidentally press accept immediately. Shit.

'Hello?' I say.

'Ella, hello,' she says. It's so weird to hear her voice. 'Sorry, were you at work?'

'I'm taking my break,' I reply. 'Is everything all right? Are the kids OK?'

'Oh, yes, they're fine, we're all fine,' she says. 'And you?'

'I'm doing great,' I lie.

'Taking care of yourself?' she goes on.

I sigh heavily, but not so she can hear.

'Yes, I am,' I reply. 'So, what's up?'

The phone goes silent for a few seconds.

'Emma? Are you still there?'

'I need a big favour,' she eventually says. She sounds rather casual, for someone who just used the words 'big favour'.

I'm a little taken aback. Emma needs a big favour from me? What on earth could she need from me? What could I possibly do for her that no one else could do? Oh, God, you don't think she needs a kidney, do you? That's all I can think of, that she needs me for my DNA. Ergh, I'd have to give it to her as well, wouldn't I? We might be estranged but she's still my sister. It's just that, if there's anyone on this planet who needs both their kidneys, surely, it's me? With my terrible luck, I need a back-up everything. If I'd had a back-up flat, car, or job I might not be sitting here right now.

'Oh?' is all I say. I don't try and make a case for needing both my kidneys just yet, instead I wait and see what she says.

'I've got myself into a spot of bother and you're the only one who can help me,' she explains, still so casual. 'Basically, I'm going to prison.'

I laugh wildly.

'Emma, look, I'm sure it's wine o'clock and you're bored about the house, but some of us live in the real world and have jobs we have to do. I'm really not in the mood for jokes right now,' I tell her.

'I'm not kidding,' she says quickly. 'Ella, seriously, I'm going to prison.'

'What on earth are you going to prison for? Did you use self-raising instead of plain at a WI meeting or something?'

She doesn't laugh at my joke.

'Ever since we got the new Range Rover, I don't know, it's massive, I have trouble parking it,' she says. 'So, I started trying to see what I could get away with, parking on a double yellow here and there – but only where it wouldn't cause any problems for anyone. I had a few fines come through, but I read online that you could just ignore them, and they were too minor for them to chase up... but I guess that's not true.'

'Oh my God, Emma, you're literally a millionaire, just pay your fines,' I say.

'Honestly, it's too late for that,' she replies. 'This went on for quite a while. I was way into double digits as far as offences went and the fines really mount up when you don't pay them, and saying I would pay them all immediately didn't help, it just made it seem like I thought I had enough money to put me above the law. The judge is making an example of me. He's given me six weeks. My sentence starts tomorrow.'

'Holy shit, seriously, I wish Mum were alive to see this,' I blurt. 'If either of us was going to end up banged up she probably would have bet every penny she had on it being me.'

'Ella, this isn't funny,' she says. 'I need you to come here and be me.'

'To what?'

'You know how important image is here in the village – no one in the community can know I'm going to prison, and I certainly don't want the kids knowing. I'm mortified and it sets a terrible example. I need you to come here and fill in for me while I'm away. I've had a word with Rich and he'd really appreciate it too. With the amount he works, he can't run a house and look after the kids too.'

Ah, good old Richie Rich. Emma's childhood sweetheart who she wound up marrying at eighteen. Hilariously, Rich was my first boyfriend, but when we were ten, so I don't hold it against either of them that they got together when they were teens.

'So, you want me to pretend to be you?' I ask. 'Will that even work?'

Wow, she really does want me for my DNA.

'Of course, it will – you haven't shown your face here for a decade. Most people I know don't even know you exist. Henry is nine and he's never even met you. Millie doesn't remember you and, anyway, she's like any nearly sixteen-year-old – she hates my guts and she doesn't look up from her phone. She's basically you when you were that age.'

'Oh my God, is Millie sixteen next?' I say.

It doesn't seem right, that my niece is a teenager. The last time I saw her, which is the last time I saw my sister, I think she must have been four or something like that. I always send them birthday cards but I guess I hadn't been counting just how many I'd sent over the years.

'Yep, it's been a while,' Emma says. 'Only Rich would be able to tell you weren't really me, and Rich will be in on it... so... what do you think?'

'God, Emma, I'd love to help you out,' I start as I search for the right words. 'But, honestly, I don't know the first thing about looking after kids, or a house. My flat was literally destroyed by a fire this morning.'

Emma laughs.

'Emma, I'm serious,' I insist.

'Where are you living?' she asks.

'I'm going to check into a hotel tonight, just while I find a new job – I mean a new flat,' I quickly correct myself.

'Ella, are you homeless and unemployed right now?'

She asks me in such a parental way, and as if she knows the answer is yes.

Ergh, she is literally going to prison tomorrow, for being an entitled idiot, and somehow, I'm the one coming across as the worst right now.

'Only temporarily,' I say. 'You worry about your own problems.'

'But our problems have lined up – it's perfect,' she enthuses. 'I need someone to fill in for me, you need a home and a job. Live in my house, look after my kids, turn up to my social events. I have a digital assistant that will keep track of everything for you. I'll pay you, put you on my car insurance, and so on. I mean, unless you want to go to prison for me, it doesn't seem like you have a whole lot of options right now...'

Family life or prison? I don't know which is worse. She does have a point though – I really don't have many options.

It's interesting, how our problems have aligned like this – people always used to ask us about mysterious links between twins, but I always dismissed them because we've always been so different, I just never felt it. I'm still not sure I buy into this being an act of twin-chronicity but, when you think about it, it's strange how these things have lined up.

'Look, if you don't want to do it for me, please do it for Millie and Henry,' she begs. 'We both know what it was like, growing up with a mum who wasn't always there, who left us with issues. Please help me to not screw up my kids.'

As a cold breeze rushes past me I tighten my scarf around my neck to keep the chill out. I don't know how many nights in a hotel I can afford, or how quickly I can get another job, plus, she's right. My mum completely screwed me up. Never mind that my sister's image means everything to her, just think about how Millie and Henry will be treated for having a mum who has done time.

'Please, Ella,' she says. I can hear a real desperation in her voice. This really, really matters to her. I don't know if she's embarrassed, or she feels like she's let her family down, or a combination of both, but something in her voice tells me how badly she needs me to say yes.

Thinking about it – how hard can it actually be? Take the kids to school, hoover, make them chips. Rich has always been fine, we've always got along well, and it doesn't sound as though he's in much. Emma must have one of the easiest, most comfortable lives going. It'll be the easiest job I've ever had...

'OK, sure, fine, I'll do it,' I say. 'But – did you say you're going tomorrow?'

'Yes, in the morning. I could call you later tonight and fill you in, and we could come up with a plan together?' she suggests. 'Oh, Ella, thank you, honestly, you don't know what this means to me.'

'It's fine, it will be nice to see my niece and nephew – even if they don't know it's me,' I say.

'Ella...' Emma starts.

'Yes?'

I wait a few seconds, but the call is silent again.

'Hello?'

'Never mind,' she blurts. 'I'll let you go get sorted and I'll call you tonight.'

'OK, speak to you then,' I reply.

Gosh, my sister, Amazing Emma, the jailbird. I can't believe it. I mean, prison seems a bit extreme, but it kind of serves her right, thinking she can park her big, flash car wherever she feels like parking it. I'm not surprised the judge made an example of her. The only thing more surprising than Emma heading off to prison is me agreeing to fill in for her while she's gone. Can I do this? Can I really do this? I mean, I'm sure the day-to-day will be easy, but will people actually believe that I'm her? We've spent our whole lives with basically everyone we know finding it impossible to tell us apart – it was usually our actions that made us more distinguishable – so perhaps it's all going to come down to my acting skills... if I have any.

I'm freezing my toes off out here, so I'd better go find a hotel for tonight. If it's just for the night, maybe now that I'm kind of employed again I can afford somewhere a bit nice – a sort of halfway house to prepare me for going back to the house I grew up in. Yep, it's Emma's house now, but that's another story...

4

The bath in my hotel room is nothing fancy, but it's a bath, and after the day I've had, a long soak was exactly what I needed. I laid back, relaxed, scrubbed the smoky smell out of my hair, and then climbed into bed. It would have been a completely chilled end to a totally hectic day, were it not for the fact that I'm on the phone with Emma again, planning exactly how I'm going to take over her life for her.

It's so strange, being on the phone with her, chatting – I was going to say 'like normal', but there's nothing normal about taking over your sister's life. You know what I mean though. Considering I haven't heard from her in years, even having a conversation is a big deal.

'So, my digital assistant will keep track of everything you need to do, so you don't need to worry about that, just do what it says, when it says to do it,' she explains.

To be honest, I haven't got a clue what she's talking about. What is a digital assistant? Should I be imagining a robot or human at the other end of the Internet? I suppose I'll just wait and find out tomorrow – she makes it sound simple at least, and I don't want to look stupid.

'How much do you actually do in a day?' I ask. I'm not having a go, I just can't imagine that either. I've never known Emma to have a job and it doesn't sound like she needs one.

'Oh, you know, just keeping the house clean and the kids alive,' she says.

Suddenly she makes it sound easy, but I can't help but wonder. Aren't kids supposed to be a nightmare? And I remember how big that house is...

'You don't have a cleaner like Mum did, then?' I say.

'Oh, we do, but I tend to have a pre-cleaner clean. I feel so guilty, having her come in and clean up all our mess,' she explains.

I just about manage not to laugh out loud at her for saying that.

'And you'll have Rich to help you, when he isn't working, and everything else is easy – just show your face at coffee mornings, attend a few Parents' Association meetings. None of it is a big deal, I promise.'

I like to think that, even though we lost touch, I would have helped Emma out if she needed me, no questions asked... but it's hard to imagine me agreeing to doing something like this if I wasn't completely desperate.

'Do you have any advice for me, on how to survive in prison?' Emma asks.

'Oh, charming,' I reply, although I do know that thing about punching the biggest inmate on your first day, I suppose, not that I'll recommend that to Emma.

'Hey, I didn't mean that as an insult,' she says. 'You've always been able to stand up for yourself, and for others. I remember when you nearly broke that kid's jaw...'

'He deserved it,' I insist, as I did at the time.

I've always found it hard not to call-out injustice when I see it. I remember in secondary school, one of the bigger year 11s was bullying one of the smallest year 7s I've ever seen in my life. He was in the process of tying him to a lamp post in the car park. I asked him to stop, then I told him to stop – then I guess I lamped him. His jaw healed absolutely fine though, and he never did it again. I'd punch that kid again in a heartbeat... if I was still a kid too, obviously – even I draw the line at punching kids.

'Emma, my life is not so bad that I've had to learn how to survive in prison,' I point out, because apparently it needs saying. 'Not yet.'

'Are things bad?' she asks softly.

I don't say anything for a few seconds.

'Ella, I'm so sorry about... the money thing,' she says.

And there it is, the elephant in the room, the reason we fell out all those years ago. Money. Isn't everything always about money at the end of the day?

'We don't need to talk about it,' I say.

'I *am* sorry though,' she says. 'I'll always wonder, if I handled it right...'

'Emma, can we not do this now?' I say seriously.

'OK, sorry. At least you're thirty-five soon, hey?' she reminds me.

People usually only excitedly count down to birthdays in the first part of their life. Milestones as kids, big birthdays as teens when you can finally do things like drive or drink. By the time you're in your mid-twenties, you don't count down to birthdays any more, and I'm sure no one in the history of the world has actively looked forward to turning thirty-five. It's a kind of depressing age, when you think about it. I'm noticing when I fill out forms and surveys, that when I tick the box for my age range, as soon as I turn thirty-five, that's it, I'll be in the next category. Eighteen to twenty-five is but a distant memory, and moving into the twenty-five-to-thirty-five bracket didn't bother me all that much. Thirty-five to forty-five though... that one stings a little. Not because there's anything wrong with getting older, but because I'm falling behind on where I'm supposed to be. Forty-five isn't that far off fifty, and I have absolutely nothing to show for my life – if I vanished, no one would notice. And let's not even get into the whole 'geriatric mother at thirty-five' thing... Oh, God, I'm spiralling.

The reason Emma is mentioning my thirty-fifth birthday is because it is linked to the reason we fell out.

We were teenagers when we found out Mum had breast cancer. We went from having a mum who worked all the time, who we never really saw all that much, to having a mum who was still working an awful lot – as much as she could manage – and then the only time we did see her was on her bad days, when she was too ill to do much else. I guess Auntie Angela was worried about leaving behind a world without giving all the advice she could give. She didn't worry quite so much about her daughters though.

Mum lived long enough to see Emma and Rich tie the knot at (just) eighteen, but not long enough to see Millie born soon after.

I found it really hard, during that last year. Emma was so busy with Rich, trying to throw an amazing wedding – but mostly for Mum's benefit, which made it like a weird kind of send-off party that I struggled to get on board with – and I found myself drifting further and further away from her. When it came to Mum, her end-of-life care, her funeral and so on, Emma and I could never quite agree, but somehow Emma always got her way. By the time Mum's will reading came around Emma and I could hardly look at each other. I felt like Emma wasn't including me and that she didn't care about what I wanted or what I was going through, she thought I wasn't pulling my weight or taking what was happening seriously. Our relationship really was at make-or-break point. The will reading finished us off.

When Mum was alive, she didn't really want Emma and me to feel her wealth. She wanted us to grow up standing on our own two feet. It's strange, when you're a kid, living in a big house, going to private school with a bunch of spoiled rich kids, when your mum doesn't want you to be a spoiled rich kid yourself. It was kind of like growing up in a sweet shop but being told you weren't ever allowed sweets – which we weren't. Auntie Angela did not endorse parents giving their children too much sugar. Honestly, forget smoking behind the bike sheds, I was putting away bags of Maltesers there.

I should have realised, when Mum died, that her stance would remain the same.

Mum was a bestselling author, a TV star, a newspaper columnist. She'd made a lot of money and she'd invested it well. With Emma and me not even being in our twenties when Mum passed away, we were both still living at home. We didn't have jobs yet – we'd only just finished our A levels. And, look, it's not that I just wanted to get my hands on my mum's money, of course I didn't. Even if we weren't all that close, and she was strict with me, she was my mum and I was devastated when she died. But she really did leave me up shit creek without a paddle.

You see, my mum, adamant her children must learn to stand on their own two feet – just as she'd always preached – left all her money to me and Emma equally... but she left it in a trust fund, that we wouldn't have access to until we were thirty-five. For a moment this briefly brought me and Emma a little closer together. I remember, sitting in the solicitor's office, sharing a laugh together. It was just so like her. And while I knew that the

implications of Mum's will weren't going to put Emma in any kind
of immediate trouble – she had just married Richie Rich, after all,
a boy from one of the wealthiest families in the village – when the
house immediately went up for sale I really hoped Emma would
help me out until I found my feet; found a job, found somewhere
to live.

But then came the kicker. The small print. The thing that
drove the wedge well and truly between us. The stipulation that
our money would be kept in a trust until we were thirty-five *unless*
we had kids, at which point we would get it immediately. I
suppose the idea was that she wanted her kids to learn to stand
on their own two feet, but she wanted to do right by her grand-
kids, but I just felt so royally screwed over, especially given the
fact that Emma was already pregnant. At first, I felt relieved –
Emma would definitely help me out... except she felt as if that
would be going against Mum's wishes. She said she would help
me look for a job and a flat, and I'd already delayed going to uni
because, you know, *my mum was dying.*

Of course, the first thing she did with her newfound wealth
was buy Mum's house – and it just felt like such a kick in the teeth
that in such a big house she basically wanted me out straight
away. No prizes for guessing that I didn't end up going to uni, but
I did end up packing my bags and leaving. That's when I moved
away and, other than a couple of occasions after, my sister and I
have had nothing to do with each other. And now she needs me
to help her – isn't it funny how life works out?

'You haven't done anything weird with your look, have you?'
she asks. 'Like dyed your hair jet black, cut it short, or had a lip
piercing?'

'Erm, I haven't, but, even if I had, I would just tell people, as
you, that I had changed my look – and then you'd have to adapt
when you got out of the clink,' I insist.

'Snap me a quick selfie,' she says. 'Send it over and I'll see what we're working with.'

'OK, give me a second,' I reply.

I fire up my camera and take a photo, careful to hold it a little higher and angle it down so I don't look completely awful.

'Sent,' I say.

'OK, well, the length and the colour are pretty similar – maybe people will just think I've run out of expensive toning shampoo,' she says rudely. 'But I do need you to do something for me... I had a fringe cut a couple of years ago. Do you think you could book in somewhere for a fringe, before you get here? Money is no object – throughout any of this – I'll give you a card. You can spend whatever you like on it. You just need enough to get the fringe, and to get here. Where are you, by the way?'

'I'm in Sheffield,' I admit.

'Wow, that's not far at all,' she says, with a tone that suggests if I was so nearby, I should have visited.

'And I can afford a train ticket and a fringe,' I insist. 'I'll get those things booked when we're off the phone.'

'OK, thanks,' she says. 'Just one more thing, and I hate to say it, because you are doing me a big favour but... you'll behave, won't you?'

I gasp theatrically.

'Ella, seriously,' she continues, before I have chance to say anything. 'Just... please... try and be like me. No drinking, no swearing... no bad-girl stuff.'

Ergh, she's talking to me like I'm a child.

'Emma, I'm a grown woman now. You haven't spent any real time around me since I was practically a kid. Give me some cred-it,' I say.

I do drink like a fish and swear like a sailor but I'm not exactly going to do shots with my nephew while we play Cards Against Humanity, am I?

'Sorry, OK. Well, so there's no overlap, after Rich drops me off, he's going to meet you at the station and take you home,' she says. Her voice gets higher as her sentence goes on. I think reality is setting in, now that we're through the practical side of things.

'You'll look after my family, won't you?' she says tearfully. 'Promise me.'

'Yes, I promise,' I say. 'Come on, sis, suck it up, it's only six weeks. Just keep your head down and it will be like it never happened.'

'Yeah.' She sniffs loudly. 'You're right. Ella, I really can't thank you enough for this.'

'Meh, you can return the favour one day,' I say casually.

I don't know what else to do, other than to make jokes. Saving face in the community, and with her kids, really does mean an awful lot to her. She's always worried so much about what people think of her, and I always used to tell her not to.

'Well, maybe I'll see you after?' I say. 'For the handover, when I give you your life back.'

'Oh, gosh,' Emma replies, somehow laughing and crying. 'I really hope so.'

'OK... well... see you then,' I say.

'Goodbye, Ella,' she replies.

God, she sounds absolutely terrified – who wouldn't be, I guess? I wouldn't have thought she'd last a day in prison, just because there won't be a nail bar or a sushi bar... the only bars they have in prison are, y'know, bar-bars. Still, I'm sure she'll be fine. I doubt they'll send her to a real, '*Bad Girls*' style prison; it will be one of those rich-person-rehab things, surely? Maybe I've seen too much TV... It still stinks, either way, but at least she'll make a point to learn how to park her car properly when she's out. My car might be knackered, but at least I know how to park it.

Well, I didn't think it would happen, but I have a new job already – kind of? I'm going to say yes, so that's a new record. Maybe this is just spin, from someone who really needs a break right now, but I'm going to say I got a new job offer within an hour of losing my previous job. I think that deserves a cheap bottle of wine from room service – especially if it's the last time I'll be drinking in a while.

One glass turns into two, then three, then you stop counting, right?

Oh, boy, when did trains get so expensive? Are they always this pricey or is it because I'm trying to book one at 11:45 p.m. for the next day? It's a good job this is an all-expenses-paid gig because by the time I've paid for my train and my haircut I'll be totally broke.

I head into the bathroom and hold the front pieces of my hair over my forehead, sort of like a fringe. I've never really thought about having a fringe before. I guess the beauty of having a twin is knowing that, if something suits them, it will definitely suit you too. I mess with my hair, moving it into position. I think I might like a fringe, you know. It could have been worse. She could have told me she'd dyed her hair brown or something and I would have hated that. I've been blonde all my life. Even after my hair got darker as I got older, I've always had blonde highlights. I suppose Emma did the same. Of course, they're expensive to keep up with, so I was rocking the balayage look long before it was in fashion. It turns out grown-out highlights are cool now. Luckily, though, I had mine done fairly recently, and it sounds like Emma must have too, so I should pass, if I have the fringe...

The light hits the nail scissors in my open make-up bag, causing them to catch my eye. At least I think that was what just happened – as if it was a sign. It is also, of course, possible that, fuelled by wine, I already had the idea that I should cut my own fringe, to save some money. But, really, how hard can it be?

I fire up YouTube to search for the best way to cut myself a fringe, because YouTube is so rich in content like that, and I can just put the video on in front of me and snip along with it. I'm going to save myself, what, like £40 if I went to a salon? Even with the free lecture they'd throw in about the barrage of bleach and heat I've subjected my long locks to, that's still a lot of money to someone like me.

There's a video titled 'I cut myself a fringe in lockdown', which seems like a good shout. It's a step-by-step video so I follow it to the letter. Section off the front part of my hair, twist it around into one big piece and then... cut.

Shit. Shit, shit, shit. She's cut hers too short. I've cut mine too short. Oh, God. I stop the video – well, it hasn't served me well, and in hindsight someone cutting themselves a fringe in lockdown, during what looks like the middle of the night, given how dark it is outside their window, maybe wasn't someone I should have been taking advice from. I suddenly notice the word 'fail' in the video's description, so that makes sense.

I stare at myself in the mirror. My face is so scrunched up in disgust at my new look I hardly look like me right now. I don't suppose my new, stupid haircut is helping either. Crap. Not only is it too short, but it's popping open like curtains in the middle. Like proper Nick Carter from Backstreet Boys circa 1999. I'm a couple of inches and a white suit away from being him in the 'I Want It That Way' video.

I scramble to plug my straighteners in, back in the bedroom, to see if there's something I can do. The two pieces of hair are too short but they're not *that* short. And I should get a bit of length back when I straighten it, and maybe if I put a bit of a curl in it...

It looks longer and better for me running my straighteners over it a couple of times but, no matter what I do, I can't get it to meet in the middle.

I sit down on the bed and plonk myself backwards. As my head hits the mattress my new fringe – technically my *two* new fringes – part so widely that, when I touch my forehead, it's as if I never even cut a fringe. Well, there's that at least, maybe I can just make the best of it for a few days then pin it out of the way at both sides, tell people I'm growing it out or something like that.

If this is me starting as I mean to go on, I've shagged it already, haven't I? Hopefully, I'm better at being a housewife than I am cutting hair...

5

Standing outside the station with my bags for life on the floor in front of me, and my drunk fringe fail tucked away inside my scruffy beanie hat, I cringe as I see a black Bentley pull into the car park. There's no way that isn't Rich. I would bet everything I have – which, admittedly, isn't much – that this is him. It's so on-brand for him, to have such a ridiculous car – he probably does the school run in it. He, like a lot of the other rich kids I grew up around, had a brand-new car the second he passed his driving test. Because for some people it's not enough to be rich, you have to show people that you're rich too.

Rich pulls up next to me and jumps out of the car to greet me. It must be ten years since I saw him last.

'Hello,' he says cheerily. 'Thanks so much for doing this, Ella. Emma was in a real flap about it all.'

He hurries around my side of the car where he hugs me, kind of awkwardly, before reaching for my bags.

'Wow, you travel light,' he says. 'Your sister packs more than this for a day at the coast.'

'Great to see you again, Rich,' I say.

It occurs to me to tell him he's looking well – because he is – and it feels like that's a thing people say to people they haven't seen in a while, who *are* looking well, but it feels weird. We're about to pretend we're a married couple and that's awkward.

'Yeah, you too. It's a shame it's under such unusual circumstances though,' he says as he loads my bags into the car. 'Quick, get in, it's freezing.'

As soon as we're inside I can feel that he's warmed my seat up for me, which is very much appreciated on a chilly evening like this. I practically snuggle down into it.

'So how have you been?' he asks.

'Yeah, good, I guess... you?' I reply, although it seems like a stupid question given the circumstances.

'Oh, you know,' he replies. 'I've been better.'

Rich doesn't look all that different from the last time I saw him. His blond hair is almost shaved on the sides and curly on top, just as it was when he was younger. I'd forgotten how intensely blue his eyes are, but the dark circles are new. It's only now that we're in the car that I can see that, despite looking good, he looks so stressed out. Seeing him look so worried and so tired makes me feel kind of good about turning up to help out. I still have no idea how I'm going to pull this off though...

'Do you really think this is going to work?' I ask him.

'You know Emma – do you really think she would have taken any chances, if she hadn't planned it in great detail, thought of every possible hiccup, and then every *impossible* hiccup, just in case?' He smiles to himself. 'She's thought of everything.'

'I think she's counting on no one knowing or remembering me,' I say as I stare out of the window.

It's so strange, being back here after all this time, because everything seems so familiar and yet so different. I'll just spot something I remember so vividly, only to be disorientated again by a demolished building or cluster of new-builds.

'Yeah, I don't think most people even know Emma has a twin,' he points out, plainly oblivious to the implication: that she pretends I don't exist. Then again, I don't exactly tell anyone about her either.

'Won't Millie realise?' I say. 'She knows I exist, and she's met me – I know she was really young at the time but she might figure out what's going on.'

'Millie is my daughter and I love her,' he explains, 'but she's really embracing the whole "horrible teenager" thing. She's mostly ignored us for months, she does her own thing, she's never home. Truth be told, Emma has been quite worried about her and the way she's being, but you don't need to worry about that. I remember you being similar.'

I smile.

'So, leave the teenager alone, got it,' I reply.

'And Henry is good as gold, in his own little world, all he cares about is playing football, Animal Crossing and the MCU,' he says.

'Football is the only thing on that list I recognise – and I hate football,' I reply.

'One is a video game, the other is superhero movies,' he says. 'But Emma isn't into any of those things either, so you don't need to know anything about them. Nine-year-olds just want to talk at you – they rarely check if you're listening.'

'Do I get my old room?' I joke.

'Well, your old room is actually the guest room, but you're not a guest,' he reminds me. 'We've done a lot of work to the house. The master bedroom is in the loft conversion now. It's a big bedroom with an en suite – you can sleep there. I have a bed in my office, I'll sleep in there.'

'Won't that seem weird to the kids?' I say. 'Not that I'm trying to get you into bed with me...'

When will I learn that more words rarely equal less awkward? Now it *definitely* sounds like I'm trying to get him into bed with me.

'I'm always the first one up and the last one to bed,' he says. 'And it's not unusual for me to fall asleep on the sofa bed in my office if I'm working late, so the kids won't think twice – if they realise at all. Emma really did think of everything.'

'I can't believe she's in prison,' I say.

It must have been so hard for Rich, dropping Emma off at prison, not just because her getting banged up doesn't fit the perfect family image, but because he genuinely must be so worried about her.

'You and me both,' he replies. 'The car is yours to use while you're here – just make sure you park it properly. Are you used to driving big cars?'

Christ, I'm barely used to driving working cars, let alone big ones.

'Oh, yeah, I'll be fine,' I insist, not being one to prop up the patriarchy with the myth that women are bad drivers.

I shift uncomfortably in my seat as I recognise the entrance to the street I grew up on. Even in the dark, it feels an uncanny combination of completely alien and no different from how it did fifteen years ago. As we pull around the corner and under the usually leafy canopy that cloaks the road (it's bare right now, given that it's January), it's easy to see why the avenue is the most desirable location in the village.

Behind big electric gates, at the end of long private driveways, sit a variety of massively different detached houses – the only thing they have in common being that they are massive – and right here, number six, is where I grew up.

We drive through the big gates, passing the sign for The
Willows – so they haven't changed the name of it, at least – and as
we continue up the dark driveway, I notice all the ultra-modern
spotlights that line the way, and it becomes clear that the house
itself might not be exactly as I left it.

The Willows is a large period property – I think it's Edwar-
dian, if I remember correctly. It's a huge red-brick detached house
with Tudor-style black and white cladding at the top. With it
being dark out, light beams through the large windows.
Somehow it doesn't look as cosy as it used to, which I genuinely
think might be down to modern light bulbs giving off a much
cooler light, rather than the warm glow they used to give off. I
can't see any curtains either, just California blinds in every
window, which create shadows of horizontal bars. I could make a
prison joke but that seems insensitive given the circumstances.

Once we're out of the car, Rich hands me a coat – a belted
dark green Michael Kors coat with gold detail.

'Oh, I'm fine,' I say. 'We'll be inside soon.'

'It's not that,' Rich replies, pausing as though he's carefully
searching for the next words to leave his lips. 'It's just that, well,
this is Emma's coat, and you're Emma as soon as you walk
through that door, and for the foreseeable future, and... Emma
wouldn't wear a coat like that.'

'This wasn't cheap,' I protest.

It really wasn't. I (at least it felt as if I) had paid a fortune for
my khaki-green parka with the neon-pink fur around the hood. I
suppose he's right though; Emma would never wear a coat like
this.

'OK, fine, give it here.' I give in. 'I suppose you want me to
hide my outfit with it too?'

'For narrative purposes,' he says tactfully. 'And maybe lose the
beanie.'

'If you want me to pass myself off as your wife, trust me, it's better if I keep my newly cut fringe and my hat hair concealed under the beanie for now,' I tell him honestly.

'Fair enough,' he replies. 'Just, erm, one more thing – well, two more things...'

Rich removes a wedding ring and an engagement ring from his pocket.

'Rich, please, you're married to my sister,' I joke.

He laughs politely.

'Emma said if you could wear these at all times,' he says.

'Yeah, of course,' I say, hoping they'll fit.

'You can probably put them on yourself,' he says with an awkward laugh.

'I can do that,' I reply. At least I hope I can.

I slide the rings down my finger one at a time and, while they might be a little on the snug side, thankfully they fit. Emma's wedding band is a small (probably) platinum band with a series of twinkling diamonds. Her engagement ring, on the other hand, is one hell of a rock, just the one diamond, but it's huge. This ring is probably a deposit on a house – it's probably as much as a whole house, in some areas, but not this one obviously.

'Well, that's us official,' he says. 'I'm going to sneak in with your things, hurry them up to your room without anyone seeing. Just head in whenever you're ready, OK?'

'OK, sure,' I reply, suddenly not at all confident about any of this, and Rich must be able to hear it in my voice because his face falls, just for a second, before he regains his role as a supportive husband.

'Ella... or should I say *Emma*... it's going to be fine, OK?'

'OK,' I say again – like I mean it this time.

Rich helps me on with Emma's coat, which, truth be told, feels glorious on. It's cold and dark but, not only is this coat super toasty, I feel chic as hell. I watch as he disappears inside with my bags, leaving the door ajar for me.

Oh, God, am I really doing this? Am I really going to get away with it? I can't believe it's come to this, for me and for Emma; my mum would be spinning in her grave – if Emma hadn't insisted we have her cremated, because apparently that's what she told Emma she wanted instead, in the days before she died, despite what her will said.

I belt up my coat to hide my Primark tracksuit that's seen better days and adjust my hat to hide my hair. OK... here we go...

As soon as I step inside the large hallway, I realise just how much the whole house has probably changed since the last time I was here. The original polished wooden bannister is still the same, and the cast-iron fireplace is still there (although it looks more like it's there for decoration than for use) but otherwise everything seems ultra-modern. Brilliant white walls, patterned 'feature floor' floor tiles, weird and wonderful (mostly weird) art on the walls. Were the shape of the room and the distinctive cast-iron fireplace not so familiar, I could think I'd just stepped foot into this house for the first time, it's that much of a departure from what it was like when Mum owned it. I guess the modern mansion matches the flash cars and the fancy coats, so I'm not all that surprised; I guess I was just expecting the place to feel a little more like home.

I walk through the door on the right, where the living room used to be, and it's still a lounge but it's like something fresh out of a catalogue. The walls are a neutral shade of grey, providing the perfect backdrop for a variety of pastel furnishings and accessories. The centrepiece of the room is a millennial pink banana-shaped sofa – not exactly the kind you'd curl up and watch TV on, but there isn't a TV in here, so I don't suppose that matters. Most notably, of course, no one is actually in the living room (it barely looks lived in at all). I wonder if they might be in the kitchen.

My mum loved her kitchen. She never really had much time to cook, not while she was travelling all over the country dishing out advice, but she always said how important it was to have a kitchen that could accommodate the whole family. I understand the logic, even if she didn't practise what she preached, because I have lots of memories of sitting at the wooden breakfast bar while our nanny prepared our food. I think, especially because the house was so big, it was nice to all be gathered together in one room, even if Emma and I were just sitting there quietly doing our homework.

As I walk through the kitchen door, I'm overwhelmed by too many things at once. First of all, I hadn't mentally prepared myself for the humongous rear extension that has opened the kitchen up into one of those massive open-plan living, kitchen, dining areas – you know the ones, the big rectangular rooms with a wall of bi-folding doors that lead out into the back garden. The kitchen area is more than anyone could dream of, with a large island and a fridge freezer bigger than the bathroom at my old flat. The dining area is just beyond it, with a large ten-seater table in front of the glass doors, and then next to that is the living space – a huge grey corner sofa with a small boy sitting on it, half pointing towards the doors and the other half facing the massive wall-mounted TV that sits above one of those trendy three-sided glass fires. The extended half of the room has a huge glass, roof lantern, window above it, which is currently jet black because it's dark outside, but it's framed with tiny spotlights. It's nothing like it was when I lived here, but I can't deny how amazing it is. This house is a dream.

I don't have time to truly take it all in before a skinny blonde with an angry look on her face pushes past me.

'Finally,' she moans as she passes me. 'I told you, I'm not your babysitter.'

She heads into the hallway just as Rich walks down the stairs.

'Where are you going?' he asks her.

'Fay's,' she replies, without making eye contact, low-key slamming the front door behind her.

'That's Millie,' Rich whispers to me as I hover in the kitchen doorway. 'That will be her out for the evening. And Henry is going over to his friend Josh's for dinner. I've got some work to do this evening so I'll pick him up on my way back. So, you'll have the place to yourself, settle in, get an early night – you look knackered.'

As soon as he says this, I get the overwhelming urge to yawn. He's right about me being knackered; I've hardly slept over the last couple of nights. I'd love nothing more than to climb into bed.

'You're going to need the energy tomorrow, trust me,' he says, before raising his voice back to a normal level. 'Henry, let's go.'

Henry must be the small brown-haired boy sitting on the sofa staring down at a Nintendo Switch.

'Hi, Mum,' he says as he shuffles past me, his eyes still glued to his game.

'Erm... hi,' I reply.

'I caught three new fish today,' he tells me.

'Oh yeah?'

Oh, God, I don't know how to sound mumsy at all.

'Yeah. See ya,' he says, heading for the door.

'OK, *Emma*,' Rich says, putting a little emphasis on my new name, but not so much Henry notices. 'We'll see you later. Oh, and I didn't see the dog anywhere, so I think he must be in the back garden, if you want to let him in.'

'OK, yeah, see you later, erm... darling?'

Rich just laughs.

I walk into the kitchen – that's what I'm going to call this room, because it's where the kitchen used to be – and, honestly, it's just so overwhelming. As I near the back doors I can see a golden retriever sitting there, waiting to be let in, patiently wagging his tail. The doors are made up of six large frames of glass. As I scan them for a handle, I finally spot one right in the centre – I should have been tipped off by the dog sitting in front of it. I fiddle with the handle and I'm relieved when I realise you can just open the middle doors like regular doors, because I was starting to have visions of the very first thing I did in the house resulting in me destroying something.

The dog runs in from the cold and bounds towards me with excitement before stopping in his tracks. Wow, I can't even convince the dog.

'You know what's up, don't you, buddy?' I say, in a whisper, because I'm that terrified of blowing my cover. 'It's OK, I'm nice, I'm going to look after you. Come here, boy.'

The dog decides I'm OK and continues over to me so I crouch down on the floor to scratch his ears. He kisses me all over my face.

'At least you love me, huh...' I fumble with his collar to look at his name tag. '... Marty, don't you?'

I yawn again. A combination of knackered and overwhelmed, I think Rich might be right: I should get an early night, ready to tackle a full day of being my sister tomorrow. I'm nervous about so many things, from how to act around the kids to how to work pretty much every appliance in the kitchen, but I know it could be worse. I could be in prison...

6

I jolt upright in bed, rudely awakened by what turns out to be the loud, solitary drumbeat at the start of 'Wouldn't It Be Nice' by The Beach Boys, before the onslaught of the first verse keeps me awake.

Don't get me wrong, I love The Beach Boys, who doesn't? I just wasn't expecting to be woken up by them at 6-fucking-30 a.m.

I scoot over to the side of the super-king bed where the noise is coming from, and notice both Emma's phone and a small screen next to the bed alive with noise and notifications. The music – which, now that I'm awake, I've realised is Emma's alarm clock – is coming out of the screen. It's a Smarty Home thingy, kind of like an Alexa, I guess, but I've never used one.

I notice the button, to make the alarm stop going off, which I delight in pushing, but as soon as I do the screen fills with what looks like the house schedule for the day. I rub my tired, blurry eyes to get a better look and that's when I realise it's not the house schedule, it's my schedule, and it is hectic. Too much to take in. My eyes can't even process it. I don't imagine Emma always puts so much detail on her day-to-day schedule – maybe – I suppose this is for my benefit, so I know where I'm supposed to be, when, and what I'm supposed to be doing, but... wow... I had no idea this was going to be such a full-time gig.

I puff air from my cheeks as I lie back down on the bed. I just need a couple of minutes, before I tackle *everything on that intensely detailed list*.

I probably should have made more of exploring the house last night but, truth be told, I was so tired and so nervous, that I just went upstairs, lay down, just for a moment, and that was it, I didn't wake up until the alarm woke me. I'm glad I managed to sleep for so long, given my very early, very harsh awakening.

I'm in Emma and Rich's bedroom – the master bedroom, another new addition to the house, in the loft conversion. Their bedroom has this sort of bright monochromatic vibe going on, shunning the soft and subtle colours of downstairs in favour of a daring cobalt-blue theme. I've never slept in a super-king bed before and it really is something. Not only is the mattress unrealistically perfect but I feel as if I could just keep rolling and rolling and never fall out.

I make myself get up and notice the dressing gown and slippers that Emma has left for me on the chaise longue at the end of the bed – I feel as if I'm in a fancy hotel.

I take off the clothes I accidentally slept in and slip on the fluffy robe and slippers. Around a corner in the bedroom is a massive walk-in wardrobe with fitted drawers and cupboards that leads to the en suite of my dreams. There's a double sink, a big, deep bath, and a shower that could fit an entire rugby team in it – which, incidentally, genuinely would feature in my dream bathroom. One of the walls is entirely mirrored, which looks gorgeous, but I'm not sure how much I fancy seeing a play-by-play of my naked self, climbing in and out of the bath.

I wash my face and brush my teeth before looking myself in

the eye for a few seconds, silently psyching myself up in the mirror, preparing for the day ahead, which I can absolutely do. It's hard to take a pep talk seriously from someone with such a ridiculous fringe though.

I grab Emma's phone – my phone from now on – from the bedside table and slip it into my pocket.

I could tell from the signs on the doors, on the floor below, that the kids' bedrooms and Rich's office were down there. There's another door, up here on the top floor, and I can't help but wonder what's behind it. This house was already massive – I can't believe how much bigger it is now.

I open the door and feel around for the light switch. At one end of the room is a massive screen, with a series of sofas facing it at the other. A cinema. A literal cinema. Of course, they have a cinema. Gosh, how the other half live.

I head downstairs into the massive kitchen where Marty is waiting for me, wagging his tail. I pull my phone from my pocket and see that he has a little bit of food on a morning, so I give him that before searching through the seemingly millions of cupboards to find the things I need to make a cup of tea. I find everything but the kettle, which is when I realise, they've got one of those taps that gives you boiling water, well, on tap.

I sit on one of the stools at the white marble island, my mug cradled in my hands. Marty is sitting at my feet, looking up at me, steadily but constantly wagging his tail, batting it against the tiles, so at least he likes me, I guess. We always wanted a dog growing up, but Mum always said no. She never really explained why though – I suppose she had enough on her plate and didn't think Emma and I would take care of one properly.

'Morning,' I hear Rich say as he walks into the room.

'Good morning,' I say, turning around to greet him.

'Whoa...' he says when he sees me.

'Oh, God, it's my fringe, isn't it?' I reply. 'I... the hairdresser I went to cut it too short or too blunt or both, I guess.'

'It's not that – well, it's partly that – but just, for continuity, Emma usually gets dressed before she comes downstairs. You could go see Emma's hair stylist,' he suggests, obviously trying to sound helpful. 'Which reminds me, these are for you...'

Rich places car keys and a purse down in front of me.

'Here,' he says. 'I've left the car out front, all the necessary paperwork is completed for you to drive it – assuming no one has taken your licence off you?'

'Har-har,' I say sarcastically.

'And there's a credit card in there – I've stuck a Post-it on it, with the pin number, if you can memorise it and get rid of it asap. Feel free to go get your hair done – her stylist's number will be in her phone – and feel free to spend whatever you like on that card, money no object. We're so grateful for everything you're doing for us.'

A phrase like 'money no object' is really quite vague – there's a difference between buying a purse and a car and a house, although it's probably not that different in this household.

'Thanks,' I reply.

'And obviously, all the shopping and everything, just stick that on there too,' he says. 'Have you got the kids up yet?'

'Got them up? Do I have to wake them? I thought I just had to help them get ready,' I say. I really should read the notes Emma leaves with the reminders.

'They're kids, Ella, they'll sleep forever if you leave them to it,' he replies. It makes me laugh, the way he speaks normally but then says my name under his breath.

'OK, well, I'll go do that, then,' I say.

'I'm going to grab a coffee and get to work,' he tells me. 'So, I'll see you at dinner this evening – good luck, I guess.'

'Thanks,' I reply with a laugh. He says that as if it's going to be hard but, really, how hard can it be? Now that I'm here and I'm settled in, surely, I just need to drop them at school, make them some chicken nuggets later and boom – parenting!

'Well, Marty, let's go wake up the kids,' I say to my new best friend, who seems eager to go wherever I'm going, even if he has no idea what I'm talking about.

'I'm sorry but "wake up the kids" is not an action I am currently able to perform.'

A smooth woman's voice comes out of the device on the kitchen wall.

I stare at Rich.

'Yeah, you're going to have to get used to that,' he says with a laugh. 'The Smarty thinks you're talking to it when you're talking to Marty – and vice versa.'

He whispers both names, not wanting to trigger either party.

'We had the dog long before the devices,' he says. 'So, we can't really change his name, and it's the only command that works the device… so… just be aware.'

'Well, that is absolutely ridiculous,' I tell him as I make a move for the hallway. 'One of the most middle-class problems I can think of.'

Rich just laughs.

'See you tonight.'

I walk up the large curved staircase with Marty at my side. The wooden bannister is one of the few things in this house to give me a genuine nostalgia hit, because it's one of the few things to remain the same.

The first door I come to is Millie's and suddenly I'm a little nervous about seeing her again – properly this time. There's a piece of A4 paper stuck to the door with the word 'KNOCK' written on it in capital letters – somehow even the writing looks angry.

I knock, as instructed.

'Millie... Millie, time to get up,' I say as softly as I can, given that I'm calling through a door.

'Oh my *God*, I am *up*,' she snaps back, putting an angry emphasis on some of her words in that way moody teenagers always do.

Wow, they told me Millie was difficult, they didn't tell me what a dick she was. I don't care if she's only fifteen, I call it like I see it. She's sixteen in few months. I remember thinking I was so grown up when I was sixteen – I thought I was an adult – but when I look back at pictures of myself from then, I look like a baby. A chubby little kid with too much blue eye make-up and gothy Tammy Girl outfits that made me look like my number one choice on UCAS was Stripper University.

Henry doesn't have an aggressive note on his door so I open it slowly and peep inside. He's still fast asleep, bless him. I only wonder how best to wake him up for a couple of seconds before Marty takes the initiative and jumps up onto the bed, kissing Henry until he's awake. Henry just giggles.

'Good morning,' I say to him.

'Morning, Mum,' he replies.

'Do you want to get ready and come down for breakfast?' I suggest. It didn't say anything in the notes about him needing any help with anything but, truthfully, I don't remember being nine, and I have no idea how capable nine-year-olds are of anything.

'OK,' he says, still giggling as he plays with Marty.

At least this one is cute. I can't believe they called him Henry though. That's Rich's dad's name, except I've never heard anyone call him anything other than Hank, which really does sound like an old man's name.

'OK, kid, see you down there,' I say, relaxing into the part a little.

As I head back downstairs, I remove my phone from my dressing-gown pocket and look at the notes under breakfast. It says...

Henry: Cereal combos
Millie: Anything you can possibly get her to eat, she thinks she's fat

Wow, Millie is absolutely not fat, not by any stretch of the imagination. So, I just need to get her to eat something and for Henry... cereal combos? What is that? I've never heard of it.

I hurry into the kitchen and begin searching through the cupboards – there are so many cupboards, and most of them are seemingly hidden – until I find the large pull-out one with the cereal boxes in it. I start at the top, scanning my way down past the boxes, looking for whatever combos are.

'What are you doing?' A voice from behind me snaps me from my quest.

'Millie, you made me jump,' I tell her, turning around, seeing her sitting on the other side of the island. 'I didn't hear you come in.'

'OK, are you like depressed or something?' she says.

'What? No,' I reply quickly. 'I'm fine, why do you ask?'

'Well, you're not dressed, you look like you've been tearing your hair out, and you were on the floor when I came in,' she tells me.

Millie is intimidatingly mature. Not only does she seem way older than I was expecting her to seem, but she doesn't look like the awkward chubby teenager in the blue eyeshadow that I was. She has perfectly sculpted eyebrows and contoured cheeks. Her long blonde hair is poker straight. She looks a lot like her mum did at that age, apart from being taller, and boasting the polished appearance of one of the Kardashian-Jenners. Kids should not be allowed to grow up this attractive; it is character building to look completely ridiculous when you're young. Millie isn't going to be embarrassed of her leavers' prom pictures – she'll probably frame them.

'I was just looking through the cereals,' I reply by way of a perfectly reasonable explanation.

'Whatever,' she replies.

'Anyway, what can I get you?' I say. 'Cereal, toast...'

Ah, the two blandest breakfasts I can name; that's not exactly going to inspire her to eat, is it? But I haven't had time to riffle through all the cupboards to see what else there is.

'I'll grab something at school,' she says.

'Yeah?'

'Erm, yeah,' she replies. 'Stop being weird.'

'OK, well, I'll get Henry something, get dressed and we'll get going,' I tell her.

'I'm totally walking,' she informs me with a semi-scowl. 'You look so embarrassing.'

Wow, I can't believe she actually talks to Emma like this – and Emma must let her get away with it. Unbelievable. Can you tell your own teenage kids to fuck off or is that considered some kind of child abuse? Because it would be on the tip of my tongue if I wasn't trying to pass myself off as my sister. If Emma takes this from a teenager, she really won't be having a fun time in prison, even if she is in some low-security rich-person prison. I can't help but wonder how she's getting on.

'OK,' I say, leaving it at that.

'Mum, before I go, don't freak out, OK?' she starts, and I am kind of freaking out, but only because it sounds like she's about to tell me something that is going to need some actual parenting, and I don't have a clue where to begin with that. I can't even find a box of cereal in, frankly, the smartest, most efficient kitchen that has ever existed.

'OK,' I say. I'm saying OK quite a lot for someone who isn't at all OK.

Millie steps down from the stool and steps out from behind the kitchen island.

'Cute skirt,' I tell her, noticing the blue and green plaid mini she's paired with her navy school jumper.

Millie goes to the same private secondary school I went to – Hammond Hall – where you can basically wear whatever you want, providing you wear a school-branded jumper or something similar.

'You're not freaking out about it,' she points out.

'It looks fab,' I say, but then I suddenly realise that maybe Emma wouldn't want her wearing such a short skirt, so maybe I shouldn't have signed off on it.

Millie sighs dramatically.

'Don't try and pretend you're cool,' she says before grabbing her bag and walking out.

As she passes through the doorway, she meets Henry, who she pretty much shoves out of the way.

I frown. I might have been a horrible teenager, of sorts, but I was never like that.

'OK, kid, breakfast,' I say. 'Cereal combos...'

'Today I want Coco Pops, Weetos and...' he thinks for a moment '... Krave.'

OK, now 'cereal combos' makes sense – he mixes a few up. Damn, that actually sounds kind of nice.

'Coming right up,' I say. 'In fact, I think I'll join you.'

'But I thought you only ate grapefruits,' he replies as he eagerly watches me combining the three cereals in two bowls.

'That's what Josh's mum eats too, and he says it makes her grumpy all the time.'

Seriously, Emma? Grapefruit for breakfast? I'm not taking this gig *that* seriously, ergh.

'Well, I fancy cereal today,' I tell him.

We sit together, silently other than the sound of us crunching our breakfast, with Henry oblivious to the fact I'm not his mum, and me thinking about what a peculiar way this is for me to meet my nephew for the first time. He looks like a mini version of Rich but his eyes are all Emma. It's almost spooky, looking into them; I feel as though it's Emma watching me.

'Are you looking forward to school today?' I ask him.

Henry goes to – just let me peep my notes – Oakley Primary – also a private school, but not one that was around back when I lived here.

'A bit,' he says with a shrug.

That seems fair.

'Well, I'll just go get dressed and then we can get going,' I tell him. 'Good plan?'

'Mmm,' he says through an especially large spoonful of cereal.

'OK, back in a sec,' I tell him.

I make the trek to the dressing room just off my bedroom, where I find a note on the dressing table from Emma telling me to help myself to her make-up and clothing. This is really generous of her, but I imagine it's also because she thinks I'll embarrass her with my own things.

Luckily, I brought my own dry shampoo with me because Emma doesn't seem to have any. I give my hair a generous spray before repeatedly wrapping my new fringe around a big round brush, to try and give it some shape, but it just keeps popping apart in the middle. Emma got the good fringe genes, it turns out, I got the... I'll get back to you on that one.

I notice a framed photo of her and Rich on the dressing table. God, she looks amazing. She's in great shape, her hair is so sleek, and she and Rich look so impossibly in love – the pair of them look so good you could be convinced this is just the photo that came with the frame.

I look at myself in the mirror. I'm a little rounder than my sister, and my hair has certainly seen better days – to be honest, I've got more split ends than I've had boyfriends, and I've had a fair few of those, no childhood-sweetheart husband for me.

I don't think I look bad, not at all – someone once mistook me for Margot Robbie in a bar, although he was pretty drunk, and probably just trying to sleep with me. But having a twin is like having a mirror that shows you what you could look like, and be like, if you really tried. Or, in my case, looking at this picture of Emma is like looking into a funhouse mirror, one of the ones that makes you look thinner.

My phone makes a noise in my pocket so I quickly remove it, almost terrified of what it's going to tell me.

Set off for school now

Shit, shit, shit. This early? I thought I had loads of time. I thought kids started at, like, nine at the earliest?

I scrape my hair up into a messy bun on the top of my head – a very messy bun – before throwing on my own tracksuit and hurrying downstairs.

'Come on, kid, we're going to be late,' I tell him.

Henry turns off his Switch and reluctantly mobilises.

I grab the keys from the kitchen worktop, say goodbye to Marty, and head for the car.

Once we're outside I notice there's a child car seat in the back of the car around the same time I see Henry walk up to the door next to it. Do nine-year-olds have to go in those? Is that right? Sure enough, that's the side he's getting in on, so that's something new I've learned today. I follow his lead and help him get strapped in.

I've never driven a Range Rover before – because of course I haven't – and I'm kind of amazed by just how big it feels. I knew they were big cars but I feel as if I'm driving a tank.

I set off cautiously, trying to adapt to driving a car twice the size of my old banger, making small talk with Henry as I go.

'Why are you using directions?' he asks me.

That's a good question, and the answer is because I don't know the way, and because I really didn't think he would notice.

'I'm testing out a new app,' I tell him.

That reply seems to satisfy him. I don't think he's on to me, or anything like that, I just think that nine-year-olds notice a lot more than people give them credit for, and that they ask a lot of questions.

Outside Henry's school is like the queue to get into Disneyland. There are cars everywhere. As we get closer to the front of the traffic, I notice that different cars are driving up different lanes, marked out with different-coloured mini cones.

'Henry, wouldn't it be funny if Mummy forgot what colour road we drive up?' I say with a fake chuckle.

'Yes,' he replies, laughing, but not saying much else.

I imagine this particular bit of information was in the notes on the schedule, but I didn't have time to read the notes before we left and I can't look now that I'm driving.

We're the next ones to turn onto the school driveway, which deviates two ways around a roundabout, with two lanes on each side.

'What, er... what would you say to Mummy if she did that?' I ask him.

'I'd say it's the blue ones, silly,' he tells me, just in time for me to quickly pull into one of the right-hand lanes, because obviously the school drop-off process has to be so needlessly confusing. I drive around the roundabout, turning left before I get to the school building. But it's only as I do that, I notice the blue cones on a different lane – the way I didn't go. The route I've taken actually has purple cones, which, in my defence, do look blue, until you see them in comparison to the actual blue cones.

'Sh...' I stop myself swearing, but I hear Henry laughing behind me.

I don't need to panic, I just need to turn around, go back the way I came and then I'll be back on track.

I pull off onto what looks like a dead end, and begin reversing back onto the road I just drove up, trying to turn myself around.

'What are you doing?' Henry asks me, as someone beeps their horn at me.

'I just missed our turning,' I tell him casually, but as I try to reverse this monster of a car, to head back down the road, I realise that there's a queue of cars wanting to get past me, all beeping their horns at me. I don't think this is what Emma had in mind when she asked me to protect her reputation – then again, driving doesn't exactly sound as if it was her strong suit so maybe people won't be surprised.

One of the high-vis drop-off attendants comes running up the road towards me.

'You're going the wrong way down a one-way system,' she shouts at me angrily. 'Parents are explicitly told that they have to follow the one-way, colour-coded system—'

'I know, I'm sorry, I made a mistake,' I tell her.

Jesus Christ, she's so angry she looks like she's going to

explode. She's small and kind of round, and in her yellow high-vis coupled with her large, round-rimmed glasses, she looks a bit like a Minion. A really angry Minion.

'Parents are explicitly told that they have to follow...'

Oh, God, she's just repeating herself, only twice as loud, all while I am trying to manoeuvre this humongous piece of metal out of the way of an army of angry parents. Two thoughts: one is that I will never, ever, judge Emma for having trouble parking this thing again, and two is that I really wish this woman would move because, God forbid, I run her over.

'Hey, go easy on her, Lesley,' I hear a male voice call out.

I glance out of the window to see a man standing outside his open driver's side door.

'Parents are explicitly told...' she starts up again.

Does no one ever make a mistake in this village? Does she not realise that if everyone did this perfectly every single day she would be out of a job?

'Stand down,' he tells her with a playful bat of his hand. 'She'll struggle to move with you breathing down her neck.'

Lesley's shoulders drop. So does her face. She doesn't look happy but she retreats.

The man, who is maybe in his late thirties/early forties, smiles widely at me. He's a good-looking fella – he's almost got a little bit of a Robert Downey Jr thing going on – with dark hair, brown eyes and thick black rimmed glasses.

I mouth the words 'thank you' at him. He just smiles and gets back in his car.

'I think you're having a bad day, Mum,' Henry tells me.

'I think you might be right,' I reply as I finally straighten up and get back on track.

And, somehow, I don't think things are going to get much easier.

7

While some might say me waking up in a strange bed with my arms around someone I don't remember falling asleep with might not sound all that out of character for me, it does take me by surprise for a few seconds, until I realise I've just woken up from a nap in Emma's bed, and the dog I'm waking up with is an actual dog – Marty – who has taken it upon himself to spoon me while I sleep.

Emma's schedule certainly didn't mention anything about day naps, but I genuinely don't think I've ever felt so tired.

I don't know how she does it. I really, *really* don't know how. What could my sister possibly have in her genetic make-up, in her system, that I don't have? Because I am knackered already.

Getting up at 6.30 a.m., it turns out, does not agree with me, and I certainly don't agree with it either, but that's what I have to do every weekday, apparently.

I didn't actually intend to have a proper nap, it just sort of happened. As soon as I got home, with the house to myself, I curled up on my bed – just to rest my eyes – and fell asleep. But now I'm way behind schedule so I jump up and head for the car before making my way to Buckley's to do the shopping, which I need to get done in time to pick Henry up from school. I'm even more tired just thinking about it.

Buckley's is basically a supermarket except everything costs around four times as much as it does in a Tesco, but God forbid we'd have a Tesco in the village. If Tesco so much as tried to set up shop here the locals would run them out of town on day one. So, I'm here, sticking out like a sore thumb in Buckley's, except I left home without my/Emma's phone, so I'm pretty much freestyling it, just buying the staples, playing it safe. I'll give it at least a week before I make them my favourite dishes, like grilled cheese sandwiches with pineapple in them – that's always a crowd divider.

Buckley's is perfect. So clean and tidy. Everyone is so civilised. As I push my trolley around, barely needing to move a muscle to weave in and out of people like I often have to do in the shops I usually visit, I feel fresh out of that scene in the supermarket towards the end of *The Stepford Wives* – the 2004 comedy remake, not the original horror version from 1975. However, I look nothing like tall, slim, beautiful, blonde-haired Nicole Kidman – I'm a Bette Midler with a chip in my head, tops. Everyone else here seems positively perfect, and that *is* like something out of a horror movie for me, because you know the classic anxiety people talk about where you're having to give a speech in front of a bunch of people and then you realise, you're naked? Well, I feel kind of like that now, except it would probably be less embarrassing if I were naked. I'm certainly the only one in here in Primark's finest, and I can't help but notice the strange looks I'm getting – although the fact I didn't wake up too long ago, coupled with my bird's nest hair, probably isn't helping either.

It's not all bad though. To someone like me, who usually has to think about how much they are spending, this is like a dream.

The feeling of walking around a supermarket, just throwing things in the trolley – branded items, foods that are typically expensive, anything and everything, straight in the trolley, because today I am Emma and Emma doesn't need to worry about whether or not she can afford one of the pizzas in the fancy black boxes instead of the ones wrapped in plastic from the freezer – it feels amazing.

As I browse the organic chicken nuggets in the chilled section, I hear someone calling my name – well, my sister's name. Do you ever feel as though you're not going to like someone based on nothing but the sound of their voice? Because this does not sound like my kind of person at all.

'Emma? Oh, Emma, is that you?'

I glance up to see two women with trolleys heading straight for me. One is a skinny blonde in her late twenties who would have WAG written all over her if her clothes didn't already have Balenciaga printed all over them. The other is more likely in her late thirties. She has voluminous brown curls with one big streak of grey hanging down on one side of her face that must be intentional, because it looks too perfect to be natural. Her eyes are so big and round. They look almost glazed over as she stares at me, smiling the worst fake smile I have ever seen in my life. Actually, I think it might be genuine; she looks almost intensely pleased to see me...

'Oh, Emma, love, are you OK?' she asks me with a sort of playfully concerned look on her face – the kind you usually reserve for kids with bumped elbows as you offer to smack the coffee table that wronged them after they ran into it. 'What on earth has happened? Did little Henry cut your hair while you were sleeping?'

She reaches forward to touch my fringe but I weave out of her way.

'Oh, no, I've just been to the gym,' I say by way of an explanation.

'I see, didn't have time to shower?' she says with a nauseating bob of her head.

'Didn't have time to blow-dry it,' I lie. I don't want her thinking I'm some kind of slob.

'Well, good for you, going to the gym,' she says. She looks down at my stomach in the most unsubtle way. 'It will do you good.'

I self-consciously tug on my top to try and get a little slack around my middle. I'm wearing Emma's belted coat over my tracksuit but to fasten it now would be me too obviously trying to hide my body. I don't want them to think they're getting to me. I don't even know how they're getting to me. If I were me right now, I would tell them to piss off. I suppose that's the problem. I'm not me right now. I'm Emma. And Emma probably doesn't clothes-line what appear to be her best friends into the quiche display.

'You look tired,' the blonde says. 'Don't you think she looks tired, Jessica?'

'You look exhausted,' Jessica says. At least now I can put a name to her – my new least favourite person in the village. 'And we heard about the drama at drop-off this morning. Sounds like you were having a bit of a 'mare.'

'I'm fine,' I insist, trying to put an end to whatever this is, but they're relentless.

'The only time I looked like this was when I was... Oh my gosh,' the WAG blurts. A huge smile spreads across her face. 'That explains why your hair looks so dry too!'

I have no idea what she's talking about, but Jessica appears to because she starts grinning too.

'Emma... This explains everything! When were you going to tell us you're expecting again?' Jessica asks.

I hate her. I hate her so much. I hate both of them. There is no way on earth I look pregnant. I'm half a stone heavier than Emma at best, I reckon – the amount I weigh more than Emma is probably what my own weight can fluctuate by, because it's the time of the month or because I ate too much pasta. Sure, I'm not as toned as my sister appears to be in her photos, but that doesn't automatically equal pregnant, does it? WAG might be a bit of a bimbo, but I reckon Jessica knows exactly what she's doing...

'Not pregnant,' I say firmly and finally. I keep my face neutral and my clenched fists inside the excess of my long sleeves.

Jessica looks down into my trolley, pulls a face at my shopping, and then looks back at me with a knowing grin, implying that she thinks I'm getting fat because I'm eating shit.

I meaningfully grab two more boxes of chicken nuggets and place them in my trolley with a smile.

'I'd better get going,' I say through gritted teeth and the best fake smile I can muster.

'Well, it was lovely seeing you,' she says. 'Don't forget our coffee morning this week.'

'Wouldn't miss it for the world,' I reply, fake smile still firmly in place. It drops the second I turn my back on them.

The high of being able to buy a load of shopping and pay for it without wondering if my card is going to be declined is somewhat dampened by the encounter I just had with the yummy mummies my sister – for some reason – calls her friends. She needs to get better friends, or take a leaf out of my book and have no friends at all. My non-existent friends have never insulted me by suggesting I was pregnant when I so clearly wasn't.

I load my shopping into the boot, sling my coat in the back of the car, hop into the driver's seat and head for Oakley Primary to pick up Henry.

Seriously, how does Emma do this? I'm knackered, I'm

running around like a blue-arsed fly, and do keep in mind that I had a nap through – what Smarty tells me was – my suggested house-cleaning time, and poor Marty is way overdue his afternoon walk.

Now that I'm more familiar with how the school drop-off and pick-up system works, I manage to make it to the collection point for Henry's year with minimal trouble. I wedge my monster car into a space and realise that I'm actually somehow ten minutes early, which means I finally get to catch my breath.

I recline my seat, ever so slightly, just so that I can rest my head back a little. Enough to relax but not so much I can't eat the £4 bag of chocolate-covered honeycomb pieces I just bought from the shop.

As hard as I try to relax, I can't help but feel as though this is the calm before the storm, and that this evening is going to be non-stop too. This almost certainly requires chocolate. I pour a little handful out and toss them into my mouth. Mmm, they're so good. If looking 'not pregnant' means stopping eating things I like then consider me eating for two.

I glance down at my chest and notice a few pieces that I dropped so I pick them up and throw them into my mouth – right as I hear a knock on the window next to me. It's a man – or at least it is as far as I can tell. I can't see him properly from this angle with where he's standing. Am I parked in the wrong place again? This is ridiculous!

I hurriedly mess around with the car controls to get the window open.

'Look, I followed the blue cones, I parked here – what on earth have I done wrong now?' I blabber.

The man moves forward to lean just inside the car window, so I can see him. Christ, he's gorgeous. What is it with all the dads at this school, that they're all so ridiculously good-looking? He's tall and broad – so broad he couldn't lean further into the car if he tried, and these are big windows. He has dark brown, slightly wavy hair that's blown back, and a stubbly beard... maybe... It's so short I can't tell if it's a short beard of if he just hasn't shaved. Either way he looks great, and he looks even better when he smiles, when he flashes those dimples...

'Hi,' I say, retreating a little now I've got love hearts for eyes.

'Hi, Emma,' he says, with an amused grin. Well, of course he's amused, he just watched me eating chocolate off my own boobs. 'Henry left this at Josh's last night.'

As he hands me a knitted Captain America hat through the window our hands touch for just a second and all I can think about is having him ravish me right here on top of the blue cones. But I really don't think the car-park monitor from earlier would be too happy with me if I did – that would definitely stop traffic more than a Range Rover going the wrong way.

'Oh, right, thank you,' I say. I need to snap into polite mumsy mode. 'Most kind of you, much obliged... er...'

Not only do I sound like a character from *Oliver Twist*, but I just made out like I was going to say his name, and obviously I don't know his name.

'Marco,' he reminds me.

'Marco,' I say back to him. 'I was just going to say that.'

He looks confused as he laughs at me.

'OK, well...' Marco reaches into the car and steals a chocolate from the bag. 'See you around, Emma.'

'Yeah, see you later,' I call after him.

God, I really would like to see him later. But I'm pretty sure Josh's mum would have something to say about that.

8

The kitchen here is somehow a confusing combination of simplicity and complexity.

Reasons it's so easy to use range from the sheer number of appliances and gadgets, coupled with the fact that – and even a novice like me can tell – someone has put a great deal of care and attention into where every single thing has been placed. Everything just makes sense, which makes using the kitchen feel a little bit like dancing, as you move gracefully from one point to the next.

The downsides – which are glaringly obvious, and exclusive to me – are that for the most part I don't know where anything is and/or I don't know how to work it. But for everything I can't figure out – like what the hell actually is an Aga? I can't even work out how to control it, I just know that I love standing next to it to keep toasty – there's always a plan B.

Tonight, I have made the organic chicken nuggets I picked up earlier, cooked in the regular oven, along with some curly fries and baked beans. So at least I got to dance from the freezer to the oven effortlessly. I absolutely loved eating stuff like this growing up – and I still do, to this day.

I hear Marty barking before the front door opens and closes. That must be Rich home from work.

I know that Rich works in finance, and that he makes a shit-load of money, but that's the extent of it. It makes sense though, right? If there's money in any industry, it's the money industry.

'Wow, dinner smells good,' he calls in from the hallway. 'Is it ready now?'

'Just putting it out,' I call back.

'Kids,' I hear him shout upstairs. 'Kids... Henry... Dinner's ready, tell your sister to come down too.'

By the time Rich has entered the room he's already discarded his coat, jacket and tie. He unfastens his top button as he heads for the table.

'Thanks so much for doing this,' he says quietly. 'I had an awful feeling today that you might not be the kind of girl who cooks.'

I wonder if perhaps Rich sees me as quite immature, reading between the lines there. I suppose I am, and I'm happy with that, but for the sake of the part I am playing, it just makes me want to try even harder to get this right.

'Have you had a good day at work?' I ask him – ever the dutiful wife.

'Yeah, not bad,' he replies. 'But I'm shattered now. I think I could do with an early night.'

'Ergh, that's so disgusting,' I hear Millie chime in. She must think that was a euphemism. 'I'm putting my AirPods in.'

'No, you're not, you're sitting down for dinner with your family like a human would,' he tells her.

'No one wants to think about their parents having sex before they eat,' she complains as she sits down.

Henry snorts to himself as he takes a seat too.

Christ, do nine-year-olds know what sex is?

'We'd wait until after dinner,' Rich jokes. 'Now, can we just have dinner like a normal family, please?'

Right on cue I start placing items in the centre of the dining table. I head back to the kitchen island, to grab the sauces, but by the time I get back I can tell something is really wrong.

'What?' I ask.

'Mum, are you having a meltdown? Seriously?' Millie asks. 'Like, do you want us to get fat and die?'

'Millie, don't be so hysterical,' Rich tells her before turning to me. 'This is, er, quite the departure from our usual dinners, Emma...'

I shrug.

'I thought you guys might fancy a change,' I say, although I have no idea what kind of things they usually eat. Not chicken nuggets and curly fries, I'll bet. Perhaps there was something in the schedule but I haven't exactly had time to read the detailed notes on everything.

'You never call Mum "Emma",' Henry points out as he loads up his plate. 'Why aren't you calling her "Emmylou"?'

I glance over at Rich because I don't know what to say to that. This only raises Millie's suspicions.

'Oh my *God*, he's right,' Millie blurts. 'It's embarrassing AF but it's true – are you getting a divorce?'

Henry drops his fork.

'No, don't do that, please don't do that,' he protests.

'Kelly Barker's mum and dad got divorced and now she and her brother have to go stay with her dad every weekend – *in a flat*,' Millie tells us, as if it's genuinely the worst thing she's ever heard in her life.

'Oh my God, not a flat,' I reply sarcastically.

'I know, right?' she says, not detecting my tone at all. 'And Henry has a friend with divorced parents and he's miserable too.'

'It's not Josh's parents, is it?' I can't help but ask. Of course, I immediately wish I hadn't, because surely, I – Emma – would know such a thing.

Rich stares at me.

'Just a joke,' I insist, not explaining the punchline.

'Josh's mum and dad really love each other. They're always kissing – it's gross,' Henry informs me.

'That's nice,' I reply dutifully. Nice, but a tremendous shame for me, because Josh's dad is *hot*.

'Millie, give it a rest, OK,' Rich interrupts. 'One minute you think we're getting an early night, the next you think we're getting a divorce. It's neither. Now, eat your dinner.'

'I'm not eating that,' she insists.

Rich sighs.

'I could make us a couple of omelettes, then?' he suggests.

'Fine,' she replies, staring at the ceiling.

I feel relieved that she's almost too self-involved to find any of this suspicious. Emma was right about her.

'Well, I'm eating this,' I say.

'Me too,' Henry replies, messily sucking a curly fry into his mouth like it's a long wiggly worm.

I pick up a chicken nugget in my hand and hold it towards him.

'Cheers, kid,' I say.

Henry laughs as he grabs one of his own nuggets, clinking it with mine.

'Cheers,' he replies.

I know you're not supposed to have a favourite child, but Henry is definitely mine.

9

In a disturbing plot twist that I did not see coming at all, it turns out that Emma likes to be woken up by 'Wouldn't It Be Nice' by The Beach Boys booming out of the Smarty at a deafeningly loud volume at 6.30 a.m. every damn day. The gentle little guitar intro is so soft and so easy to sleep through, which means it's always the bang of the drum before the passionately belted-out first verse that wakes you up, like waking up to someone throwing a brick through the window before loudly singing you a love song.

Still, the alarm went off, so I got out of bed, headed for the en suite and jumped into the shower. I absolutely hate showering first thing on a morning, just minutes after getting out of bed; it gives me this icy cold shiver all over my body, no matter how hot the water is.

By the time I stepped out of the shower and slipped on the fluffy dressing gown I realised that the underfloor heating had turned on, which was absolutely glorious. I'm tempted to drag my duvet in there tonight and sleep right there on the hot floor – not that the house is cold, not like it used to be when I lived here, but just because it feels so good. The version of this house that I grew up in is long gone in favour of this swanky modern pad. If I hadn't known what it was like before I never would have believed it.

I decided, when I woke up today, that I needed to up my game. Yesterday did not go to plan at all. I don't think I did a single thing right, and the thought of struggling through today too sounds far more exhausting than trying harder to get this right does. I really did think this was going to be a walk in the park, but it turns out I'm going to have to try a bit harder if I want to convince people I'm Emma. So, no more dry shampoo – not more than a couple of days in a row, at least – and no more scruffy tracksuits. I'll have to think of some different things to make for dinner, because if I suddenly can't cook, that's not going to check out, and I need to make more of an effort at school, to show people that it's business as usual.

So, I dried my hair with the fancy Dyson hairdryer, and I used Emma's posh make-up (to the best of my ability), but while the bags under my eyes may be covered, the fringe is still giving me a hard time. I'm going to head to the salon later, but in the meantime, I've used bobby pins to grip it to the sides, as though it were never there, which begs the question, why did I need to bother in the first place, if I could have just made out like it was gripped?

I decided to raid Emma's walk-in wardrobe for something to wear and, oh... my... God...! She's got some serious designer gear in there. Dresses, shoes – things that are way sexier than anything I have ever seen her in, and the pictures I've seen dotted about the house of her confirm the same. Emma has always been like that though; she's collected things she had no intention of using. It's so like her to have this epic wardrobe but to never have the confidence to wear most of the stuff in here. She's always played it safe – unlike me.

After finally picking out an outfit, I managed to drop Henry off at school without a hitch, and with no 'hot dad' sightings unfortunately. I was looking a little more the part perhaps, in a pair of black skinny jeans, a red top, a leather jacket, and the most enormous Burberry scarf I have ever seen – it's practically a Burberry blanket – teamed with a pair of black biker boots and a decent face of make-up. I don't look quite so much like the poor sister today.

I'm back home now, currently juggling launching a tennis ball repeatedly through the back door for Marty with trying to work out how to use this pod coffee machine. I've used a few different ones, at different places I've worked at, but there never seems to be any consistency in how each of the machines work, so I'm having to learn from scratch how to work this one.

'Someone is at the door,' the Smarty announces suddenly, causing me to jump out of my skin. Christ, why do I feel as if I'm in a *Purge* movie all of a sudden? Do I need to go and open it or do I ask her to open it? Surely technology isn't there yet?

I try to force my game face to engage – whatever that looks like – as I hurry to the front door.

'Oh, hi,' I say when I see Josh's dad standing there. Was it Matt? No, it was Marco. Sexy Marco.

'Hey,' he says. 'Can I come in?'

'Oh, yeah, sure,' I reply. 'Come through to the kitchen.'

I've no idea if Emma calls it a kitchen – there's probably some name for these rooms I'm not aware of – but hopefully Marco isn't so finely in tune with Emma's vocab.

He is wearing what I like to call a handsome man coat – you know the ones, long, black material, stiff collar. They're smart, with big black buttons. They're usually worn by dishy businessmen over designer suits but when Marco removes his I can see that he's wearing jeans and an oversized, kind of scruffy jumper. Wow, I've only walked a few steps in my sister's actual shoes and I'm already judging people's clothes.

'Making a coffee,' Marco says – just stating a fact, or is it a hint?

'Yes, would you like one?' I ask, although I really hope he says no, because I haven't quite figured out how to use it yet.

'I'd love one,' he says. 'Thank you.'

Ah, just wonderful.

'Coming right up,' I say. 'Take a seat on the sofa.'

'It's OK, I'll sit here, so we can chat,' he says as he sits on one of the island stools.

I really don't need an audience. Things are going to seem off if I can't work my own coffee machine.

'So, what can I do for you?' I ask.

I pick up one of the coffee pods and click it into place. Then, with one random push of a button, the machine springs to life. Oh, thank God.

'A couple of things,' he starts, tapping his hands on the worktop in front of him, almost like a drumroll. 'First of all, are we still car-sharing for the boys' rugby away game?'

'We certainly are,' I tell him with a completely unjustified confidence. 'If that's what we said we'd do, that's what we'll do.'

'Great,' he replies. 'We appreciate the lift. Will 7 a.m. give us enough time?'

7 a.m.... 7 a.m.! Christ, I imagine this is going to be a weekend thing, and so setting off at 7 a.m. means getting up way earlier than the 6.30 a.m. weekday Beach Boys wake-up. I was hoping I'd get to lie in on weekends – well, I wasn't just hoping, I was relying on it to recharge.

'It sure will,' I reply, safe in the knowledge Emma will have left me detailed instructions and reminders in the Smarty app. 'I'll let you know if anything changes.'

I can't help but smile at how well I'm doing. Wow, I am *so* convincing, even I'm impressed. Perhaps my mum was right all along; if I just applied myself, blah blah blah...

'Great, thanks' he says, as I hand him his coffee. 'The other thing – and the main reason I'm here – is to borrow the skimmer you said you'd lend me.'

'The skimmer,' I repeat back to him, trying not to seem at all like I don't have a fucking clue what a skimmer is. What *is* a skimmer? What room would it even be in? Is it a kitchen thing? 'Of course, I'll just get it for... oh, my phone is just vibrating, excuse me.'

I pick up my phone – that wasn't vibrating at all – from the worktop and try to look as though I'm reading some kind of important message, but I'm actually frantically searching online to find out what a strimmer is.

I look up from a page of what appears to be garden tools and notice Marco laughing at me. I feel frozen on the spot.

'What?' I ask him. Shit, I feel as though he can see straight through me. He can't though, can he? Of course not...

'Are you looking it up on your phone?' he asks with a laugh.

Shit, maybe he can see straight through me.

'Erm, no,' I insist, snorting out a laugh to show just how ridiculous I find the concept. I quickly lock my phone and place it down on the worktop in front of me. 'Of course not.'

'Well, you won't mind showing me what's on your phone screen, then, will you?' he says. He looks *so* smug right now.

'Except what's in my phone is private,' I remind him. 'Didn't your wife teach you better than to go through a lady's phone?'

'I don't have a wife,' he says with a smile. 'I thought you knew that?'

Shit, he and Josh's mum must not be married, but Henry did say they were always all over each other, so I'd still be ruling out the two of us falling head over heels in love with each other, if I hadn't done so already, because I kind of want to punch him in the face right now for prodding at me like this.

'Something seems off,' he says slowly, still smiling ever so slightly.

Right, I need to do something, so I'll show him my phone screen, but I'll quickly swipe away the evidence before I turn the screen towards him.

'OK, fine, I'll show you my phone,' I tell him.

I confidently and casually unlock my screen, to turn it and show him, but he's around to my side of the island in a flash. I swipe it away, but I suspect it's too late.

'I said skimmer, not strimmer,' he says with a laugh. 'You're so busted.'

'OK, you need to leave,' I tell him, trying not to sound as if I'm panicking. 'Come on, let's go.'

I usher him into the hallway, towards the door.

'Hang on, let's talk about it,' he says.

'Nope, I'm not talking to you any more, you're harassing me,' I tell him. 'My husband would be horrified...'

'*Your* husband would, would he?' he says, almost laughing, stopping dead at the front door. 'I don't think he's your husband at all, just like they're not your kids.'

'Oh yeah, how'd you figure that one out?' I ask him.

I'm trying to sound as if I think he's being ridiculous but, also, it would be really helpful to know how he figured that one out because he obviously has.

'The boys don't even play rugby,' he informs me. 'And Lord knows what a skimmer is.'

I feel my jaw drop, ever so slightly, but I'll bet I've got a big, dumb look on my face that is a lot more obvious.

'Don't worry, your secret is safe with me, for now,' he teases me. 'I'll get going. But let me know when you fancy that chat.'

I open the door and gesture for him to walk through it.

'Wow, Josh has a real dick for a dad,' I say, to myself, so that he can hear. Well, he already knows I'm not Emma, so I can't resist saying something.

Marco just heads off back down the driveway.

'I'm not Josh's dad,' he says as he walks away. 'I'm his uncle.'

Oh.

A notification grabs my attention. I scowl at my phone instead of Marco and see the first reminder I actually set myself: my hair appointment. I'm going to get my hair sorted so that it isn't quite so tragic, and to do a better job of looking like my sister, because Lord knows I need the extra help now.

How the hell did Marco rumble me? I know how he confirmed his suspicions but how was he on to me in the first place? I just need to hope he doesn't tell anyone, because can you imagine if I failed on the second day? That's exactly what my sister will be expecting me to do, and it's exactly what my mum would expect me to do if she were still here. Nope, I can't let that happen. I'll just have to give that Marco a taste of his own medicine, get some dirt on him too; that way he can't tell anyone.

I want to do a good job at being Emma, I really do, but perhaps Ella needs to rear her head, just for an afternoon, just to level the playing field with Marco a little. Then it's straight back into mum mode, I promise.

10

Harris, Emma's hairdresser, is screaming. Actually screaming, like a little girl in a haunted house. I'm talking a proper, shrill, lengthy, blood-curdling scream, and it's all because he's just clapped eyes on me.

'Emma... no... no... what have you... how have you...? Oh, Emma,' he rants without taking a breath.

Harris has an accent I can't place and one hell of an angry look on his face. His own hair is longish and perfectly wavy, and so glossy the light bounces right off it. I suppose that's one of the perks of being a hairdresser, having perfect hair – I'd be worried if he didn't.

'What do you mean?' I say innocently.

'What do you mean?' he says, not so successfully mimicking my accent. 'What the hell have you done to your hair since I last saw you?'

'Erm, nothing, I don't think,' I say, keeping up the act. 'I maybe used a different conditioner... maybe the Dyson malfunctioned... it's hard to say.'

'You look like you've used a *de*-conditioner,' he tells me. 'And the only Dyson you've been using on that hair is the bloody vac.'

I feel my eyes widen. So much for the customer always being right. I thought I was coming here for a haircut, not a dressing-down.

'Well, if you could just—'

'Who is he?' Harris asks.

'Who is who?' I reply, confused.

'You've been with someone else – someone useless – someone who has destroyed your fringe,' he says. 'Oh, for God's sake, just sit in the chair. I can't even look at you any more. I need to put this right. Immediately.'

I allow his assistant to tie me up in a silky black gown before I sit down in Harris's chair, low-key fearing for my life.

Harris mutters to himself as he examines my ends. It's almost funny, watching him short-circuit over how on earth I could have shagged the ends of my hair so terribly since he saw Emma last. It's years of cheap bleach, multiple hairdressers and scorching-hot hair straighteners that are actually to blame, but Harris thinks I've had some kind of incident, and/or cheated on him with a lesser stylist.

'The most disgusting fringe I've ever seen in my life,' he mutters to himself.

'It just keeps parting,' I tell him. 'Just... anything you can do to make it look nice.'

'Bridget,' he calls out. 'Bridget!'

He's near hysterical by the time he has to call her name a second time.

Bridget appears with a wrinkle in her nose. It's like no one here can stand looking at my hair for too long; it offends every inch of them, so much so they can't hide it.

'Bridget, get me basically every bottle of Olaplex we have,' he tells her. 'And a huge glass of white wine.'

'Oh, I'm driving, I'm fine for a drink, thanks,' I tell him.

'It's not for you,' he replies solemnly.

Harris messes with my hair in his fingertips before puffing air from his cheeks.

'OK, so we're going to treat it, try and sort the condition out, and we're going for more blonde highlights, tone the brassy ends into something that doesn't make me cry and, as for the fringe, just... leave it with me, OK?'

'OK,' I reply. I daren't say much else.

After what seems hours in the chair I look like a different woman. Not myself. Not my sister. A whole new person.

'Oh my gosh,' I say as I look in the mirror and run my hand through my hair. 'It's so soft... it's so soft I can hardly feel it...'

My hair is the brightest, lightest blonde it has ever been. Despite having length taken off, it somehow looks longer, and it looks so much healthier, and it feels amazing! As for my disastrous DIY fringe, it's a thing of the past. I now have a super-stylish curtain fringe – apparently the key to my having a good-looking fringe was to have even more cut, purposefully parted in the middle, gradually blending it into the hair that hangs at the sides of my face. Think Tahani Al-Jamil from *The Good Place*, even though I'm way more of an Eleanor, and I'm definitely living in the Bad Place at the moment.

'Do me a favour,' Harris says as he takes the payment – which is *loads*, but he's earned every penny. 'Whatever you did, don't do it again, OK?'

'I won't, I promise,' I tell him confidently, because I'm safe in the knowledge I'll never see him again.

It turns out the salon is owned by Harris and his wife, Bernice. Bernice, who gave me a spectacular set of acrylic nails while I waited for my peroxide to take effect, also asked me if I wanted my Botox topping up. I mean, she offered because she said I'm looking more wrinkly than usual, but that's not the point, she said 'topping up', which means that Emma has been having some chemical intervention to keep looking so young. I don't feel half as bad for looking so rough around the edges now – well, maybe I looked rough before I got here today but now, wow, I can't believe this is my hair. It's so beautiful I decided not to take up the offer of Botox (but if I'm being honest, I'm way too scared of it going wrong to give it a go anyway).

Spurred on by my new look – which is new for both me *and* Emma – I decide that what I need is to buy some new clothes. Something that incorporates both of our personalities – the part of Emma that wishes she had the confidence to wear sexy designer clothing and the part of me that wishes I could afford them. What Emma has is nice, really nice, but what she needs are a few pieces with a bit of edge, with some extra style. Even if I don't dare wear them now, at least I can leave them in her wardrobe for her, for when she gets back. Or maybe I'll slip into something slutty and go pick up the kids from school, because if you can't look sexy for the school run, when can you? You never know when you're going to bump into a hot dad – or a crazy uncle, like Marco, who I'm going to have to talk to at some point, before he blows my cover. Don't think I've forgotten about that time bomb but, now that I've got my sexy new hairdo, maybe I can finally use my sexuality for good, huh?

11

I top up my bright red lipstick in the rear-view mirror as I wait for Henry. I swear, every other child appears to have rushed outside and they're halfway home by now, but not Henry... The area clears of kids and parents but there's still no sign of him at all.

Safe in the knowledge that I'm not going to bump into Marco, I get out of the car and head for the school entrance.

It's a modern building – practically space-age looking. I can't even imagine what primary school must be like these days; it must be so hi-tech, nothing like when I was at school. I don't think I touched a school computer until I was in year 4, or something like that, and I must have been a teenager before we were using the Internet. I am that age where things were just starting to change, so Internet browsing at secondary school was pretty open. These days I'll bet the filters are so strict, you can't get away with anything – I doubt you'd be able to sit on MSN Messenger all day, like I used to (not that MSN Messenger even exists any more).

I'm approaching the door when a twenty-something woman

in a tight white shirt and a black pencil skirt shuffles out with Henry in tow.

'Ah, Mrs Cooper, I was just coming to find you,' she says. 'The deputy head would like to see you about Henry.'

I thought this was supposed to be the good child!

'Oh, OK,' I say. 'And the deputy head is...?'

'In his office,' she says. I must be staring at her blankly. 'A left, to the end of the corridor, then a left again.'

'Right, OK, erm...'

'I'll keep an eye on Henry,' she tells me.

I look at him as I pass him, hoping he'll give me some indication of why I'm being summoned, but he's nine years old, he has no idea how to convey a variety of signals with his eyes alone, although he does look puzzled by my new look.

I wander down the corridor, until I happen upon the deputy head's office. His name is on the door: Christian Clegg. At least I'm going in knowing his name.

Mr Clegg's door has a big glass window in it, which he's covered from the inside with black paper to give him some privacy. It creates a sort of mirror on the back of the door, and when I catch sight of my hair again, I can't help but admire it. It just doesn't look like my hair, and I could never have afforded an outfit like this – I can't stop looking at myself, not because I think I'm some super babe, but just because I really do look so different, and I feel different too. I wasn't exactly lacking in confidence before, but my new hair makes me feel kind of invincible.

I knock on the door.

'Come in,' Mr Clegg calls out.

'Oh, hello,' I say as I enter his office.

He flashes me a bemused grin, probably because I just said that like I recognised him, because I actually do, but of course Emma would recognise him.

'Hello, Emma, how's things?' he asks. 'Come in, sit down.'

Christian Clegg is the hot dad I saw yesterday, when I had my drop-off disaster – he's the one who stood up for me. And now he's talking to me as if he knows me, like we already have a friendly rapport, so he and Emma must be on good terms.

'I'm doing great, thank you, how are you?' I ask as I take a seat at the messy desk opposite him.

'Oh, you know, knackered, bored out of my skull this afternoon, frustrated from trying to get ten-year-olds to read lines of dialogue from Macbeth – the joys of being a drama teacher in a primary school,' he says with a smile. 'You've changed your hair – it suits you.'

'Oh, thank you,' I say as I self-consciously run a hand through my hair, because apparently having confidence in your new look vanishes the second someone compliments you on it.

His desk is a mess of papers, wrappers and no less than three coffee cups. There's a framed picture of him and a little boy, who looks around Henry's age, so he must have a child that goes here, as well as being the deputy head.

'I just wanted to see if everything was OK with Henry,' he starts, snapping into teacher mode.

'Oh, yes, he's fine,' I insist as casually as I can. I'm sure he is?

'Well, it was most unlike him, but he fell fast asleep in English today, which is usually his favourite subject. His teacher asked him why he was so tired and he said he was up until 3 a.m. playing Animal Crossing...'

I laugh theatrically – perhaps too theatrically. I imagine Christian sees better acting from the kids.

'Oh, that boy,' I say, laughing still. 'Such an imagination. No, no, Mr Clegg, of course he wasn't playing games all night. I put him to bed, as I always do, tucked him in, watched him fall asleep

– I even prod him, to make sure he is actually asleep and not faking.'

OK, first of all, I thought I was just supposed to send him to bed, not actually put him to bed, and second of all the prodding thing sounded like a great parent-type thing to say in my head, but out loud it sounded completely weird.

'Call me Christian,' he insists with a laugh. Emma must already be on first name terms with him. 'Well, don't worry, I didn't think it would be true. I know what a fantastic mum you are. I remember Calvin doing something similar once – of course, he wasn't sleeping properly because it was while his mum and I were divorcing.'

Christian pulls a face, as though he's got a horrible taste in his mouth, but in a playful way.

It's only now that I notice he isn't wearing a wedding ring. Ooh, so he's a hot single dad. Interesting.

'Anyway, I'll let you get home. I'm sure you're making something amazing for dinner, putting us all to shame,' he says with a smile.

I'm so glad Henry isn't here to bring up the curly fries.

'OK, well, thanks for being so concerned about Henry,' I reply.

'I'll see you at the fundraiser meeting next week,' he says. 'Unless you cause any car-park pile-ups in the meantime.'

He flashes me a cheeky smile.

I laugh.

'Sure, see you next week,' I reply – no idea what he's talking about though.

I retrieve Henry and head for the car with him.

'So, you fell asleep, huh?' I say, ruffling his hair.

'I didn't mean to,' he says. 'I was just so tired.'

Uh, boy, same.

'And you didn't take my Switch off me and I didn't realise the time,' he continues.

Oh, so I'm supposed to take it off him? Right, OK, I can do that tonight.

'Well, we all make mistakes,' I tell him as I help him into the car.

'I thought you'd be more shouty,' he tells me.

This is why I'd make a terrible parent, because, looking at his adorable little face right now, I couldn't possibly imagine even raising my voice to him.

'Well, we'll be home soon,' I tell him. 'I just need to stop at the supermarket.'

Yes, I know I went shopping yesterday, but now I know I need to up my game with dinner, so I'm going to find a recipe online and I'm going to cook it for everyone tonight. Rich and Millie might have expressed their displeasure last night, because I basically served them unhealthy kids' food, but tonight I'm going to knock their socks off... hopefully...

'I'm supposed to be going to Josh's to play before dinner,' Henry informs me.

'Oh, OK,' I reply. 'Well, I can drop you off there and then I'll go shopping, go home, start dinner...'

God, now I want to fall asleep.

After searching through Emma's phone in the twenty minutes (I'm lucky I managed that long) I was in bed before I fell asleep last night, I discovered that she's got a section on locations, which thankfully includes Josh's house. I double check where it is. It's not far from here so I memorise where it is, lest Henry pick up on me using the satnav again.

Josh, it turns out, lives on the next street along from us, on another picturesque street with big detached houses hiding behind large electric gates.

I help Henry out of the car but then send him on his way.

'Go ahead,' I tell him, because the last thing I want to do is bump into weird uncle Marco. 'I'll have your dad pick you up on the way home.'

Henry charges off up the pathway. I keep eyes on him, all the way to the door, ducking out of the way the second I see the door opening.

I get back in the car and start looking through different recipes on my phone. I refine my search a little, to look for healthy recipes, and sure enough I find one for a lighter take on spaghetti and meatballs, so that's what I'll make. I'll pop to Buckley's to get everything I need and then I'll go home and get started.

After the epic fail that was last night's dinner, I need to pull something out of the bag tonight, and weirdly enough my new hairdo gives me confidence. Not because I think having nice hair will make me better in the kitchen (although hydrating *my* ends does appear to be the work of magic, so you never know), it's more that my fringe was an epic fail too, and if that can be flipped into something amazing, then perhaps I can turn my cooking around as well. All I can do is try, and hope I don't burn down my second property of the year in the process...

12

Is cooking stressful or relaxing? Because I've heard it both ways.

On the one hand, I do feel kind of relaxed, and there's something therapeutic, and completely satisfying, about measuring things and following instructions. It's like painting by numbers – basic effort for maximum results. You don't really need to know how to cook to follow a recipe, you just do as you're told. But on the other hand, I appear to be lacking the knack, the certain something, whatever it is that naturally talented or well-trained chefs have. Just when I think I'm getting somewhere, I'll read an instruction like 'chop the garlic' and I'll start second-guessing myself. Is there a particular way to do it or do you just chop blindly away at it? It suddenly occurs to me that I don't actually know what garlic looks like inside.

'Smarty, how do you chop garlic?' I ask, but I don't think it can hear me over the TV. One of the best things about the configuration of this room is that I can watch *Hollyoaks* while I'm cooking, on the big screen, so I can see and hear it perfectly, but the downside is that the Smarty is having trouble hearing me.

'Smarty,' I say with a raised voice, but this just causes Marty to come running in the room, barking excitedly because now he's here, he can smell the mince for the meatballs.

'Marty, be quiet,' I shout over his barking.

'OK. Smarty muting,' the device replies as the light on the top turns from white to red.

'What? No! Smarty...'

The dog barks.

'Smarty...'

He barks again.

'Oh, Marty, come on,' I blurt angrily.

'Smarty turning on,' the device announces in that creepy female AI voice that could almost pass for sinister, depending on what she's saying.

Oh, God, why do I want to burst into tears? It all seems like such small things but I feel so overwhelmed right now. I lean forward over the worktop. My hands are covered in meat so I rest my head on my forearms.

'Is everything OK?' I hear a voice ask.

I look up and see Marco standing there. For a second, I just stare at him, but then...

'Oh, for fuck's sake,' I blurt. 'What are you doing here? Just fuck off.'

'I brought *your son* home,' Marco tells me. 'Don't worry, I sent him upstairs, he didn't hear your F-bombs. And if I wasn't already sure you're not who you're claiming to be, I'm certain now. I don't think I've ever heard Emma swear – especially not at guests. She'd have set me a place at the dinner table by now.'

I get the feeling from his generally playful personality that Marco doesn't take too much too seriously.

'I thought Rich was going to pick Henry up?' I say, ignoring all of that.

'I offered,' he tells me with a smile. 'Look, I feel like we got off on the wrong foot earlier. I'm sorry. I didn't mean to take so much delight in rumbling you – life is just really boring here.'

'So, you thought, oh, I don't know, you'd just blackmail the neighbours?' I ask. 'Because, I don't know if you've connected these dots, Einstein, but if I'm not who I say I am, then I don't have her money, do I? So, you're not going to get much.'

I wipe my hands on a tea towel, turn around and slide down the side of the island until I'm sitting on the floor. I pull my knees close, hugging them as I bury my head.

I don't look up but I feel Marco sit down next to me.

'Your hair looks nice,' he tells me.

I don't say anything.

'And dinner is...'

'Dinner is fucked,' I tell him. 'I'm having a meltdown because I'm getting bogged down in how you chop fucking garlic, because I've never done it before, and the smart speaker is not as fucking smart as it fucking thinks it is, and the fucking dog...'

Marty is still barking in the background.

'Give me a minute,' Marco says, placing a hand on my shoulder for a split second.

I hear the TV switch off before I hear the back door open. The room finally silent, I dare to look up. Eventually Marco steps back in front of me.

'Come here, take my hand,' he instructs.

I notice that he's taken off his coat and his scarf.

Oh, at this stage, what else do I have to lose? I grab his hand and let him pull me to my feet, which he does with a reassuring ease.

'OK, watch me,' he says.

He rolls up the sleeves of yet another tired jumper and washes his hands before taking out a knife and standing in front of the chopping board.

'You squash the whole thing with the flat side of the knife,' he tells me, as he shows me how to do it. 'You'll feel it crack. Next you peel the skin away with your hands, and then you chop it, horizontally, then vertically, until it's small. Done.'

'You make it look so easy,' I tell him with a sigh.

Marco just shrugs.

'What are we making?' he asks.

'We?' I reply in amusement. 'I was trying to make spaghetti and meatballs. And I wasn't doing a very good job of it, and you clearly know what you're doing, and now it feels like you're making me my last meal, before you expose me, but I really wish you wouldn't do that.'

'Emma... Emma clone... whatever your name is,' he starts, placing down the knife, turning my body to face his so he can look me in the eye. 'I was never going to tell anyone. This was my ill attempt at... making a friend.'

'You want to make friends with me?' I say with a scoff. 'Why?'

'For the same reason I knew you weren't Emma,' he tells me. 'I can spot a con artist when I see one, trust me.'

'A con artist,' I say softly. 'Some con artist – today is only my second day. You rumbled me on day two!'

'Technically I rumbled you on day one, then,' he points out, 'but that's not the point. Look, let's start again. You're doing a great job with those meatballs. Let me make the sauce and you can tell me all about all of it – I'm really interested to hear where you were manufactured.'

I laugh.

'OK, deal, but you have to promise to keep this between us,' I tell him, brandishing a dirty spoon at him.

I'm relieved Marco – who clearly knows what he's doing – thinks I'm doing a good job with the meatballs because I'm so out of my depth. I read that, if you want to make them less bad for you, you combine lean minced pork with green lentils. I'm not even sure if I've eaten lentils before, which seemed like all the more reason to use them, because if I don't usually use them then my sister probably does.

I don't know what it is about Marco – or if I'm just desperate for someone to talk to – but I want to trust him. He is helping me out of a crisis, I suppose, and to be honest, I have nothing to lose. Perhaps a little honesty might convince him not to blow my cover, if he knows it's for a good reason...

'I promise,' Marco replies.

'Emma is in prison,' I blurt immediately.

'No!'

Marco can't believe his ears.

'Emma? Perfect housewife Emma?' he replies. 'Lisa – who is my sister-in-law, Josh's mum, if you don't know that already – is always moaning about how *amazing Emma shows everyone up* by *being so bloody perfect*.'

I imagine those are direct quotes because he says them in a high-pitched voice.

'What did she do?' he asks.

'She's been parking her car wherever she feels like it, and ignoring the fines, so the judge made an example out of her – she got six weeks,' I say.

'Typical rich people,' Marco says. 'Bloody hell. I take it you're not a robot or an alien. Although if you were AI you probably wouldn't know, and if you were an alien you probably wouldn't tell me...'

He narrows his eyes with faux suspicion. Marco seems like a kind of a nerd, and I kind of like him, now I know he isn't trying to blackmail me.

'I'm Emma's twin sister, Ella,' I tell him. 'Lesser known, less successful, less attractive.'

'I don't know, you're not the one that's in prison, and your new look really suits you – not that you didn't look good before,' he insists. 'Anyway, nice to meet you, Ella.'

Marco heads to the fridge. He searches around in there until he re-emerges with a bottle of BBQ sauce and the sugar jar from next to the coffee machine.

'I have Italian grandparents on my dad's side of the family,' he tells me as he sprinkles sugar into the pan of tomato pasta sauce. 'My mum, who is as English as fish and chips, would cook Italian food for my dad, me and my brother – Ant. But over time my mum would go off page, trying different things, and if there's two secret ingredients she swears by in her tomato sauce it's a little sugar and a squirt of BBQ sauce.'

The bottle makes a comedic noise as he squeezes a little BBQ sauce into the pan.

'Sounds interesting,' I say. It certainly smells amazing. 'So, when you said you know a con artist when you see one... Are you a police officer?'

'Erm...' Marco laughs to himself for a moment. 'I'm closer to being a criminal than a law enforcer.'

'Oh, boy, if you're going to murder me, can you at least let me take credit for this pasta first?' I ask, totally joking, unless I'm not...

'Don't worry, I'm more of a cybercriminal,' he reassures me. 'I'm a freelancer, working with companies to find vulnerabilities in their systems.'

I must look puzzled.

'I'm a computer hacker who uses his powers for good,' he explains. 'A sort of bug bounty hunter. So, companies will hire me and ask me to try and hack them or, sometimes, businesses will offer rewards to anyone who exposes a vulnerability in their system. I'm working on hacking a... erm... you see that smart device over there?'

Marco nods towards the Smarty – obviously not saying its name because it will trigger it.

'They're offering £50k to the first person to hack it,' he tells me, widening his eyes for dramatic effect. 'And I really need it too. I got fired recently. It was silly really. Let's just say a company tried to get out of paying me for some work so I hijacked all of their computers, saying I'd let them back in if they paid me what I was owed... they didn't, and they called the police, it was a whole thing. Then my girlfriend threw me out, so I was kind of homeless for a minute. Bottom line: I'm living in my brother's house now, sleeping in the spare room, acting as a sort of manny to the kids to earn my keep. I must sound like such a mess.'

Wow, Marco and I really aren't all that different. In fact, he's probably worse off than I am, because it sounds as if he got his heart broken too. I think he needs a friend as much as I do right now.

'I was sacked recently too, because I accused the boss's nephew of burning my flat down, and apparently I kept mixing people up and eating their birthday cakes,' I explain to make him feel better. 'I'm just pretending to be Emma while she's away. She really, really didn't want anyone knowing the truth. Honestly – she sounded so embarrassed she was practically in tears.'

'I really could do with an identical twin. It would get me out of so many scrapes,' Marco muses as he puts a pan of water on to boil for the spaghetti.

He grabs a piece of the Mediterranean bread I cut earlier, tears a bit off and dips it into the sauce.

'Mmm, amazing,' he says. 'Here, try.'

He dips another bit of bread into the sauce before offering it to me. I raise my hand, to take it from him, but it's so saucy I'm worried it will fall to pieces or I'll spill sauce everywhere, so I lean forward and eat it straight from his hand.

'Oh my God, Mum, that's so weird,' I hear Millie say.

'Millie, hi,' I say, in a kind of high-pitched voice, as if I've just been caught in the act.

'Your hair looks dope,' she tells me, not all that enthusiastically though. 'And your clothes. Not totally embarrassing for once.'

Marco smiles and nods approvingly.

'Dope,' he says, amused. 'OK, well, I'll leave you guys to it.'

Millie goes and plonks herself down on the sofa and turns on the TV.

'I've really enjoyed talking to you,' he tells me quietly. 'How about we hang out again some time? It's nice, spending time with someone else who doesn't find this world easy.'

'Yeah, that would be great,' I tell him. 'Perhaps you can help me be a bit better at it, less likely to get caught out again.'

'Sure,' he replies. 'I'll text you – don't worry, I have ways of getting your number.'

I must look worried.

'I'm joking,' he insists as he smiles. 'I have Emma's number, and she has mine, so if you need me, call me.'

'I will do, thank you,' I reply with a smile. Suddenly I feel so much better.

Henry walks in, his eyes glued to the Switch I absolutely need to remember to confiscate before bedtime, with Rich close behind him.

'Cheers for bringing him home, mate,' Rich tells Marco, patting him on the back in that way men do.

'Yeah, no worries,' he replies. 'Well, I'll see you all later.'

'Yeah, see you around,' I tell him.

'Great idea changing the hair,' Rich whispers to me once we're alone in the kitchen area. 'No one was ever going to believe Emma had hair like yours.'

I think this is supposed to be a compliment, for showing initiative or something, but it's definitely offensive.

'Cheers,' I reply, semi-sarcastically, but not so much Rich notices.

I open the packet of fresh spaghetti and place it into the now boiling water.

'If everyone wants to sit at the table,' I call out. 'Dinner is ready in less than five.'

Everyone does as they're told, assembling at the dining table, waiting for their food. Henry is still playing on his game and Rich and Millie are both lost in their phones.

I finish up dinner and, honestly, wow, it looks as if a professional chef has made it. Maybe. It's certainly the most professional dish I've ever made.

I place a bowl in front of each of the three of them before grabbing one for myself and sitting down. I wait, nervously, for someone to try it. Eventually everyone is tucking in, I'm just waiting for the first bit of feedback, so I can relax, before I eat mine and... Hmm. No one is saying anything. Everyone is eating, and no one was shy last night when they thought dinner was crap but now, because they seem to like it, that's it. Not a word of praise. Not even a thank you. Is this what this is like for Emma, no one appreciating her? I worked hard to make this dinner – I almost had a mental breakdown making this dinner!

'How was work?' I ask Rich.

He stares at me, almost suspiciously, for a second before he replies.

'Fine,' he says. 'Have you had a good day, er, h-honey?'

'Fine,' I reply, echoing his level of detail.

'Kids... have you two had a good day?' I persist.

'You don't need to do this, Mum,' Millie tells me.

'Do what?' I ask.

'Pretend you care,' she says.

I look over at Rich for support, but he's looking at something on his phone and grinning like an idiot. I know that face, I've made that face – admittedly not recently, but there's only one reason people stare at their phones like that. Suddenly Rich's phone starts ringing and his expression changes.

'I'd better take this somewhere else,' he says, with a serious, almost nervous look. I swear, his eyes dart from side to side, as though he's worried about someone seeing his screen.

'Work?' I ask him.

'Yep,' he says, hurrying out of the room entirely before he answers it.

With Millie eating with one hand and scrolling her phone on the other, and with Henry's eyes firmly fixed on the TV, I decide it's probably fine to check my phone, to see what's on the agenda tomorrow.

A few taps on the screen confirm the worst. After I drop Henry off at school, I have a coffee morning with Jessica, Abbey and Cleo booked in. Jessica is the one I met yesterday, in the supermarket, and what a bag of laughs she was. I find Abbey and Cleo in the contacts and peep at the images assigned to them. So, Abbey is the other person I met yesterday, that's good to know. It's always good to put a name to people you don't like.

At least I've had my hair done now, and I'm utilising Emma's wardrobe to the max, so I won't feel quite so vulnerable.

I just can't believe these are my sister's friends. Each to their own and all that; I might not have much in common with them, but they don't even seem like nice people. And now I get to have coffee with them – oh, joy. Let's just hope no one makes any snide comments about the fact I'm going to order the biggest piece of cake they have because, honestly, it's the only reason I can stand to go. At least if I have something in my mouth, I'll be less likely to break character... hopefully.

13

The last time I was in this café – which was probably in the nineties – it was called Tea Time. Everything in it was a shade of brown, apart from the teapots, milk jugs and cutlery, which were all a dull silver colour. I always used to marvel at how many little tiny scratches were all over the metal teapots – there must have been thousands, after years and years of people using them. Pensioners meeting up in the day, families out for lunch on weekends, friends meeting up for a chat. I remember so vividly I would always have one of two things. Either the kids' lunch boxes, which were these little cardboard things shaped like animals, with tiny sandwiches, crisps and a juice carton inside, or I'd get toasted teacakes with butter, except I'd always leave a pile of dried fruit on my plate, because I would pick it out while I was eating. I loved the taste of the teacakes but I've always hated dried fruit.

Tea Time is no more. Instead, where it used to be, is Frothy Coffy, a modern café with so much going on, it's almost void of personality at all. Suddenly, Tea Time feels like something I saw on TV – it's hard to imagine it ever existing.

Everything here is grey, because isn't everything always grey these days? Tables look as if they're made out of recycled wood, none of them match, and there isn't a single chair in this place (unless you count the decorative one on the wall – what the fuck?) in favour of wooden benches that are not playing ball with the dress I'm wearing today; I just can't seem to get the leg span needed to make myself comfortable.

The café has those lights where light bulbs hang from wires pinned to the ceiling, looking almost like a spider. I hate them. I hate everything about this place. Well, everything but the 'frothy coffee' and the massive triple-chocolate brownie I have on the table in front of me. Incidentally, I find it absolutely hilarious that they call a cappuccino a frothy coffee here. Well, everyone seems like such a ridiculous snob, and yet here we are, calling cappuccinos frothy effing coffees, and my common arse is the one taking issue with it.

It's funny, how things can be classy or trashy, depending on whether you're rich or poor. All sorts of things – everything from wearing a full tracksuit, to day drinking, to not paying taxes.

Anyway, here I am, with my frothy coffee. Jessica stares down at my brownie and then back up at me, her smile not faltering.

'It's nice to see your hair back to normal,' she says. 'I see you've gone for something more… young.'

I wonder if that's a dig – I'm sure it is.

'Thanks,' I say, before taking a meaningful bite of my brownie.

The conversation with Jessica, Abbey and Cleo is so impossibly dull. Abbey, the WAG-looking one, is kind of a bitch. All her stories usually result in her passing comment on someone, and it's usually a harsh comment, usually about something people can't control, like their appearance.

Then there's Cleo, a short woman with an Essex accent who

has semi-recently tied the knot with Ed Allen, of Allen Construction – which I think is supposed to mean something to me, as if he's local rich royalty or something – and all she talks about is their wedding last year, as well as complaining about how much they want to install a pool in their basement, but they can't, for some reason, I don't know, honestly, I keep just tuning out.

And then there's Jessica, the clear queen of the Yummy Mummy Mafia, the one who is always quick with a snide remark, or a not-so-subtle criticism, the one clearly running the show around here – I think the other two might be scared of her.

'Rich is so lovely,' she tells me.

'Oh, isn't he just?' I reply enthusiastically, pausing for a second to sip my drink. 'I'm lucky to have him.'

'I'm so relieved to hear that,' she says. 'Because we'd heard there was trouble at home, hadn't we, ladies?'

The ladies, who are on the edge of their bench, waiting for gossip, nod wildly.

'Oh?' I say casually.

'Yes,' Jessica replies. 'I've heard Millie is going off the rails and—'

'Oh, she's fine, she's just a teenager,' I insist. 'I'm sure you ladies were horrible teenagers too... or maybe not.'

Judging by their faces, I don't think they think so.

'And Elsie Barnes told Joan Carr, who told Roland the butcher, who told Abbey, that Henry has been falling asleep in school and I thought that, coupled with you taking a step back from your job on the Village Echo, meant, well, that maybe you can't have it all.'

'Oh, no, everything is fine,' I insist. 'And as for taking a step back, well, does that sound like something I'd do?'

I have no idea what the Village Echo is, but that feels like the right thing to say.

'Well, I thought not,' Jessica replies. 'I know it's only pocket money to you, but I thought you loved your job running the village website. I was surprised to hear you'd made such a sudden decision – and then I heard about the meeting, today, to figure out what they're going to do about replacing you.'

'Hmm, maybe someone got the wrong end of the stick?' I say.

'Well, I saw Arthur on my way here, and he said he was heading for a meeting at HQ now,' Abbey chimes in. 'So, it certainly seems like they're replacing you.'

'And obviously John works there,' Jessica reminds me. 'And his favourite thing to do in bed at night is tell me all about the website.'

Well, John needs to get a life, or some little blue pills, clearly.

'Probably not his favourite thing,' Cleo jokes, but I can see something behind Jessica's dead eyes that makes me think it might actually be true.

I've just realised what's going on. Emma trusts me with her house, her kids, her husband... but the one thing she thought I could never do, in a million years, was fill in for her at work. Unless she's hiding something... How did Jessica describe it, as pocket money for Emma? It's not as if it's what pays her bills, then, is it? And I actually think I'd be really good at something like that. Either way, it's my excuse to get out of here.

'Well, it was lovely seeing you ladies, but I'd better head over to HQ and sort out the misunderstanding,' I say. 'But we must do this again soon.'

'Well, we've got the fundraiser meeting next week,' Jessica reminds me.

'Can't wait,' I say, carefully standing up from the bench.

I drain the last of my coffee from my cup and pop the last bite of brownie in my mouth before heading for the door.

'Nah, I don't think she's pregnant,' I hear Cleo whisper to the other two under her breath. 'Eating for two maybe though.'

I bite my tongue and remove my phone from my pocket to call Marco.

'Hello, *Emma*,' he says. I feel as if I can hear him winking. 'What can I do for you?'

'Do you want to cause some trouble?' I ask him.

'I'll get my coat,' he replies.

It turns out the Village Echo is a website for all things local – and it seems like it's kind of a big deal too.

Marco looked at some stats on the drive over to HQ (which is actually in the back rooms of the community centre) – publicly accessible ones, he assures me, and he told me that a large proportion of the village view the website daily. It has news, stuff about local businesses, announcements – it even has a message board, and an active one at that.

Looking at the 'meet the team' section I can see that Emma is the editor, the manager, the big boss. And now that I know she didn't want me assuming her role, I'm curious to find out more about what she does.

I've brought Marco with me because he knows all things local, and he knows all about the site, and if I have any glaringly obvious gaps in my knowledge, well, he can fill them in for me.

To be honest, I think Marco is so bored here, that he would have pretty much agreed to do anything I suggested.

'So, what's the plan?' he asks, opening the community-centre door for me, gesturing towards the back of the room to where the offices are.

'No plan,' I reply. 'I guess I just want to be nosey.'

'Emma, hello, what a surprise,' John says. 'Wow, look at your hair, and your clothes... you look... amazing...'

I smile, kind of graciously and kind of awkwardly, at John's compliment.

I know who everyone is from the 'meet the team' section of the website.

John is in charge of the running of things – keeping the website online and updated with all the latest, etc. The tech guy, basically. Then we have Arthur, who is the local know-it-all, who keeps the info up to date. He's probably in his early seventies, and has lived here all his life. He holds his non-smart phone as if it's a dog turd – a dog turd that might have a bomb in it, perhaps, because he eyeballs it so suspiciously. Actually, I think he might just be squinting to see it better.

'You text me and said you were taking some time off,' Arthur tells me.

'Oh, yeah, but just like a couple of days, not like a long time,' I say.

'I'm looking at your message and—'

'Oh, it was probably wine o'clock when I sent that,' I explain. I wonder how much I can get away with by claiming wine o'clock. 'Anyway, I'm here now, and I've brought Marco – he's a tech expert. He's going to look over everything, see if he can't offer us some advice. He's going to make sure we're not hackable.'

'Who on earth would hack a village website?' John asks – I think rhetorically – with a mocking laugh.

I think John must feel a little put out, because I've turned up with Marco, bigging him up as an expert.

'Oh, you'd be surprised,' Marco tells him seriously. 'I'm also going to make sure the website is compliant – GDPR, clearly labelled advertisements, and so on.'

Ooh, he sounds so professional. I don't know if that stuff is true but it sounds good. You'd never believe, hearing him speak, that this is all just a front for me to have a snoop around, because I'm so curious as to why Emma wanted me to fill in for her in all aspects of her life apart from this one...

I glance around the room, where I notice a door with Emma's name on it.

'We'll just pop into my office,' I say, eagerly heading straight over there. 'We'll give you a full report when we know what the deal is.'

'Well, do let me know if you need anything,' John calls after us. He doesn't sound very happy.

'Will do, mate, cheers,' I hear Marco call back.

Once we're inside Emma's office I close the door behind us.

'OK, let's figure out what she's hiding from me,' I say.

'How do you know she's hiding anything?' Marco asks with an amused chuckle as he watches me riffle through a filing cabinet.

'Because I know my sister,' I tell him. 'Do you really think she would leave me looking after her kids, sleeping in her marital bed, with a free run of the house, her credit card, her car – all of that stuff – if she didn't trust me? No, no. It's not that she doesn't trust me here, it's that she's hiding something. Definitely.'

'Well, if you say so,' Marco says. 'Although I don't know how much you can even hide, somewhere like this, unless she's embezzling or something fun like that.'

The computer on the desk is old. So old the monitor is box-shaped, rather than a flat screen, and if there's one thing working in digital agencies has taught me, it's that screens have not looked like this for a long time.

I fire up the computer, only to be hit with a password screen –

crap.

'She's got a password,' I tell Marco.

'Here, let me,' he says.

I shift out of the desk chair so that Marco can sit down. I suppose I'll just keep searching through drawers while he...

'I'm in,' he announces casually.

'Oh my God, that was fast. Did you hack the mainframe or something?'

'I don't know what you think that means,' Marco replies with a laugh. 'But, no, I just guessed her password. You'd be amazed how many people have "1234567".'

Oh, I hope he's joking.

'OK, let's have a look, see what's going on,' I say.

'What kind of thing are we looking for?' Marco asks as he goes through the motions, firing up different programs, all the usual sorts of things you'd open if you were sitting down to work.

I know she's hiding something from me, I just know it... but I have no idea what.

I start scanning through her files, trying to get a feel for what she does here.

'I'll know it when I... oh my God,' I blurt. 'So *that's* what she's up to.'

I can't help but smile to myself – and I'm not surprised she didn't want to tell me.

'What are we looking at?' Marco asks.

'My sister is the agony aunt for the website,' I tell him, a combination of shocked and amused.

'Is that bad?' he asks.

'Our mum was an agony aunt – a famous one, actually,' I say.

'Unless your mum was Jerry Springer, I'm not sure there are any famous agony aunts,' Marco replies with a laugh.

'She was called Auntie Angela,' I tell him.

'Oh, shit, no, I have heard of her. Probably one of the first pair of boobs I ever saw – I remember being off school and seeing her getting a breast exam live on daytime TV.'

He finds this funnier than he does awkward, thankfully.

'Yep, that's my mum, mortifying as ever,' I say with a sigh.

Christ, it's been a long time since anyone mentioned that to me. I think I'd repressed it.

'That's pretty cool though, she helped a lot of people. How's she doing?' he asks.

'She died,' I said bluntly. 'Breast cancer.'

'Shit, that's fucking horrible, sorry,' he says.

I can see how uncomfortable he is from the tightness of his face. It's like every muscle he has is suspended in time, cringing, just waiting for a way for him to figure out how he can go back in time and not mention it.

'It's hilarious that my sister thinks she's qualified to give advice,' I tell him, changing the subject. 'She probably thinks it's in her DNA, like she's inherited the ability to give good advice. She probably got that in the will too.'

'OK, I'm sensing some tension regarding that,' Marco points out bravely. I'm sure he'd rather this conversation just ended.

'Oh, it's nothing, old news, I'm over it,' I tell him. 'Basically, we were still teenagers when my mum died, so she put our inheritance in trust until we were thirty-five – she wanted us to make our own lives, not live off her money – which is fine, except she put in this clause that if either of us had a child, we'd get our money. Emma had a baby pretty much straight away, meaning she got her money, but I got nothing, and I thought she might help me out when all of a sudden, I was basically homeless and jobless, but, nope. Honestly, it's so bloody backward, I'm being punished for not using my womb.'

'A lesser person would have had a baby, just to cash-in,' Marco says. I think this is supposed to be a compliment.

'Yeah, I don't think Emma would have been shocked if I had, but no,' I say confidently. 'I've heard when you have a baby you've got to keep looking after them until they're at least eighteen...'

Marco laughs.

'Is that so?'

'Just what I heard,' I joke. 'So, it didn't seem worth the risk.'

I fire up the website to see what sort of advice Emma – or 'Ask Alison', that's what her title is – is giving out.

'Oh, God... Emma, no, what are you thinking?' I say to myself. 'Someone wrote in asking for advice because she thought her husband might be cheating and Emma is telling her to leave well alone – no! That's awful advice. I could definitely do better than that, look...'

I open up the incoming letters and select the newest one.

'OK, let's see what the problem is here...' I say, before reading aloud. '"Dear Alison, I hope you can help me, as I'm having trouble with a house guest. My brother-in-law recently lost his job after a run-in with the police and now he's living in our spare room..."'

'Is that...?' Marco glances at the sender. 'It is! That's my sister-in-law! She's talking about me! "He keeps going on about this big pay-day that's coming. It sounds like a pipe dream. I think he needs to get a job, and that we need to show him tough love and throw him out, but my husband says it's his brother and we have to give him another chance." Absolute crap. Run-in with the law? She makes me sound like a criminal, and I'm basically the help in that house, but free, obviously. Unbelievable.'

'Sorry,' I tell him. 'This is probably why we shouldn't be looking... Shall we just—?'

'You should reply,' Marco suggests eagerly. 'Reply and tell her not to kick me out.'

'OK, so I'm not exactly the CEO of ethics, but even I know that's kind of wrong, and manipulative,' I point out.

'That's a strong ethical stance from someone tricking a nine-year-old into thinking she's his mum,' he teases with a cheeky smile.

I shoot him a look.

'Sorry, just a joke, but, OK, tell me this – what advice would you give my sister-in-law?' he asks. 'And you can be honest.'

'Well... knowing what I know about you, it sounds like you need support right now. You've lost your job and – whether your plan to make money is going to pay off or not – tough love isn't going to help you, it's just going to make things even harder, and the longer you're down, the harder it is to get back on your feet, I know. Of course, Emma would probably tell her to kick you out, because that's basically what she did with me, and it fucked me over so... Yeah.'

'Two things,' Marco starts. 'Obviously it's in my interest for you to tell her that, because I really don't have many options right now, but also, you clearly are much better at giving advice than she is. You should do it. Take over from her for a while – you'd be doing her a favour.'

'Do you really think so?' I ask.

Could it actually be good for Emma, if I step in and try and keep things going here?

'Definitely,' he replies. 'And, if you want some honesty from me, this website is really bad.'

'Is it?' I ask.

I mean, I know it looks bad, kind of old-fashioned, not very exciting. It seems to be doing its job though.

'There's so much wrong with it,' he tells me. 'For one, it isn't even responsive, so it won't scale down for users on mobile devices.'

I just stare at him for a second.

'All websites these days fit to whatever screen size they are being viewed on, and having to zoom in and out of the page to browse content really hampers the user experience,' Marco explains.

'I think that guy out there, the younger one...'

'John,' he reminds me.

'Yeah, John,' I continue. 'I think this is all his handiwork. But imagine, if the two of us started making changes, if I tackled the content, and you made the website better... it could be amazing.'

'Well, it couldn't be worse,' Marco says with a laugh.

'Plus, think about it, if we can get you some work here, then you can start saving. It will get your sister-in-law off your back,' I say. 'It must make money, right? Jessica said Emma was paid for it.'

'It's monetised,' he says. 'Not well – I could get it making more money, fast – but it has adverts on it, and I'll bet they sell ad space to local businesses and so on.'

'OK, follow my lead,' I say before heading back out into the main office.

'So, are we compromised?' Arthur jokes.

'I didn't even get that far,' Marco tells him. 'I was too distracted by your UI.'

I don't think Arthur knows what that means – I know I don't know what that means. It sounds almost funny.

'We're in luck, gents, because Marco here is going to work with us to revamp the site, make it more user friendly, make it work on mobiles, get more revenue coming in,' I tell them.

'And are you going to give him your wage, or pay him out of your own pocket?' Arthur asks, sounding rather ticked off.

'I'll work for free, to start with,' Marco says. 'I'm that confident I can turn this website around, but I'll wait until we get results.

Then you can pay me out of all the extra money coming in. Sound good?'

'John, what do you think?' I ask him.

He looks at me, then at Marco, then back to me.

'Well, if you vouch for him, and he'll work for free, then sure, why not?' he says, although he doesn't sound too happy about it either.

'OK, fab, well, we'll head back into my office and make a plan,' I say. 'And we'll take it from there.'

I give them both a huge smile as I clap my hands together, almost signalling an end to the conversation.

'I'm not sure they're happy,' Marco says once we're alone.

'They don't seem like the sort to be happy,' I reply. 'But they'll come around, once what you do starts working, *if* it starts working...'

'Oh, it will,' he tells me. 'You just focus on giving advice to other people, I'll take care of my end.'

'Which reminds me,' I start, sitting back down, clicking back to the agony-aunt emails. 'I'd better email your sister-in-law.'

'Thanks,' he says. 'And thanks for the job.'

I shrug my shoulders.

'We'd only be getting in trouble here if we were bored, right?' I say.

I know I've only known him a few days, but Marco seems a lot like me, kind of down on his luck, a bit of a wild card at times, but ultimately a good person.

What he needs right now is a good friend and, to be honest, so do I. And at least now I've got someone else in on my little secret. I know they say that the more people know a secret, the harder it is to keep, but I can't imagine Marco giving the game away. I'm probably doing a brilliant job of that all on my own.

15

Is it weird, that I'm excited about the website? I know, I probably have enough on my plate right now, and Emma did keep it from me, but only because she didn't want me finding out she was playing agony aunt to the whole village. Man, I can't believe it. We were always both so adamant we weren't going to grow up to be like Mum and yet here she is, living in the same house, giving out advice, with one nice child and one not so nice one.

Henry is lovely, just like his mum was at that age, such a sweet and thoughtful child, never putting a foot out of place (I don't blame him for the gaming all-nighter he pulled; that was me dropping the ball). Millie is... kissing a boy!

I slow the car down, keeping just enough distance between us and them, so that I can see them but they can't see us.

'Why are we stopping?' Henry asks.

I forget how many questions kids ask.

Henry had an afterschool club today – football practice. It has become clear, on the drive home, that Henry absolutely hates playing football, and going off what he's said today it sounds as if he's really bad at it, but that his dad likes him to go, so he goes.

I remember Mum making me go to ballet classes when I was younger. Emma loved them but I found them so boring. It was too stiff for me – and so straight-faced. I always preferred drama to dance, which my mum eventually said made sense, and so she let me quit ballet, but I never quite heard the end of it.

I find it hard thinking about my mum sometimes, my thoughts caught in a middle ground between what a nightmare she was and how she only had my best interests at heart. I would prefer it if she hadn't got her boobs out on TV though, even if it was for a good cause.

We were only just around the corner from home, when the most obnoxious car caught my eye. Lime green with matte black detail. Exhausts so big you could fit your feet in them. The sickening display of wealth you expect, driving around these parts, but while it was the car that caught my gaze, it was my niece stepping out of it, with a boy clearly much older than her, that kept it. And they're kissing, and I mean *really* kissing.

He's obviously dropping her off around the corner so that her parents don't realise she has a boyfriend. God, I wonder how old he is. He's a confusing mixture of clearly way too old for her, but he still looks like a kid. Still, he must be at least seventeen, to be driving that car, which was no doubt gifted to him via the bank of Mum and Dad.

Their lips finally part. Millie heads off on foot, in the direction of home, whereas the boy leaps into his car and speeds off in the other direction.

I feel parental rage – and for a child that isn't even mine. See, I was right, it was never worth getting knocked up for the money, because kids are nothing but trouble.

'What's wrong, Mum?' Henry asks from the back.

Oh, Henry. Sweet Henry. Even a cute kid like him would probably betray me one day. It will only be a matter of time before he's the one driving far too fast around these streets, harassing someone else's underage daughter.

'Everything's fine,' I tell him. 'Just… promise me you'll always be a good boy.'

Henry laughs.

'That's weird, Mum,' he says. 'But OK.'

I hover for just a few more minutes, giving Millie time to get home, because for some reason I find it embarrassing that I caught her out. Well, I'm not her mum, am I? I'm supposed to fill in for Emma, but I'm not supposed to be tackling big stuff like this, and, sure, I could tell Rich, but he's clearly got enough on his plate right now.

I'll just keep a very close eye on things and see how they play out. I'm definitely the person for the job; I was just like her when I was that age. Well, like a version of her who couldn't contour away her chubby cheeks or get the boy she liked to text her back.

At least it's finally the weekend tomorrow. No kids to get ready in the morning, no school run. I had a quick chat with Rich this morning and he said that, although he was pretty busy with work this weekend, moving forward he was going to try and be around more, to take the pressure off me as much as possible, which sounds great. In the meantime, I'll just look forward to my lie-in in the morning. I've definitely earned it.

16

The good news is that I absolutely do get a lie-in on a Saturday. The bad news is that I only get to lie in until 7 a.m. Big whoop, an extra half-hour. Honestly, I don't know how Emma keeps up this pace. When does she sleep?

As 'Wouldn't It Be Nice' boomed out of the speaker, just as it does every day, two things occurred to me. One: wouldn't it be nice if The Beach Boys *shut the fuck up*? Two: while I've heard the song a million times, I'd never really considered what it was about. But now that I've heard it so many times in a row, every day, I can't help but really hear the lyrics. A young couple in love, talking about the future. Ergh, young love. I really hope Millie knows what she's doing.

I couldn't get back to sleep so I went downstairs and made myself a coffee – because, honestly, now that I can work the damn machine I'm making barista-quality coffee – and now that I've drained every last drop I figure I might as well take advantage of that massive bath in the en suite while I've got some downtime.

As I head back upstairs, I notice Rich's office door is open. I peer inside and see that he's gone to work already. Wow, money really doesn't sleep, does it?

Curiosity gets the better of me, as I wonder whether or not the terrace is still the same. When I lived here this room was the guest room, and it had a little outdoor terrace, just outside a set of patio doors. The original doors have been swapped in favour of something more modern and energy efficient, but as I approach them, I can see that the terrace is still there, still the same. I guess I'm just surprised – I thought they would have turned it into a helipad or something. The house really doesn't have all that many original features left – if things don't match the new aesthetic, they're gone.

I let myself outside and take in the view of the back garden. It's massive, and completely private thanks to all the trees and bushes that grow around the perimeter. All the houses on this street are like that, tucked away behind a big gate and walls of trees. It could feel quite lonely here when I was a teen, if I was ever the only one home, especially at night. Well, a teen alone in a big house, completely hidden away from the outside world – that has all the makings of a horror movie, doesn't it?

It's funny, I used to use this terrace to sneak back in here, late at night. I knew that whoever was downstairs would hear me arrive home and head up the front stairs, so I figured out an alternative route in. It wasn't anything fancy, I'd just climb onto the patio furniture, up onto the pergola, then onto the terrace. My mum was a worrier, but only in the oddest ways, so rather than hide a key under a plant on the front doorstep in case of emergencies, she hid one up here, under a... oh my God, it's still there. The little decorative stone my mum used to hide the key under. I pick it up and turn it over, and there it is, the little silver key, attached to the stone with a blob of white tack. Wow, the apple really hasn't fallen far from the tree, has it?

I put it back where I found it, just as I used to, and head back inside.

Rich has a wall of floor-to-ceiling bookshelves in his office. There are so many books, you can safely call it a library – they're even sorted as they would be in a library. Fiction, sorted alphabetically, and by genre, then there's non-fiction, and there's even a little section for Mum's books, like a weird little shrine.

I scan their spines, gently running my fingertips across them as I refresh my memory. Whatever you thought about Auntie Angela, she certainly won't ever be forgotten. People still buy her books, even now, long after she stopped appearing on TV. More than anything, I think it's just so amazing that she's been able to leave something behind like this. She's made her mark on the world and, while we all might have moved on after her passing, we'll always have her books. I'd wonder what I'll leave behind when I die, but I already know the answer: three bags for life (the big ones though) and... wow, no, that's actually it. So that's a bunch of worn high-street clothes, some ancient GHDs that stink of scorched hair the second you turn them on, and my investment coat with the pink fur, that probably cost, oh, I don't know, maybe 5 per cent of what the coat I'm currently wearing of Emma's cost her.

There is one other thing though. As I near the end of the Auntie Angela section of the library, I notice two copies of her final book. She signed two copies, one for Emma and one for me, and gave them to us just before it was published.

One Last Thing...: Advice from a Dying Woman, unsurprisingly, is not something I fancied reading all that much. Well, it sounds like a drag anyway, and that's without it being written by *my* mum. Plus, I'm sure she found some last-minute way to embarrass me unnecessarily.

I pull out a copy and open it. On the title page it reads:

To Ella. Something to remember me by. Love Auntie Angela.

It's so strange, seeing her handwriting, it's like seeing a ghost.

When someone dies, they usually say you only remember the good stuff. With my mum, it's different; I find it hard to focus on anything but the bad, because that was what she left me with: one big, final act of forcing my independence on me. And I get it, she wanted me to turn out self-sufficient, but life isn't always that easy, is it? I know people have much rougher starts to life than I did, but I think that's half the problem. I had a comfortable life and then all of a sudden, I didn't, I was out on my own, and I've never quite been able to get myself sorted.

If I force myself to focus on the good times, they're not all that hard to find. I don't think things were as bad when we were younger, and I don't think Mum was quite so uptight. I don't remember how often – it felt like loads – but the three of us used to get in the car and drive to Blackpool for the day, and I still remember it being the most fun I ever had as a kid. We would walk around, for what seemed like hours, past all the gift shops, out to sea, around the Pleasure Beach – for what felt like miles and miles before we would finally stop for our much-needed fish and chips and one of those bottles of pop with the panda on, that I'm not even sure if you can buy any more. We would admire the illuminations before heading home in the dark. I would always get one of those deep pink sugar dummies, and I would suck away on one until my hands and face were sticky, before falling asleep in the car. All in all, an absolute dream day out for a kid.

Of course, the trips got fewer and fewer as we got older, and Mum got busier, and then cheap and cheerful days out in Blackpool weren't good enough. While an annual holiday in the Bahamas might sound like a dream as an adult, I always found beach holidays so boring when I was a kid. I would have swapped it for Blackpool in a heartbeat.

I take the book with me when I leave the room. Well, if I'm going to be dishing out advice on the village website, it might do me good, to see what my mum would have said – and then I'll write the opposite, I imagine. Hell, I might even try – or not try – some of it out for myself. Now that I'm here, and I'm bored, it finally feels like the right time to rip off the plaster and see what's inside my mum's final book.

'Hi, Mum,' Henry says cheerily.

I jump out of my skin, not expecting to find him standing just outside his bedroom door.

'Morning, kid,' I say. 'What are you doing here?'

'I was looking for you,' he says. 'To find out what we're doing today.'

'What we're doing today,' I repeat back to him, as though I know what he means by that.

Hang on minute – am I supposed to actually entertain the kids on a weekend?

'Are you going to play your game today?' I ask with an encouraging nod.

Henry looks puzzled.

'I thought I wasn't allowed,' he says. 'Because it's family time and we do fun stuff.'

Jesus Christ, does Emma not let the kid play video games on a weekend? I know I'm supposed to be pretending to be her, but that seems a bit tight. I'm not sure I can enforce that one.

'Do you want to play your game today?' I ask him.

'Maybe,' he says. 'After the fun stuff.'

OK, so I just need to think of some fun stuff to do with him for a bit, and then I'll sit him down with his Switch and something with loads of sugar in it, and then I can sit and read for a bit. I really, really need some chill time. I'm still not used to the pace of being a full-time mum.

I've got it!

'Have you ever been to Blackpool?' I ask Henry, because I'm a total fucking idiot. Luckily, he doesn't think anything of my question.

'No...'

'Shall we go today?' I ask.

'Is it fun?' he replies.

'It's tons of fun,' I tell him. 'You're going to love it.'

I think I'm going to as well. Blackpool is barely more than an hour's drive from here, although it always felt like so much longer when I was a kid, and not only will it be fun for Henry but it will be a real nostalgia hit for me – a good one, from good times. Everything else so far has been a sinking feeling in the depths of my stomach.

I knock on Millie's bedroom door.

'Hey, Millie... Millie, wake up... do you want to come to Blackpool for the day?' I ask.

'Mum, that's mortifying,' she calls back.

'Mum, that's mortifying,' I say quietly, mimicking her high-pitched voice.

Henry laughs.

'Ooh, would you like to invite Josh?' I ask him. 'We could see if Josh and his uncle Marco want to come with us?'

'Yeah!' he replies enthusiastically.

'OK, you get dressed, I'll make the call,' I say giddily.

It's hard to tell who is more excited about a day at Blackpool with their friend: Henry or me. At least I feel as if Marco is my friend – I've never had a hot friend before, so that's new. I thought he was just my accomplice, my partner in crime, but now that I'm inviting him for days at the seaside, sure, why not? Let's say we're friends.

I run up to my room to grab my phone, and to start getting ready. Perhaps I really am the person who is the most excited!

17

It is possible that, in an attempt to preserve some of my few happy family memories, I have been remembering Blackpool in a more favourable light than is probably accurate.

Henry and I got ready, put our things in the car and headed over to pick up Marco and Josh, who had a similar spring in their steps. The drive was actually quite pleasant – my childhood memories usually involved sitting in traffic for what felt like forever – with the boys nattering about all sorts in the back, and Marco and I chatting away in the front. There wasn't really any traffic, and we found a parking space (and it was even one I could fit the Range Rover into without having a panic attack) – it was shaping up to be a great day.

I should have known, the second we stepped out of the car, when it started raining, that it was a bad sign. Still, it's January, we knew we weren't going to be getting a tan, so we arrived wrapped up nice and warm in our coats. That said, I don't think we'll be bothering with walking on the beach at any point today – it's just too miserable.

I did wonder, as we walked along the street – which seemed to be lacking the frantic but fun frenzy I remembered being everywhere as a kid – whether or not the Pleasure Beach still runs as normal when it's raining. Can roller coasters run in the rain? I'm sure they can, otherwise you wouldn't be able to leave them outside, and, anyways, it's not even raining that heavily.

Turns out it doesn't matter because, obviously it being January, the Pleasure Beach is closed. I didn't stop to think about whether or not Blackpool might be, shall we say, dormant at this time of year, but of course it is.

Now that we've been here a little while, seeing the place through adult eyes, it has to be said, there's something inherently disappointing about Blackpool. I'm not actually surprised my mum stopped bringing us here. Firstly, it didn't actually seem all that easy, to see the sea when we first got here. It feels really touristy, and not in the good way – I'm sure it's great for a hen party, what with all the raunchy giftshop tat (most of it penis-shaped) about. I don't know if the donkeys work at this time of year but I'd probably burst into tears if I saw one because what always seemed like an adorable concept when I was younger probably hasn't aged well.

We're currently inside Pirate's Cave amusement arcade taking shelter from the rain. You know the type of place, an open-fronted space full of arcade games like penny machines and those electronic horse-racing games, things like that.

Marco and I are figuring out what we can actually do here for fun, given that most of the big stuff is closed for the season, while Henry and Josh charge around the arcade, which is also surprisingly empty. But while there might not be anyone here, the machines are alive and the club music is blaring out of the tired old speakers. It's like a ghost town – if the ghosts forgot to turn the electricity off.

'Mum, Mum,' Henry starts breathlessly, having just worn his

little legs out running over to me, to tell me something clearly very important to him. Sometimes it takes me a few seconds to realise he's talking to me when he says Mum. 'If you get enough tokens you can trade them for walkie-talkies. Can we try, can we try?'

'Of course, you can,' I say. Well, look at them, look how excited they are. They actually look as if they might be on the verge of having fun.

I take a £20 note from my purse and send them to the booth to get what they need to start playing.

'Are you any good at stuff like this?' I ask Marco once we're alone.

'No one is good at stuff like this,' he tells me with a smile. 'But if you were your sister, you'd probably say it was the taking part that counted... not that I think your sister would be here in the first place. To be honest, I don't think my brother and sister-in-law would either – you should have seen the look on their faces, when I told them what we were doing.'

'Snobs, the lot of them,' I joke. 'Unless they just know something we don't...'

'Like Blackpool being almost entirely closed in January?' Marco teases. 'I didn't really think about it either.'

I notice Henry and Josh heading back towards us with a plastic tub that, on closer inspection, is full of pennies.

'What have you got there?' Marco asks them.

'This is what she gave us,' Josh explains. 'We said we wanted to win the walkie-talkies.'

'Well, you can't do that in those God-awful penny machines,' Marco says, his brow furrowing angrily. 'Come on, let's go back.'

We march over to the booth angrily with our kids in tow. With each step I take, my boots stick to the carpet. I meaningfully tear them off the ground, one at a time as I walk, which must only make me look angrier.

'Hello, there's been some sort of mix-up,' Marco tells the women in the booth.

She's an older lady... I'd say she was in her seventies, but she might just have had a hard life, and be younger than that. Her face is scrunched up and her eyes dart between us casually. She takes a drag from the cigarette that I'm not even sure she's supposed to be smoking in here, before blowing smoke rings at us, which would be much more impressive if she wasn't sitting inside a metal cage, because the bars ruin it.

'No refunds,' she says in a raspy voice. Wow, not only is she a genuine villain but she's a living breathing (just about) advert for not smoking.

'The boys want to win the walkie-talkies,' Marco explains.

'You need tokens for that,' she says.

'Yeah, so they didn't want pennies,' Marco continues. 'They wanted pound coins or whatever.'

'You buy game tokens to play those games,' she explains.

'Wait, you buy tokens to play the games and you trade tokens to win the prizes?' I ask.

'Different tokens,' she says casually as she exhales more smoke.

I subtly edge the kids away from her a little more.

'So, you won't let us swap them? What are we supposed to do with all these pennies?' Marco asks. He seems kind of annoyed, but he's still so calm, as if it doesn't ultimately matter. I suppose it doesn't, the kids have parents who could buy them iPhones, never mind walkie-talkies, but it's the principle of the thing.

The woman just shrugs.

'OK, well, I guess we'll take £5 of game tokens,' he says plainly, which surprises me. He doesn't strike me as the kind of person who likes to be screwed over.

The woman's face twists into a smile as she takes his money. I can see why they call this place Pirate's Cave now: she's an absolute crook.

We shuffle off, back into the heart of the arcade.

'Why don't you lads go offload these pennies into the machines?' Marco suggests. 'See if you can get anything good out of them, OK? And while you do that, I'll try winning you some walkie-talkies.'

'OK,' they both say excitedly, almost in sync. They hurry over to a penny machine and begin dutifully feeding it coins. All you can win, other than a couple of different keyrings and some sweets, is more pennies. Honestly, these things are a total rip-off – in fact, this whole place is like one big scam. And we've given them £25 already. I'm sure walkie-talkies don't even cost that much.

'Do you really think you're going to win enough tokens with a fiver?' I ask him in disbelief as I follow him to a machine nearby, where we can still keep an eye on the kids.

'How do you feel about breaking the law?' he asks me, stopping dead in his tracks in front of a claw machine.

In the most Blackpool way imaginable, this claw machine is for over eighteens only, although I'm not sure how they police that, with only that little old lady in the money booth, and no one else seemingly around. I dread to think what's inside these anonymous prizes, hidden inside wrapping paper with the 'over eighteens only' symbol all over them.

'How do I feel about breaking the law?' I repeat back to him. 'Erm, surprisingly, that's more my sister's arena. Why?'

'This whole place is a scam,' he tells me. 'It's almost impossible to win anything good, because the machines are rigged to only pay out every so often. No one is winning anything because they're good at it.'

'So, the chances you'll win walkie-talkies with a fiver...'

'Slim to none,' he tells me. 'But not impossible... so... how do you feel about breaking the law?'

He's got a cheeky smile on his face, which I really like; it makes me feel excited. Marco feels like a lit firework that I'm just waiting to go off, to see what happens.

I smile at him.

'This feels like a Robin Hood type situation,' I reply, justifying whatever he's about to do. 'So... cautiously... do what you want to do.'

My permission makes him smile.

'Right, OK.' Marco claps his hands together, before glancing around the room to make sure no one is looking. 'Let me show you on this machine – and make sure I've still got the knack. Basically, if you know which buttons to punch, you can just put these things into maintenance mode. So, the claw is programmed to only work every so many times – a really small number. But once you do this...'

I watch Marco subtly fiddling with the machine before something seems to change with it.

'OK, have a go,' he tells me.

I smile as I nervously approach the machine. I've never been any good on these things – or so I thought. With a couple of pushes of the buttons I've got myself a prize!

'Oh my gosh,' I say quietly. 'That's amazing. Can I do another?'

'Sure,' he says. 'We need to get your £20 back somehow. While you play with that, I'm going to go work my magic on a different machine, get just enough for walkie-talkies, and then let's get out of this shit hole.'

'Sounds like a plan,' I say with a big grin.

I have a few more goes – it's even more addictive, when you know you'll win – before calling it a day at five prizes, which I quickly stash in my bag, reminding myself that they're strictly for over eighteens. I highly doubt I've made my money back, but at least it's something.

'How's it going, boys?' I ask Henry and Josh.

Their penny tub is running seriously low and it seems that even when they do manage to get some out, it takes far more than they've put in.

'I don't think you win anything from these,' Henry says. 'It seems like everything is stuck down.'

'I'm pretty sure it is,' I confirm. 'Come on, let's go find Marco.'

We eventually catch up with him on his way to the booth.

'I actually won more than we needed,' he whispers quietly. 'But I'm not trying to clear them out, I just want to get the boys their walkie-talkies.'

Marco absolutely fascinates me. His skill set really isn't something I've even encountered before – usually you only see hackers in corny action thrillers, which is where I learned the term 'hack the mainframe', which is probably why Marco was so amused when I said it. But while he might be able to hack into pretty much any system put in front of him, whether it's the latest operating system on a PC or a claw machine in Blackpool's least reputable arcade (of all the ones we walked past, we just had to walk into this one), he does only seem to use his powers for good reasons... or at least morally justifiable ones, like avenging scammed kids or making his employers pay what they owe. I just... I just can't figure him out. Is he a bad good guy or a good bad guy?

Marco strolls up to the booth and delicately places the strip of printed tokens on the counter in front of Blackpool's biggest super villain. He smooths them out with his hands, all smiles, before pointing out the walkie-talkies on the prize sheet next to her.

'We'll take the walkie-talkies, please,' he tells her.

The woman's twisted smile drops when she sees the tokens, but it quickly returns. She hobbles down off her stool and into the back room before returning. She takes the tokens and replaces them with a walkie-talkie – a single one.

'Oh, come on,' I blurt.

'That's the prize,' she says with a smirk. 'You want two, you need double the tokens.'

God, I can feel such an anger bubbling up inside me, making me so mad. I've been trying to keep a pretty Emma-authentic persona, but I want to go full-Ella right now.

'You know what,' I start, as I feel the words rushing to the tip of my tongue. They're angry, sweary, shouty words that I know I probably shouldn't say in front of the kids, but with the bad taste this woman has left in my mouth, my only option is to spit it all out.

'OK, we'll take another one,' Marco says casually, stopping me before I get into it with this vile woman. 'And... hmm... we'll take a couple of those giant Minions too.'

Marco slaps his pile of tokens down on the counter in front of her.

I know he said that he only wanted to use the tokens to get the walkie-talkies, but he's clearly just trying to teach this woman a lesson now. And she deserves it.

She hops down from her stool again, this time with less twisted delight, moving in near to slow motion as she retrieves a second walkie-talkie, which, surprise, surprise, is alone in the box she took the other one from. She also hands over the two life-sized Minions through a large hatch next to her. It's kind of like the ones they have in post offices, where only one side can be opened at a time. I suppose you do need to worry about your safety, and keep yourself securely tucked away behind metal bars, when you're ripping people off all day long.

Marco hands the walkie-talkies over to the boys (who are so excited they look as if they're going to explode) before handing me one of the Minions. He carries the other one himself, because they really are massive. I say they're life-sized, but I'd imagine they're much bigger than an actual Minion would be, if they were in real life. These things are nearly as big as the boys.

'Erm, do you like Minions?' I ask him as he walks out of the door, back into the rain.

'No, not at all,' he says. 'I just wanted to take something big from her. She needs reporting.'

'She really does,' I reply. 'Listen, thanks for all that. You definitely saved me from dropping a few F-bombs in front of the kids.'

'Ah, it was nothing,' he says casually. 'But you're welcome – I saw the shape your lips were making. I thought it was going to be worse than an F-bomb.'

He laughs. I think Marco might be having more fun than anyone.

'So, what's next, lads?' he asks them.

'I want to go here,' Henry says, holding up a flyer he must have grabbed from the arcade.

Marco takes it from him to have a look before turning to me.

'What do you reckon, shall we go to Anderson's Amazing Weird and Wonderful World?' he asks. 'It's a museum.'

'If the kids want to go to a museum, I say let's go,' I reply. 'I certainly never wanted to go to museums at their age.'

'OK, let's do it,' he says. 'But let's drop the Minions off at the car first, otherwise we'll have to pay admission for them too.'

'I have no idea where you're going to keep those in the long-term,' I say with a laugh as we head back in the direction of the car.

'One of them is yours,' he points out with a chuckle. 'Friend-ship Minions.'

He says this in a high-pitched, teenage-girl voice.

I cackle with laughter.

The only way I can think of to describe Marco is a handful – which is how people usually describe me. It's nice though, not being the only messy person in the room – or the only person running along the promenade in Blackpool, in the rain, clutching a giant Minion, as the case may be today.

It just goes to show that the days are what you make them. We might have picked the worst day to come here, at the least opportune time of year, but we're making our own fun now. Perhaps that's why I loved coming here so much as a kid, because it's easy to make the best of somewhere like this. It isn't a perfect beach in the Bahamas, it's a roller coaster of a place, no matter what time of year it is.

I really am so glad we came, and I'm so glad Marco came too. It wouldn't have been the same without him.

18

I've always struggled to believe the unbelievable.

Well, life hasn't been too cracking, so that doesn't exactly give me the feeling of someone watching over me, or karma seeing me right. Then there's the fact that I am the least Virgo-y Virgo (I'm not tidy or organised or patient), so that's got to be a load of crap, right? Statements like 'you often wonder if you have made the right decision' or 'you see the weaknesses in your personality' could apply to absolutely anyone, and be applied to absolutely any situation.

I think psychics work in a similar way – or at least I hope they do...

I don't know what I expected Anderson's Amazing Weird and Wonderful World to be, but I don't think any leaflet could have prepared me for what it actually was.

Weird? You bet. Wonderful? Erm... I'm not sure about that one. Imagine a cross between a fun house, a ghost train and a freak show and you're someone in the right area.

The place was divided into three sections: fun, future and

freaks – or, as I prefer to call them, the good, the bad and the ugly.

The fun section was fine, if not a little creepy at times. From optical illusions (which I loved) to the Room of Bears (literally a room full of creepy old stuffed toys, which I hated), yes, I suppose fun seems like a fair title.

The future section was a peculiar combination of technology and astrology – a jarring mixture, I'm sure you'll agree – with the star feature being the fortune-telling Mystic Molly, who looked very much like a cheap beach-side caricature of a fortune teller.

Mystic Molly would bestow a glimpse into the future upon anyone who passed her table, and when I passed her, she simply stared into my eyes and said: 'You're pretending to be someone you're not.' Of course, the boys thought nothing of it, they were too excited to get to the freak show, but it gave Marco a little chuckle, and after the split second of horror I felt at being exposed, it was amusing to me too – and very much just one of those broad statements that apply to absolutely everyone.

Then it was on to the freak show and the less said about that, the better. It was all models, or people in prosthetics, but it was completely disturbing. Needless to say, the boys loved it.

After that we went for fish and chips, which we ate while it got dark – and of course there are no illuminations at this time of year, so we just bought a bunch of sweets and then headed for the car. That's where we are now.

Henry and Josh are in the back of the car, eating overwhelmingly sugary-smelling sticks of rock that come with a sherbet dip, that Emma absolutely would not approve of – I know this because I know my sister, but also because of the look in Henry's eyes when I told him he could have it. He looked a combination of confused and excited, as if he were pulling a fast one. They are each holding a walkie-talkie –obviously they didn't come with batteries, but given that they almost came without a corresponding receiver, that's no surprise. Still, even though they're not working yet, the boys are clutching them proudly.

It's a dark drive back home but I'm buzzing from such a fun day, and Marco is keeping me on my toes, so I hardly mind. Usually I hate driving at night; there's something about the extra responsibility that makes me nervous. Of course, I've always driven piece-of-shit cars that break down if a slight breeze dares to brush by their bonnet, so that might have something to do with it.

'Hey, did you open those eighteens-only prizes we won?' Marco asks me in hushed tones as the boys chat away in the back.

'I didn't,' I say with a laugh. 'They're by your feet, in my hand-bag, if you want to have a look.'

Marco roots around in my bag until he finds the wrapped prizes.

'Well, these two are T-shirts,' he starts, sounding ever so slightly disappointed. 'We'll open those and see what's on them later, shall we?'

'Perhaps our Minions can wear them?' I suggest.

'Good shout,' he replies. 'This next one is... it's a sugar dummy—'

'I'll take it,' I interrupt quickly, memories of my childhood flooding back. 'Can I have that, please?'

'It's shaped like a... erm...'

Marco holds the horrendously detailed penis-shaped sugar dummy so that only I can see it.

'I'll still take it,' I say with a shrug of my shoulders. 'You can have whatever the other one is.'

'You dirty girl,' he teases. 'But OK, deal, that means I'm getting... a... erm... vibrating ring.'

I love how Marco is choosing his words, careful not to say anything that will make little ears prick up and tune in.

'Well, you'll find more use for that than me,' I reply.

'Newly single,' he reminds me.

'All the more reason,' I insist.

'Your dimples deepen when you're being cheeky,' he points out. 'It's cute.'

'Well, your dimples are on show 24-7, so what does that tell you?' I reply with a raised eyebrow.

He just smiles.

'You're a real mystery, you know,' I start bravely, double checking in the rear-view mirror that the boys are still finding us too boring to listen to. They're not paying attention at all; they're playing with some bit of tat puzzle game Marco bought them when we exited through Anderson's amazingly expensive gift shop.

'How so?' he replies.

'Well... you're obviously a tremendous geek,' I point out. 'Like, you should be living in your mum's box room, trolling people on the Internet. Not looking like Henry Cavill's stunt double and being all cool, going around teaching people lessons...'

'I mean, first of all, I'm living in my brother's spare room, so that's not too different, and I do get into the occasional Twitter spat, but don't we all?' he says. 'And anyway, you want to check your facts, because Henry Cavill is a PC nerd – and a gamer.'

'No way,' I scoff. 'The man is a god. There's no way Superman plays Call of Duty in his spare time.'

'Well done for naming a game, I suppose.' Marco chuckles. 'But honestly, he is, he builds PCs, he games – you shouldn't be so quick to prejudge.'

'Well, that's me told,' I say. 'I suppose next you'll be telling me that—'

'Mummy...' I hear Henry's voice from behind me. My Henry, obviously, not Henry Cavill, although I wouldn't be against that in theory.

'What's up, kid?' I reply.

'I'm going to... I think I'm going to be sick...' he replies, absolutely sounding like he's on the verge of chucking.

'Oh, crap, OK, what do I do?' I ask Marco.

'There's a petrol station coming up,' he says after a few taps of his phone. 'So, if you can just hold—'

The sound of Henry vomiting fills the car.

'Oh, God,' I blurt softly. 'Sorry, kid, I'm pulling in now.'

I'm just finding a parking space when I hear him throwing up again.

'Oh, that's Josh at it now,' Marco announces kind of casually.

I stop the car and hurry out. I help Henry out of the car while Marco gets Josh. Both boys are covered in purple puke.

I quickly pull Marco to one side.

'Oh my God, do we need to call an ambulance?' I ask, panicking. 'If they're both being sick, and it's *purple*.'

'Ella, relax,' Marco whispers, rubbing my shoulders. 'Josh has this thing where, if anyone throws up in front of him, if he sees sick, sometimes even if he just hears sounds like someone puking – he throws up. He's just really sensitive. And Henry threw up because he's eaten loads of junk, which he probably isn't used to, and they both threw up purple because of those massive purple slushes they had with their dinner, so just relax, OK?'

I puff air from my cheeks.

'Whew, you're right, OK,' I reply.

'Look at them,' Marco says, turning me to face the boys, who are laughing at each other's sick-covered clothes. 'See, they feel much better now they've puked.'

'They're still covered in it though,' I point out.

'Chuck me those T-shirts we won,' he suggests. 'I'll take them into the gents, get them cleaned up. We're not far from home anyway.'

'Thank you,' I say gratefully – of course it does leave me with the job of cleaning the car.

Remarkably, despite the car stinking of sick, I can't actually see any, so I wind down all the windows and leave it to air out a bit.

I plonk myself down on the kerb and meaningfully suck on my penis-shaped sugar dummy, hoping a sugar hit will make me feel better, but I possibly suck it a little too meaningfully, as a man in a Volvo drives ever so slowly past me. I wait until he's gone before having any more.

Eventually Marco returns, with a nine-year-old in each arm.

'You don't waste any time,' he jokes, nodding towards my sweet.

I shove it back in its packet and chuck it in the nearest bin.

As Marco places the boys down on the ground, I notice they're wearing matching 'Suck my Blackpool rock' T-shirts.

'They haven't noticed,' he whispers to me with a smile as he chucks a carrier bag full of vomit-stained clothes into the boot.

As we strap the boys back in, Henry yawns.

'Why don't you two snooze the rest of the way?' I suggest.

They don't take much convincing.

'Thanks for sorting that out,' I tell Marco quietly once we're back on our way.

'Ah, don't worry about it,' he says. 'My last trip to Blackpool ended exactly the same way for me.'

I laugh quietly.

I still don't know if Marco is a bad good guy or a good bad guy, but I don't suppose it matters. He's a good person, no matter whatever else he gets up to.

We drop Marco and Josh at their house before making the short journey home.

I lift Henry out of the car, although he is nine, and I'm nowhere near as strong as Marco, so I don't find it quite so easy.

'About today...' I start as we head for the front door.

'Today was the best,' Henry replies, his walkie-talkie clutched tightly in his hand. 'Thanks, Mum.'

'You're welcome, kid,' I reply, smiling to myself.

As long as the kids had fun, that's all that matters, but I now fully understand why my mum started taking us to the Bahamas instead.

19

Another weekday, another early morning start, another rude awakening by The Beach Boys, another failed attempt at getting Millie to eat any breakfast. It was cereal combos for Henry – and he's up to five different cereals now – so his sickness was short-lived.

I get changed before I head downstairs now, which means no more frantically getting dressed to take the kids to school in the few minutes before I need to set off, and the school run itself goes without a hitch, now I know which lane I'm supposed to stay in.

What's different today is that I have a meeting at Henry's school. A Parents' Association meeting about (do keep in mind I'm having to figure it out as it's happening) the fundraiser for the drama department.

Yes, I find it baffling too, that Emma and Rich pay so much money to send their kids to private school, but that they still need to hold fundraisers to pay for things. Of course, I don't mind too much, because the head of the drama department/deputy head of the school is chairing the meeting – Christian.

My good friend Jessica is here, of course, motor-mouth

herself, trying to hijack the meeting any chance she gets. Most of the mums and dads are keeping quiet – I get the feeling she's the queen bee, and that everyone is sort of scared of her. Even Christian seems to back down when Jessica wants to speak.

'So, we've got the outdoor quad and the main hall space,' Christian explains.

God, he's handsome. Even when he's talking about boring shit like this, it's hard not to start playing out hot-single-dad fantasies in my head. There's something about maturity that's so sexy, isn't there? Then again, maybe I just find the stability attractive because I usually only date men who let me down and mess me around.

'We'll have food and drinks,' he continues. 'A band, a dance floor – and I think Jessica wanted to make a suggestion for the theme.'

'Yes, I did,' she says, pulling herself to her feet to speak, yet again, even though there's only like ten of us here. 'So, as you all know, my ancestors are the famous Lord and Lady Darnbrocke, so I thought that might make a pleasant theme.'

'Wait, what?' I blurt.

Suddenly everyone's eyes are on me. I don't think that was a very Emma outburst.

'Emma, what's wrong?' she asks seriously.

'Sorry, I'm just confused. The theme is like, what, your gran and grandad?' I ask.

'Emma, you sound like a stroppy teenager,' she points out. 'Did they remove your filter when they gave you that midlife-crisis haircut?'

I notice Christian wince, just a little, at her words. Of course, no one says anything, they're all too scared. The room is so silent you could hear a pin drop. It's like a scene from a western.

'I'm just baffled by your non-theme,' I persist, because I'm not scared of her. 'How would it even work? What do we wear?'

'I mean, first of all, they're not my *gran and grandad*,' she says, mocking my voice. 'And we would wear period wear.'

'What's that, big knickers and sweatpants?' I joke. I get a few quiet laughs from around the room but Jessica has a face like thunder.

'I suppose you have a better idea,' Jessica says.

It's more of a statement than a question but I can't help but wonder how much Emma would want me to get involved in this. I'm sure the brief told me to just turn up to these things and smile and nod but...

'I'm thinking,' I start. 'If this is for the drama department, why don't we have a drama theme? Like musicals!'

'Emma, that's nasty, and tacky, and I won't plan it,' she tells me firmly. 'If that's what you want, but I won't facilitate it, and there's only a matter of weeks to go...'

'I'll do it,' I suggest. 'If everyone else likes the idea...'

I glance around the room at the few nervous smiles. It's as if people want to speak up but they daren't.

'Perhaps we could have an anonymous vote?' Christian suggests. 'Everyone write down which idea you prefer on a piece of paper and we'll go with the majority.'

'Sounds fair to me,' I say.

'OK, fine,' Jessica says, reluctantly taking a piece of paper and a pen from Christian.

Everyone folds up their paper and drops it into the cardboard box that Christian has found for the occasion. He takes them out one at a time before announcing the result.

'I'm really sorry, it's nine votes to one,' he announces.

'Ha!' Jessica cackles.

'No, it's nine votes *for* the musical theme,' he corrects her, and

I haven't seen a human that shade of purple since Henry puked that purple slushie down his front.

'Well, like I said, I'm not lowering myself,' she eventually comments, her eyes fixed on the ceiling.

'I meant what I said. I'll do it,' I say with a shrug.

'You'll do it?' she asks angrily, looking right at me now. 'You'll do all of it alone? Or are you going to make all these busy parents take on even more?'

I shrug again. How hard can it be?

'I'll help her,' Christian offers, quickly adding: 'If it's what the group want?'

'That's settled, then,' I say.

'OK, well, this was the final meeting, so if I don't see you before, and everyone knows what their individual jobs are, see you on the day for the event prep,' Christian says. 'Class dismissed.'

I hang back, until it's just the two of us in the meeting room. The second we're alone together Christian drops to his knees and bows down theatrically at my feet.

'Oh my God, Emma, what was that?' he asks.

'What?' I laugh.

'You, finally standing up to Jessica,' he says excitedly. 'You're a hero. Her theme sounded crap – yours actually sounds fun. We're actually going to have a fun fundraiser for once.'

Christian looks so excited and it only makes him all the more attractive.

'Thanks for saying you'll help,' I say.

'Hey, anything for the hero of the hour,' he replies, grabbing my hand to give it a playful, meaningful shake.

My hand is only in his for a second but, I swear, it sends a little tingle through my body.

'Do you want to go for lunch with me?' I blurt.

'What, me?' he replies.

'Yeah... you know, to talk about the fundraiser,' I say, back-tracking a little, because what the fuck am I doing asking him out for lunch?

'OK, sure,' he replies. 'That would be great. Does tomorrow suit you?'

As I make plans with Christian, I can't help but think about how this is not a very Emma thing to do, but I wasn't thinking like Emma when I asked him, I was thinking for myself.

'OK, well, I'll see you later,' he says.

'Yep, see you then,' I reply casually, but as I walk to my car, I can feel a big smile on my face. Oh, God, do I have a crush on a teacher?

There's no point worrying about it; it's just lunch, to talk about the fundraiser, and he thinks I'm Emma, and Emma is married, and blah blah blah, but still. I'm really looking forward to it. I just need to remember who I am... or who I'm pretending to be, anyway.

20

'I think I have a bit of a crush on one of Henry's teachers,' I blurt.

'Oh, God, that's kind of gross – which one?' Marco replies.

We're currently sitting on the sofa in the kitchen, watching daytime TV, and eating instant noodles, straight out of their plastic tubs, because when Marco asked me what I wanted for lunch, they were the first things that sprang to mind. Well, I have to make real food here, so my usual culinary favourites are severely lacking from my life.

'It's not gross. He's not *my* teacher,' I insist with a slightly embarrassed giggle. 'Whoops.'

A string of noodles slips from my fork and lands on my T-shirt. During the day, when no one else is around, I like to slip out of Emma's clothes and into my own comfy ones. Today I'm wearing my scruffy trackies and – mostly just to make Marco laugh – one of the smutty Blackpool T-shirts.

'*That's* gross,' he points out with a laugh. 'So, go on, which teacher? I feel like I've spent my life talking to teachers since I took on manny duties. They really want you to feel like you get your money's worth, don't they?'

I smile. It's nice to have a friend to confide in. I never thought I'd have someone here I could talk to like this.

'Mr Clegg,' I confess.

'Oh, Ella, no, come on,' Marco says. 'He's a drama dork.'

'Are we not grown adults now?' I remind him. 'And are you not a dork?'

'I'm a nerd, nerds are cool,' he points out.

'Sure, sure... anyway, I asked him out for lunch tomorrow,' I say.

Marco gasps.

'Ella Emma Cooper, you are a married woman,' he teases me, as though ticking me off with my full name is best done with my name and my sister's name mashed together.

'It's just to plan the fundraiser,' I tell him.

'Is that what the kids are calling it these days, you dirty girl?' he teases.

I lift the noodle off my top and lean over to drop it in his tub. Then I drink from mine, as if it's a cup, to get the last of it out.

'Erm...'

A voice snaps us from our conversation.

'Rich... hi, erm, what are you doing home?' I blurt guiltily, as though I were his actual wife, and he'd just walked in on me with another man.

'Can I have a quick word with you?' he asks me. 'In the hallway?'

'Yeah, sure,' I say.

As I head for the hall, I notice a look on Marco's face – sort of like when you were at school and another kid would be in trouble, and you'd want to laugh your head off, but you didn't want to get in trouble too, so it would be more like an amused grin.

'What's up, hubby?' I joke.

'*What's up?* What's *he* doing here?' Rich replies.

'Marco?' I reply. 'We're friends... look... he knows the truth.'

'He knows? How does he know?' Rich asks, panicked.

'Listen, don't worry, he rumbled me pretty early on, but now he's helping me, OK? It's going to be fine,' I insist.

'Ella, he's a criminal,' he tells me, in a somehow raised whisper.

'OK, first of all, he was never charged, so that's not strictly true,' I point out. 'Second of all, snobby much? Your wife is literally in prison right now.'

Rich places his head in his hands.

'Rich, seriously, he's all right, I promise,' I remind him.

'Regardless, this... this won't do,' he says.

'What?'

'You look like a student, you smell like a student, you're acting like a student,' he rants. 'You look nothing like Emma right now and, worse still, it's going to look weird, if you two are hanging around like that – people might think you're having an affair!'

'Rich, chill,' I insist. 'First of all, no one would ever think Emma was having an affair, because she obviously never ever would. Secondly, I promise you, I'm staying in character when it matters, OK?'

'This is really important to your sister, Ella,' he reminds me. God, he looks frazzled.

'I know, I know – anyway, what are you doing home from work at this time?' I ask him.

'I forgot my bag,' he tells me.

I notice a sports bag, over by the table where his phone is. He must have come back for it and then heard me and Marco joking around and decided to investigate.

I grab his bag and his phone.

'Listen, get back to work, don't worry about things here,' I insist, but as I hand over his phone for a split second the screen springs to life, and it's in his hand before I know it, but I could swear I saw a love-heart emoji on his screen.

'Erm... yeah, don't worry...' I continue, as I try to compose myself again. 'Marco is helping me. It's all going to be fine.'

'Yeah, all right, OK,' he says. 'Sorry. It's just hard.'

'I know,' I tell him, squeezing his shoulder reassuringly.

'OK, see you tonight,' he says as he slips his phone in his pocket.

'Yeah, see you later,' I tell him.

I head back to the sofa and plonk myself down next to Marco.

'Wow.' He laughs. 'You'd think he thought you were having an affair.'

'You would,' I reply.

And now I can't help but wonder if he might be...

21

I arrived for lunch with Christian in the most Emma outfit possible. Something a little more sensible than I've been opting for recently, but still stylish, none the less. It's going to be really hard going back to my high-street wardrobe when all this is done. By the time I get my inheritance, I'll probably blow the lot on clothes, and do you know what? I wouldn't even mind. I suppose thoughts like that are why I'm always skint.

We're at the cutest little café called Joan's, not too far from the school, which I kind of remember being here from my childhood.

It's like a proper café, if you know what I mean, not one of those quirky, modern ones with odd themes and meta names and seventy-eight different coffees to choose from.

A very smiley woman, in a navy-blue Joan's branded polo shirt, carries our food over towards us.

'Fantastic, I'm starving,' Christian says, almost excitely.

The woman places my cheese and pickle sandwich down in front of me. Next, she presents Christian with an omelette and the biggest bowl of curly fries I have ever seen in my life.

'There you go, Mr Clegg, my love,' she tells him.

'Ah, Shirley, you're a star,' he tells her. 'Thank you.'

'Are you a regular here?' I ask him once we're alone.

'It's embarrassing how often I eat here,' he says as he sprinkles pepper on his omelette. 'I'm trying to go for healthier options though.'

I imagine he's talking about his omelette but, erm... I just stare at the curly fries.

'I said trying.' He laughs. 'I don't ask for so many, that's just what they give me. They're such friendly ladies here.'

I notice Shirley smiling over at Christian. When her gaze meets mine her smile drops. Wow, is she jealous? It has to be that, unless perhaps Emma has been in here and given her a lecture about frying food in the past.

'How's your sandwich?' he asks me. 'I love the sandwiches here – proper old-fashioned sarnies. Not a panini in sight.'

'Yeah, it's really good,' I reply. 'Cheese and pickle is my favourite – it could have more pickle in it for me, to be honest.'

'Uh-oh,' he replies. 'If pop culture has taught me anything about women and pickles...'

'Oh, God, you don't think I'm pregnant because I'm looking fat too, do you?' I blurt.

'What? No! God, no!' he insists. 'Sorry, that was an ill-judged pickle joke. I had heard the rumours that you and Rich were trying for another though. I always wish I'd had more than one.'

Wow, it's astounding how personal information is passed around this village. I'm not surprised Emma was so desperate to keep her time at Her Majesty's pleasure out of the public domain.

'Well, no, not pregnant, and I can confidently tell you that we won't be trying any time soon,' I point out firmly, suddenly so awkward at the flicker of the suggestion of me and Rich having sex, even though, obviously, Christian thinks I'm Emma.

Instead I focus on the disappointment in Christian's voice, when he says he wishes he'd had more than one kid.

If this were a romcom, and I were a somewhat unsavoury leading lady, this would be about the time in the movie where I suggest to Christian that I'll give him another kid, if he helps me get my hands on my inheritance. We'd be in love by the end of the movie, so I hopefully wouldn't be too unlikeable for my actions, but we're about ten years too late for me to consider it (and ten years ago I probably felt as if I had all the time in the world). Even if I would consider it, which I really, really wouldn't – yep, even me – there's no point now. My birthday is nine months away. I'd probably have the birthday before the baby.

'At least you've got your little Ch-uhh, your little angel,' I reassure him.

Was his kid called Chad? For some reason I have Chad in my head.

'Yeah, I love Calvin, don't get me wrong,' he says.

Calvin! Not Chad! I really should be writing these down.

'He's just... he's so quiet, and I'm not sure he has any real friends at school. I think he finds it hard.'

'Oh, no,' I say. 'I totally feel for the kid. I didn't have many friends at school – and it carried on into secondary school for me.'

'Really?' he says, his eyebrows shooting up. 'You seem like the kind of girl who would have been really popular at school.'

Right, that makes sense, because he thinks I'm Emma, and Emma was the most popular girl in my year, and, no, that didn't help my social standing at all.

'Thanks, I think,' I reply with a smile.

'It's been a year or so, but you can tell he misses his mum,' he says. 'But she'd rather be living in London, with her *banker* boyfriend.'

He grits his teeth as he says the word 'banker', as though he wishes he were pronouncing it with a different letter.

'What kind of things does Calvin like?' I ask.

'He's really into nature. Loves being outside, fascinated by bugs. He's such a curious kid. Does Henry ever mention him?' he asks. 'They're in the same classes, so perhaps he notices things?'

Oh, OK, so Henry and Calvin are in the same year. In that case...

'Why don't the two of you come over for a play date?' I suggest, hoping a play date is a real thing people say and not just something I've picked up from American TV shows.

'What, really?' Christian says as his face comes back to life. 'Emma, that would be amazing. I think that's all he needs, just a chance to make some proper friends.'

'Yeah, no worries,' I say with a bat of my hand. 'Henry is always happy to have friends over, so...'

'Well, maybe we can use the time while they're playing to do some proper planning,' he suggests. 'Because we've just chatted this lunch away.'

I look at my watch.

'Oh my gosh, we have. It's just flown by,' I say. 'I'm supposed to be meeting Marco in ten minutes, to do some revamping of the village website.'

And I'm pretty sure Emma wouldn't ever be late.

'Marco...' Christian starts. 'Hmm, is that Joshua Mancini's uncle?'

'Yeah,' I reply – I didn't know his last name, but he's definitely Josh's uncle.

Christian scrunches up his face.

'Watch that one,' he says.

'Watch him?' I reply.

'Yeah, I've heard some rumours about him, sounds like a

shady tosser,' he replies. 'And he sent Joshua to school with an Easter egg in the first week of term.'

'God forbid,' I say with a laugh, quickly stopping as soon as I realise, he isn't kidding.

'Well, yeah, thanks, I'll watch my back,' I say, but I'm not going to cry if he gives me an Easter egg. It's not like the shops aren't selling them already.

'I tell you what, I'll give you my number,' Christian says. He searches for a pen in his pocket and writes it on one of the cheap serviettes. 'We have literally no life, at all, so just call us when you think is best to get the boys together, and then we'll talk about the fundraiser... which is just before half-term, remember. It will sneak up on us in no time.'

It certainly will, because I genuinely have no idea when half-term is. Will I even still be here then?

'OK, great, I'll give you a call. We'll put something in the diary,' I reply – something I've also heard on TV.

'See you next time, Shirley,' he says as we walk through the door. 'Excellent curly fries, as always.'

'And, I'll be seeing you soon too,' he says to me as he walks me to my car. 'Again, thank you so, so much for your offer. You don't know what it means to me.'

Christian pulls me close and hugs me. He squeezes tightly, just for a second, before quickly letting go of me and putting a few feet of distance between us. He looks at his feet, as if the reality of him hugging a parent has just set in, before he politely says goodbye and heads off towards the school.

I hate to say it, because I know I shouldn't say it – I shouldn't even be thinking it, but... it's true. I have a crush on Christian.

When he touched me just now, I felt a shiver down my back and heard a voice in my head that told me that a man like Christian is exactly the kind of man I need in my life. Someone normal

– but not perfect; I mean, he swears quite a lot, he eats shit, and his office is a genuine dump – but he's nothing like the hot messes I usually date.

If anyone is my usual type, it's Marco. Crashing with his family, jobless, chasing some ridiculous get-rich-quick dream, while possibly the police are chasing him. Sure, he's gorgeous, and a lot of fun to be around, but it also sounds like he's had his heart broken, and he's got a bit of a time-bomb vibe – which is usually how people describe me, which is all the more reason I need someone like Christian in my life. Someone sensible and stable – both qualities I've always lacked myself, and I've never found in a partner, or even a friend.

OK, how about I tell myself this: Christian is exactly the kind of person Emma would spend time with, and helping out a kid with no friends is probably a very Emma move, now at least – she didn't care too much how unpopular I was when I was at school.

I just need to forget the crush, forget how good Christian could be for me, and just get on with the job I came here to do.

Speaking of jobs, I'm going to be late to meet Marco if I don't set off now. I've got the work emails coming back through to Emma's phone now – it turns out she'd disabled her notifications – and I've been mentally planning all the things I'm going to do to make the website better, with Marco's help, of course.

I'm just going to focus on that for now, because I'm only meddling with the website to make it better, but otherwise I'm just supposed to be keeping Emma's life the same.

Potentially making it worse is absolutely not an option.

22

I don't know why I was expecting Marco to be workshy... I suppose it's the semi-slippery nature of the way he operates, and the big pay-offs rather than a steady wage, that tricked me into thinking he wasn't the type to sit around and put in the hard work. Turns out I had him all wrong.

Marco is currently showing me the new website – live – because he's been working on it at home, in his free time, for no money – and, wow, it looks amazing.

'The new design is really polished,' he explains as he navigates me around the site. 'It's the perfect balance of minimal design and punchy, visual calls to action, leading your eyes instantly to the most important bits of information.'

I don't completely understand what he's saying but it sounds good, and the website certainly looks good. And Marco seems so proud of his work, which is just so nice to see. He comes alive when he knows what he's talking about. He's already a pretty confident person anyway, but when it's his time to shine, it's as if a few extra light bulbs flick on, and it's ridiculously sexy... even if it is totally nerdy.

'You've done such an amazing job,' I tell him. 'The guys out there aren't going to be able to say a bad word about it.'

'There's more to do, too, that will make it run even better. SEO, finding better ways to monetise it... I'll crack on with it now, if you like?' he suggests.

'You're a dream,' I tell him. 'Thank you. I'm just about to submit my replies to some of the latest problem letters. It's funny, I found this book of my mum's – the last one she wrote before she died – and I've been searching it for answers to the questions sent in, and I just disagree with her on so many points.'

'Oh, really, like what?' he asks curiously.

'Well, like this one man who has written in, saying his son is acting up, because he feels like his parents are always breathing down his neck, and they're worried he's up to something... Going off my mum's advice, you should be in your kid's business as much as possible, they shouldn't have an ounce of privacy. And that totally checks out, because we weren't allowed a lock on the bathroom doors until we were well into our teens.'

'Weird,' he replies. 'So, what are you going to say?'

'I'm going to tell them to give him a bit of space – or at least appear to. He'll stop feeling so smothered and stop acting up, and if he is actually up to something, well, he'll get careless and they'll rumble him. It's win-win.'

'Wow, that's funny,' Marco says with a smile.

'What is?' I ask.

'That people with their lives the least together are actually the best at giving advice,' he points out.

Huh, I'd never thought about it like that, but it makes sense. I'd imagine, if I was a struggling single mum, with not much money to go around, watching *This Morning*, seeing my mum on there saying your kids should be eating freshly cooked meals every night, I'd probably just roll my eyes and change the channel.

'You're doing a better job than your sister,' he says. 'Your advice seems more well-rounded, like you look at things from more angles.'

'Thanks,' I reply. 'I'm not sure she knows what's going on in her own house, to be honest. Millie has an older boyfriend, that I'm sure Emma doesn't know about, because she didn't mention it, and... this is going to sound crazy... but I kind of think Rich is having an affair.'

'What? What makes you say that?' Marco replies.

'I don't know, just little things – like he's almost always out, like so, so much. Surely no one works that much? And he takes calls all the time, out of the room, which I guess could be work calls but then I noticed a love-heart emoji, I think in a message, on his phone screen.' I stop to take a breath. 'I don't know.'

'Look, don't worry too much about it,' Marco tells me as he heads for the door. 'Focus on your work. He's not your husband, it's not your problem, and, anyway, it was probably just an app notification.'

'That's true,' I reply. 'I didn't think of that.'

'Right, I'm going to get back to my temporary desk, as John keeps calling it, and crack on,' Marco says as he reaches out to open the office door.

'Great, I'll get back to tactfully telling people in their forties who want to sleep in separate beds from their spouses that that's probably not a good sign,' I reply.

'You don't share a bed with your husband, you hypocrite,' he teases.

'Get out of my office, and shut the door behind you,' I joke, with a faux authority that doesn't suit me.

The door is only closed for a second before there's a knock.

'Erm, yeah?' I call out.

'Emma, hi... can I come in?'

It's John, the one who thinks Marco is making a play for his job, and Jessica's poor bastard of a husband.

'Erm... yeah,' I say, which is basically the same thing I said before. I don't think my 'erms' and my 'yeahs' are very Emma-like.

'I've seen the new website... It's... it's actually looking really good. He's doing a good job,' he says, although he doesn't sound too happy about it.

'Yeah, I really like it,' I reply. 'I think it's going to make a big difference.'

'Yeah...' John sits on the side of my desk, facing away from me. He sighs heavily. 'Is he going to get my job?'

I do feel a bit sorry for him. Well, I know what it's like to lose my job, and I can't even begin to imagine what it's like being married to Jessica.

John is maybe in his early forties. He isn't a bad-looking fella, but you know in the movies, where a newly divorced woman has revenge sex with her husband's douchey friend, and instantly regrets it? John is the kind of guy they would cast as the friend.

I get up from my desk and place myself in front of John. I don't suppose comforting and reassuring people is my strong suit, not as I imagine it is Emma's, but I'll give it a go.

I keep John at arm's length, but I place a hand on his shoulder.

'John, your job is totally safe here,' I tell him. 'We still need you for keeping things updated, uploading the content and stuff like that.'

Do I sound like I know what I'm talking about? Because I'm trying *really hard* to sound like I know what I'm talking about.

'Really?' he asks. I can see already, on his face, that he's allowing himself to feel relieved.

'Yeah, definitely,' I say. 'Marco is only here on a temporary basis, to revamp and to make changes to the system. But it's still your gig. Just think of him as this super-amazing specialist.'

John's face tightens up again. So tight, in fact, I can see his muscles tense up down the sides of his neck.

'Are you fucking him?' he asks me.

'Uh…. Uh…'

Ironically these vaguely sexual-sounding noises are the only sounds I can get out. I'm totally floored.

'Are you fucking him?' John asks again, only slower this time.

'What?' I eventually spit out. 'No! Of course not! How can you even ask me that?'

I don't think he believes me.

How *can* he even ask me that? Who the fuck does he think he is? He's lucky I'm Emma right now or I'd slap him across the face for speaking to me like that.

Perhaps it's good for me, being Emma for a while, because my natural reaction to someone being gross and offensive and kind of aggressive might be to lash out, but while I'm being Emma it's teaching me to go about things differently. I need to defuse the situation.

He stares at me, clearly waiting for a 'better' answer.

'John, don't be silly,' I say reassuringly, daring to place my hand back on his shoulder. God, he must think I'm giving Marco special treatment because I'm sleeping with him or something. I suppose I get why he's mad, but, still, it seems like a bit much.

'Of course, I'm not sleeping with him,' I insist. 'I only have eyes for one man, and one man only.'

John finally allows himself to feel fully relieved, safe in the knowledge his job is secure, and that his boss isn't giving special treatment to the latest hot guy about the office.

'I thought so,' he says, but I hardly have a second to take in John's words before he's slamming me back against the wall, hard, pinning me against it with his body. In a split second he's got my wrists in his hands, pinned over my head, and I'm trying to tell him to get off me, but his lips are practically suctioned around mine, muffling my words.

John must only have me like this for a couple of seconds before – Emma behaviour be damned – I knee him in the balls.

'Emma, what the fuck?' John cries out as he drops to his knees.

'*Me* what the fuck?' I reply, nonsensically – you'll have to forgive me, I'm a little shaken up. 'What the fuck are *you* doing?'

'I thought that was what you wanted,' he says, still on his knees, holding his balls in cupped hands. 'I know after last time, you said it could never happen again, but when you said there was only one man for you, and you touched my arm, I thought you'd had a change of heart, that you wanted me again...'

Holy fucking shit. Emma was having an affair. Emma – amazing Emma – mum of the year, wife of the year, everything of the year Emma. An affair. With someone from work. I can't believe it. So *that's* why she didn't want me coming here.

'Oh... right... no... sorry,' I say. I don't really know what else to say. 'I love my husband, John. Anything else that happened was a mistake.'

It sounds as though Emma has already told him as much but – oh my God! I still can't believe it.

'Look, erm, I think I'm going to call it a day,' I tell him, grabbing my bag before stepping over him. 'You just take all the time you need in here, and we'll forget this ever happened, OK? And never talk about it again.'

'I think I love you,' he blurts. 'I know you said it had to stop, but then... you came back in here, all dressed up, and I thought it was for Marco's benefit and then I heard him say you and Rich were sleeping in separate beds and—'

'Let's just forget it,' I insist again. 'I love my husband. That's all that matters.'

I don't give John chance to reply. I make a play for the door.

'I'm going to call it a day,' I tell Marco as I pass him. 'I've got mum stuff to do, see you later.'

'Oh, OK, see you later,' he calls after me.

I hurry outside as quickly as possible. God, I am mortified. I feel like I did when we were kids, and Mum would tell an embarrassing story about Emma on TV, and someone would think it was about me and I would feel humiliated, even though I hadn't done anything wrong.

The cold January air feels good on my warm cheeks but I doubt it's doing much to take the inevitable redness away.

I can't believe John kissed me – I can't believe Emma kissed him.

I don't know what Emma and Rich's situation is, I don't know who is cheating on who, but I want no part of it. I might have dragged myself up, morally speaking, but I know that cheating is wrong. I've been cheated on before, and it's a shitty, shitty feeling. I could never do that to anyone.

I'm surprised at Emma, the dark horse. I didn't know she had it in her. Don't get me wrong, I'm not impressed at all, but it's of some comfort that she makes mistakes.

It sounds as if she's already nipped it in the bud, and it was kind of my fault things just kicked back off again, just a little, so I'll do my best to defuse things and then keep my head down. I suppose I'll have to tell her, when she gets out, but then she'll know that I know, and I really don't want that. Her image means so much to her.

I guess I'll cross that bridge when I come to it and, in the meantime, I'll try not to get kissed again.

23

I don't know how people are able to cheat, because I can hardly look Rich in the eye across the dinner table, and I haven't actually done anything wrong.

It's just me, Rich and Henry for dinner tonight. Millie sent me a Snapchat to say she wasn't coming, and that's literally all she said, no explanation, no time when she'll be home.

'You seem quiet,' Rich says.

'Oh, I'm fine,' I reply as I finish up my stew – and yes, I did make it myself. I'm getting pretty good at cooking now... well, following recipes, at least. 'It's just been a busy day.'

'I was thinking, on Saturday evening, why don't you go for a drink with some of your girlfriends?' Rich suggests. 'Millie is staying over at her friend's, and it's been ages since me and this one spent any time together.'

Henry smiles, excited to be spending time with his dad, before shovelling another forkful of dumpling into his mouth.

I wonder to myself, just for a second, if Rich might be trying to get rid of me, but I'm not sure how much he can get up to with

Henry around. Still, I would more than appreciate a night off, but to be honest I might just spend it sleeping. Sleep is the thing I miss the most.

'Sounds great,' I say. 'And speaking of fun things for Henry to do... I've got you a play date booked!'

'With who?' he asks.

'Calvin Clegg,' I reply, all smiles.

'No way, Mum,' Henry replies insistently.

'What? Why?' I ask.

'He's a weirdo,' he tells me.

'He's a nine-year-old,' I reply. 'You're all weirdos.'

Rich laughs.

'I don't want to play with him, Mum, please, he's so weird,' Henry persists. 'All he talks about is bugs.'

'I've seen you spend hours catching bugs,' I point out.

'On Animal Crossing, not *real* bugs,' he replies.

I suppose he has a point there.

'Henry, I didn't raise you to leave kids out, just because they're a bit weird, did—' I ask him, before turning to Rich. '*Did* I?'

'You certainly didn't,' he replies.

There's a knock at the door.

'I'll get it,' Rich says, placing his cutlery down, now that he's finished with dinner. 'Thanks for that, it was lovely.'

I'm a little taken aback by the thank you.

'You're welcome,' I tell him, before turning my attention back to Henry.

'Listen,' I start quietly. 'If you hang out with Calvin, only for an hour, I'll buy you any Switch game you want. How about that?'

Henry sighs. He can't resist.

'OK, fine,' he says, but he doesn't sound happy about it.

'Emma, it's for you,' Rich calls out.

I wander into the hall where I find Rich standing with Marco.

'Oh, hello,' I say.

'You forgot this,' he tells me, holding up my coat.

'I didn't even realise I'd forgotten it,' I say with a bemused laugh. I suppose I was quite warm when I left work in such a hurry.

Rich stares at us both for a second.

'I'm just popping upstairs, then I'm going to take Marty for a walk,' he tells me. Rich is used to saying Marty's name in hushed tones, so as not to trigger the Smarty. I'm getting there myself.

'OK,' I reply. 'Do you want to come in?'

'Erm, I've got to head back home,' Marco says, clearly stalling, as he watches Rich disappear upstairs. 'Hey, are you OK? You seemed a little freaked out earlier.'

'Oh my God, it's a long story,' I say quietly. 'I daren't tell you about it now – tomorrow?'

'OK, sure,' he whispers back. 'As long as you're OK. John looked like he was crying when he left your office.'

'I kneed him in the balls,' I whisper.

'You what?' Marco asks in disbelief, his voice suddenly at a louder than normal level.

'Shh,' I say quickly. 'I'll tell you properly tomorrow.'

I hear Rich walking down the stairs behind me so I quickly change the subject.

'Yes, I think that's a good shout, for the servers,' I say – no idea what I'm talking about there. I hope it sounds good.

It doesn't sound good to Marco; it amuses him though.

'OK, well, I'll do that with the servers,' he replies.

Rich stands between me and Marco, looking back and forth between the two of us before he pushes something into my hands.

'Ella,' he says quietly, but with an anger bubbling inside him. 'I appreciate you helping out, but you need to be more careful, carrying on with this one, leaving this on the bathroom floor. It's not on and I will kick you out before I'll let you set a bad example for Millie, do you understand?'

'Erm...' I glance down at what's in my hand. 'Yes, sorry, I'll be more careful.'

'You'd better,' he warns.

Rich puts Marty's lead on him, before storming out, slamming the door behind him.

'What is it?' Marco asks me once we're alone again.

'It's an empty pill packet,' I tell him.

'I suppose you can see why he's upset, with kids in the house,' Marco reasons. 'Bit harsh though.'

'I mean, it's very harsh, considering I didn't leave it there,' I reply.

'Who did?' he replies. 'Has someone been going through your things?'

'Marco, it's not mine – I'm not on the pill. It must be Millie's,' I say.

'Oh, shit,' he says slowly.

Shit indeed. What the hell am I meant to do now? I let Rich believe it was mine because I didn't want to get Millie in trouble, but is she only going to get herself in more trouble, if I don't talk to her about it?

'Are you going to say anything to her?' Marco asks.

'I don't know,' I reply. 'Fuck, I'm not ready to be a mum. I don't know what I'm supposed to say.'

'Seems like you're not the only one,' he replies. 'I'd talk to her, make sure she's OK.'

'Yeah... yeah, you're right, ergh. I used to hate having conversations like this with my mum – usually because she'd wind up talking about them on TV,' I admit.

'Well, you're not your mum, and you're not Emma, so it might just go OK,' he tells me. 'Anyway, I'll get going, see you tomorrow.'

'OK, see you then,' I say as I show him out.

'And good luck,' he tells me.

'Thanks,' I reply.

I'm going to need it...

24

Calvin Clegg is a weird kid.

I know, that's an awful thing to say about a nine-year-old, but I've spent time around Henry, and Josh, and they're exactly as you would expect them to be, but not Calvin. Calvin is different.

It's only been ten minutes since Christian and Calvin arrived at the house and I already feel terrible about asking Henry to do this, because I can already tell that they're not going to get on.

Calvin looks a lot like his dad – he also looks as if he's physically a part of him because he's been holding onto his hand nervously since they arrived. I tried to hold Henry's hand in Blackpool because it seemed like the right thing to do and he told me I was being embarrassing.

'Henry, why don't you show Calvin all of your bugs on Animal Crossing?' I suggest.

'They're not real bugs,' Calvin says. 'And they're not the right sizes. They're too big and too small.'

'It's just a game,' Henry reminds him with a sigh.

'Erm, OK, then,' Calvin says. 'I can show you my daddy.'

'Your daddy is right here,' I say with a laugh.

'My *other* daddy,' he says.

Oh, God, have I been barking up the wrong tree here? Because I feel like that would be such a me thing to do.

'He means his spider,' Christian says with an awkward laugh. 'It's in his backpack.'

'A r-real spider?' I say, trying not to show how petrified I am, but I bloody hate spiders.

Henry doesn't look impressed at all.

'It's OK, it's in a plastic container,' Christian reassures me.

I honestly don't think I'd feel safe unless he told me it was on fire in the back garden, then maybe the hairs on the back of my neck would stand down again, and I'd stop seeing things moving out of the corner of my eye. Just the mention of spiders gives me the creeps.

'Come on,' Henry says, leading Calvin over to the sofa.

'Shall we go sit in the lounge?' I suggest to Christian. 'So we can talk about the fundraiser?'

'Yes, let's do it,' he says.

'Go make yourself comfortable. I'll grab us a couple of coffees and head through,' I suggest.

I don't know if we're allowed to drink in the lounge – I'm not even sure we're supposed to sit in the lounge. I think it's more like a museum exhibit (in the Museum of Totally Typical 2020's Décor), but we need the peace and quiet to talk.

Look, I know what you're thinking, you're thinking I'm trying to get Christian alone because I fancy him, but that's not it. Sure, he seems like a dream on paper, and he's not bad to look at, and he's super charming but... I'm not stupid. He thinks I'm Emma. I am under no illusions, nothing is going to happen between the two of us, but I do really enjoy being around him, and I'm actually excited about this drama fundraiser – whatever it's for.

We sit and chat about the event – which I now know is on the evening of the Friday before the half-term break starts, which will be 12 February. With it being so close to Valentine's Day, we decided it might be fun to have a 'couples from musicals' theme – of course, if you're going to the event alone, it's absolutely fine to go as one half of a couple, so no one needs to feel left out.

'It's the closest thing I'll have to a Valentine's Day,' Christian jokes.

'Me too,' I reply with a little laugh, but then I notice the look on his face.

'You know, being all old and married and stuff,' I reason.

Have you seen that movie, *Freaky Friday*? I'm thinking specifically of the remake with Lindsay Lohan. You know how she and her mum wind up swapping bodies (as you do) and for most of the movie we see Jamie Lee Curtis's adult character with a teenager trapped inside her? That's what I feel like. I feel like a teenager in the body of a grown woman, completely out of her depth, trying her hardest to pass herself off as a real adult.

'Right,' Christian says with a laugh. 'So, who do you think you'll dress as?'

'We did a production of *Grease*, when I was in secondary school, and I was desperate to play Sandy,' I confess.

'Oh, were you into drama?' he says.

'Yeah, big time, it was my favourite subject,' I reply.

'So, did you get the part?' he asks curiously. 'You look like you'd make a great Sandy.'

'I was a strong contender,' I tell him truthfully. 'But I lost out on the part to another girl.'

'Oh no, so who did you play?' he asks.

'They said I was perfect for the part of Rizzo, which I tried not to take too much offence to – she's the best character in *Grease* anyway – but obviously Sandy is the lead, and gets to sing the most. So, I figured, OK, I can get on board with that, and I spent hours practising singing "There Are Worse Things I Could Do" in the mirror.'

'That's one of the strongest numbers in *Grease* anyway,' Christian says. 'Reckon you've still got it?'

'I didn't get it then,' I confess. 'There were... complications. It's not worth talking about.'

'Well, maybe you can be Sandy for this,' he suggests. 'I might even go as Danny, if I can get my hair to behave.'

I smile.

What actually happened was that the role of Sandy was basically mine – until Emma decided she wanted to try out for it too. And if Sandy was too pure to be Pink, then I was decidedly not pure enough to be Sandy. It was quickly suggested I'd make a good Rizzo, because of course it would be, but then they decided that because Emma and I are twins, it would be too confusing for the audience. I got shoved in the choir instead, so I was mostly off stage, apart from when they needed me for the background during the school dance scene. I resented every single move of that hand jive.

'So, you said you had a band in mind,' I say, moving things along.

'Yes, they're called The Sound of Musicals, and their speciality is performing covers of songs from musicals, so they'll be perfect,' he says. 'Did you know there are only two bands in the area who perform musical covers?'

'Only two?' I say with a laugh. 'Well, you'd better lock one in.'

'I'll get on it this evening,' he confirms.

Christian takes the lid off his pen to make more notes. The lid rolls off the coffee table and onto the floor.

'I'll get it,' I insist.

I get on the floor and feel around under there with my hand until I find it.

'Oh my God, do you have a lower-back tattoo?' Christian asks.

I reach behind myself to pull down my top, which must have lifted up when I bent over, before quickly jumping to my feet.

'Pretend you didn't see that,' I insist, embarrassed. 'When I was eighteen and rebellious, I thought a tramp stamp was the way to go. I regret it now but, you know, I don't really have to look at it.'

'How have I had you so wrong for all these years?' Christian asks with a smile. 'I hope you're not offended by this, but I thought you were just another uptight mum with a passion for the Parents' Association. You're not like that at all. I completely misjudged you.'

'Well, you know what people are like around here,' I say. 'They're not very accepting of teenage tattoos, random acts of defiance against the Parents' Association, and so on. And yet behind closed doors you just know they're all probably spilling dinner down their Dolce & Gabbana and cheating on their significant others.'

'Are those crimes that are of equal severity?' Christian asks with an amused grin.

'Probably, in these parts,' I reply. 'I'm just saying, no one is as squeaky clean as they make out they are.'

'Well, I've never seen any food on your clothes,' he points out. 'So maybe I'm just starting to learn that you're not as squeaky as you seem.'

'Maybe you are,' I reply with a cheeky smile.

We're interrupted by a scream coming from the kitchen. Oh, no, Henry, that poor kid. Now I feel even worse for making him hang out with Calvin. What on earth has happened?

We both make a dash for the kitchen, and as we get closer the crying gets louder, and now I feel even worse. Henry doesn't seem like the type to cry so it must be bad.

By the time we get to the boys I realise that Henry isn't crying at all – Calvin is.

Christian squats down beside him, rubbing his shoulders as he consoles him.

'What's the matter, mate?' he asks.

'It's him,' he sobs, pointing at Henry. 'He was trying to scare me.'

'I wasn't trying to scare him,' Henry insists. 'I was just telling him about Eaten Alive Alice, who had the bug inside her, and it ate its way out of her stomach like this.'

Henry mimes with his hands something not dissimilar to *that* scene from *Alien*.

'OK, OK,' I say, getting him to stop.

'I only told him because he likes bugs,' Henry continues.

'I don't think that was a bug, I think it was a sea creature of some kind,' I correct him – why do I correct him?

I look over at Christian, who is staring at me, clearly horrified too.

'Oh, it's just something we saw in a museum we went to at the weekend,' I say casually. 'A scientific display, about the effects of parasites.'

It wasn't at all, it was a gruesome scene of a woman with some kind of creature bursting out of her insides, but we might as well put a positive spin on it.

'I got so scared I dropped Daddy, and the tub opened up, and he ran under the TV,' Calvin sobs.

My eyebrows shoot up at the thought of a spider running free in the room. I spring up onto the sofa and tuck my legs under my body, pushing to the back of my mind the fact that spiders can climb.

'Oh, God, get rid of it,' I blurt.

'Don't get rid of Daddy,' Calvin screams. 'He needs to be back in his tub.'

'Don't worry, mate, I'll get him,' Christian reassures him. 'Under the TV, yeah?'

The TV is on the wall but there's a sleek white unit in front of it for things like the Sky box and Henry's games consoles. Christian gives it a shove – it looks bloody heavy though – moving it just enough to convince Daddy he should make a run for it. I feel a shiver run down my spine as he heads in my direction.

Daddy is a very questionable name for a spider, for so many reasons. First of all, I was expecting a daddy long legs, but no, it's one of those chunky house spiders with the thick legs. The only time I hear people use the term daddy to describe not-their-dad is in a kind of sexual way. And then there's the fact that Calvin clearly has issues since his mum left.

Oh, it's so gross. So, so gross, I just want it gone. I let out a girly little squeak, which Marty doesn't like at all, so he takes it upon himself to intervene, bounding over to the spider and smacking it with his paw, and with that one big smack, I can see from here, Daddy is dead.

Calvin screams again.

'He's dead, he's dead!'

Christian pulls Calvin close, trying to comfort him with a hug.

I get down from the sofa to grab Marty's collar and pull him away, lest he eat Daddy's curled-up remains.

'Oh, no, Calvin, he's not dead,' I lie. 'He's just sleeping. I just saw him moving, I think he's dreaming.'

'Really?' Calvin replies through his sobs.

'Yeah, totally. Christian, come check,' I insist.

Christian catches on to what I'm doing and does as he's told.

'Oh, yeah, mate, she's right,' he reassures his son. 'I'll pop him back in his tub and he'll be fine by morning. He probably just had a scare. Listen, go grab your coat from the hall while I say goodbye to Emma, then we'll get him home and get him comfortable, OK?'

'OK,' Calvin replies, wiping his snotty nose on his sleeve.

'Give him a hand, kid,' I prompt Henry, who reluctantly does as he's told. I think he's secretly finding this hilarious. I know I told him I'd buy him a Switch game for today, but I'm pretty sure he's earned at least two.

'Thanks for that quick thinking,' Christian tells me once we're alone.

'Oh, don't thank me,' I reply. 'I'm sorry my son traumatised your son, and that my dog murdered his pet spider.'

'Don't worry about it – do you know how many times I've replaced that spider?' he says with a smile. 'I'm not hugely fond of catching them, I find them kind of disgusting too, but we do these things for our kids, right?'

'Right,' I reply.

God, do you really have to? You'd never catch me catching a spider – not for anyone, even if my life depended on it!

'Well, I'll get that band booked, you practise your hand jive,' he tells me as he heads for the hall.

'Will do,' I reply.

'And I'll see you next week, for the spelling bee,' he says.

'You certainly will,' I reply. No idea what he's talking about.

I close the front door and manage to hold in my laughter until Christian and Calvin are in the car. But then I laugh and laugh and laugh – and Henry laughs too. Even Marty is barking. Well, I don't know what else to do but laugh; that was just so many kinds of messed up.

'You've earned that game, kid,' I tell Henry as I ruffle his hair. 'Just... promise me you'll never mention the freak stuff again, OK? I don't think everyone is as brave as you.'

'OK, Mum,' he says. 'Love you.'

'Love you too,' I call after him as he charges back into the kitchen, with Marty the spider slayer close by his side.

I stop in my tracks. I do love him. I really do. I've not gone mad – I know I'm not his mum – but, speaking as his auntie, I really, really do love him. And, do you know what? Maybe I would catch a spider for him – that's how much I love him.

I've not had much family around me for the longest time, and suddenly something inside me has switched on again, that unconditional love that fills your heart.

Huh. I wasn't expecting that to happen today. It feels good though.

25

Marty drags me down the driveway, eager to get going on his evening walk, even though we're, y'know, walking already. As far as Marty is concerned the walk doesn't actually start until we leave the grounds of the house.

He's suspicious at first, with it being dark out, but then he wags his tail when he realises it's Marco standing at the bottom of the driveway.

'I'm glad you're already here,' I admit. 'It's so dark, and so quiet out.'

'Oh, come on, you know there's no crime here,' he says. 'Maybe the occasional lawn growing a few millimetres too long for the local garden club to tolerate – but with that crime being punishable by death, no one takes the chance.'

I laugh.

'Marty murdered a pet spider today,' I tell him. 'Long story.'

'One long story at a time,' he says. 'I'm here for the work gossip.'

It feels so normal, to have someone to gossip about work with. I like it.

'Right, yeah, where do I begin?' I wonder out loud.

'Begin asap,' he replies excitedly. 'Do you know how long you've kept me in suspense?'

'Emma and John had some kind of affair,' I blurt.

'What? No!' he replies. 'Your Emma? Amazing Emma?'

I nod.

'I can't believe it either! I think they only kissed – I'm not sure they slept together, but still.'

'So, you kneed him in the balls because...'

'Because he pinned me to the wall and shoved his tongue down my throat,' I tell him with a little shudder. 'I think he thought my makeover was for his benefit, and he heard your comments about me and Rich not sleeping in the same bed, and I guess he ran with it. He actually thought I was shagging *you*.'

Marco pulls a face.

'Well, don't say it like that,' he says, unimpressed. 'Like it's something horrible. I'm considered attractive, in some cultures...'

'It's something horrible if it's Emma doing it,' I remind him.

'OK, I'll let you off,' he says with a smile. 'So, there's Emma's antics, your suspicions about Rich, Millie and her love life – is *everyone* at it but me?'

'And me,' I remind him.

'Am I starting to look attractive now?' he jokes.

I give him a playful shove.

'I haven't spoken to Millie yet,' I admit. 'I never really see her. I'm going to make sure I get to talk to her tomorrow, after school.'

'Yeah, sooner the better,' he says. 'Get it over with. You'll feel better once you hear her side of things.'

'Yeah, maybe, unless my fifteen-year-old niece is having sex,' I say. 'And I need to find a way to talk to her about it that doesn't make the idea of breaking the rules sound even more exciting. I'd do anything to break the rules when I was her age, but I was such a scary teen, no one wanted to sleep with me anyway.'

'Well, you're not scary now,' he tells me.

'Yeah, I don't know what my excuse is now,' I reply.

'Married,' he tells me. 'I'd cling on to that one.'

'Cheers,' I reply with a laugh. 'I've got the night off from being Emma on Saturday. Millie is staying at a friend's place and Rich is going to entertain Henry. I can't wait. I really need a break. This is exhausting.'

'It will be over before you know it,' he reassures me. 'Then you can go back to being yourself.'

It might sound silly, but, for the first time since I got here, I'm genuinely wondering about what actually happens when all this is over. Having an instant family, house, job, friends, responsibilities – I suppose I'm getting used to them. When all this is over, what do I have? Nothing, that's what. I'm really going to have to come up with a plan, but not tonight. Tonight, I need to work out how to talk to a teenager about the birds and the bees.

As soon as I'm back indoors I grab Mum's book and skim through the chapters on children. I've been keeping her book to hand, reading chapters when I have time, or occasionally just flicking through the pages to see her take on different issues.

I find it almost amusing, how hypocritical some of it is, because, while it might be excellent advice at times, it doesn't match up with the way we were raised.

Mum was somehow overly open about so many bodily issues and functions, but a total prude about sex. You would have thought giving us 'the birds and the bees' talk would be something she would have been hyped for but, if I remember right, she had the nanny give us booklets. I had to rely on school for sex ed, and we all know how lousy that was twenty years ago.

In her book, Mum talks about finding the balance between

treating your kids like they are children, but also speaking to them as if they're adults. At first this seems kind of ridiculous but, when I think about it, it makes sense. I should talk to Millie in an age-appropriate way, but I shouldn't baby her or talk down to her.

I wish Mum had talked to us like that – it certainly would have made her illness much easier to understand. It was almost as if it was taboo to talk about at times.

If I do one thing for Millie while I'm here, it should be talking this stuff through with her, and showing her that it's OK to talk about it. That way, if she does ever need any advice, she'll know she can go to her mum.

But just because it's the right thing to do, doesn't mean I'm looking forward to it...

26

Sitting outside the head teacher's office – Mrs Robinson is the head of Hammond Hall School – is something that feels like second nature to me. I used to do this all the time, back when I went to school here. They even have the same old wooden bench, fitted into a window seat across from Mrs Robinson's door, for people waiting to go in.

It was somewhat of a tradition, back when I was here, that you would scratch your name into the wood, if you were ever summoned to see the head, just as everyone else had done, for years and years.

It only takes me a few seconds of browsing to find my own name, even though it's getting pretty crowded now. I can't help but smile, even though I was only ever sitting here when I was in trouble. It makes my distant memories feel real, rather than like something I dreamt or saw on TV.

Today I'm here with Millie, who would probably be carving her own name into the wood with a drawing compass, if I wasn't here, and it wouldn't be very Emma of me to encourage her to do so, would it?

She isn't saying much, and the receptionist didn't say much on the phone when she called this morning, just that Mrs Robinson wanted to see me about Millie.

'Mrs Robinson was my head teacher when I came here,' I tell her.

'Yeah, you've said before,' she replies bluntly.

'Mrs Robinson will see you now,' a receptionist tells us. 'Go straight through.'

'OK, thanks,' I reply, but as I stand up my legs turn to jelly. God, that's weird; it's like muscle memory. I'm a grown woman – why does it still fill me with fear and dread, walking in there?

Mrs Robinson, who must have been the head teacher here for coming up to twenty years now, somehow doesn't look as if she's aged a day, but she must have. She can't have always looked this way.

Mrs Maggie Robinson is your classic private-school head-teacher type. Out of touch with practically everything – from her hairstyle (her hair is in the same low bun she has only ever appeared to wear it in) to her mentality (assuming she still vouches for abstinence as being the best and only way to go).

'Ah, Millie, Emma, come in, sit down,' she instructs.

I swear, everything in this room is exactly the same. The large wooden desk, the dark green curtains – even the floral teacup on her desk looks familiar, so familiar that, if you told me it was in the same cup, in the exact spot it was the last time I was in this room, I would totally believe you.

It's 11.30 a.m., just thirty minutes away from lunch time, so hopefully this thing won't go on much longer than that. That's the kind of thing I used to tell myself when I was sitting here, reassuring myself that I would only be chewed out for so long before it stopped. That's the great thing about school bells – whenever they go off, everyone has to spring to action, so no matter what you're doing, it stops. Bored in History? Just wait for the bell. Sick and tired of your aggressively insistent PE teacher forcing you to run into a high-jump bar again and again because 'you can do it and you will do it'? Just wait for the bell.

PE was one of many reasons why I found this school so archaic and barbaric while I was here. I would find excuse after excuse to try and get out of it. Not only was I bad at it, but it was so repetitive for the girls. Netball, hockey, badminton, athletics – that was it. We didn't get to do anything the boys got to do – and we had to do it in skirts. Mrs Jordan, my PE teacher, was especially awful. She managed to make the changing-room experience even worse than the lesson because she would line us up and have us walk naked through the showers one at a time. I'm not even sure she'd be able to get away with treating kids like that today – I didn't believe she should back then either. Protesting it was just one of the reasons I ended up outside Mrs Robinson's office.

'Today we need to talk about Millie's progress,' Mrs Robinson starts.

Oh, I know that look, those pursed lips and narrow eyes. That's her disappointed face. At least it's not her angry face. Perhaps she reserved that one just for me.

Mrs Robinson slides an iPad across her desk.

'As you can see from the chart,' she says, prompting me to pick up the iPad with a wave of her hand. I do as I'm told.

'Millie's progress last year was climbing quite quickly. She was applying herself in all subjects. She was a quiet, thoughtful student, no trouble at all, and then today... today she called Alex Partridge a...' Mrs Robinson checks her notes, '... a chauvinistic wanker.'

'Yeah, because he told everyone I was a slag,' Millie insists.

OK, two things: first of all, it will never not be funny to hear a teacher swear; I don't care if I'm thirty-four years old, that's still funny to me. Second of all, if he was calling her a slag, he was being a chauvinistic wanker.

'Obviously the swearing isn't ideal,' I say, as I imagine Emma would, but then I drift back into myself. 'But "slag" is such a derogatory name to call a young woman...'

Mrs Robinson raises an eyebrow. I look over to Millie, who is just staring at me in disbelief. I don't think she was expecting her mum to be on her side.

'Emma, you were a model student when you were here,' Mrs Robinson tells me. 'But your sister was one of the most disobedient children I have ever had the displeasure of dealing with, and Millie's behaviour is only reminding me of her.'

Oh, there it is, there's the angry face. Wow, she really does reserve it for me. Millie on the other hand, looks amused by this.

'Millie needs to focus on her exams, she needs to behave and she needs to keep her head down,' Mrs Robinson continues. 'A lack of concentration some days, swearing today – tomorrow she could be destroying a statue!'

Millie looks puzzled by this, but I know exactly what she's getting at.

'Well, don't worry, we'll have a chat about things today,' I assure Mrs Robinson. 'Everything from revision to how best to handle the patriarchy.'

'Millie, you need to change course,' Mrs Robinson tells her directly. 'You want to grow up to be like your mum, don't you?'

Millie just smiles politely. I can tell the last thing she wants is to grow up to be like Emma.

'OK, you can go,' she tells us. 'But think about what I said.'

I don't know who wants to get out the fastest – me or Millie.

I've left Marco, who tagged along for the ride, waiting in the car for me, but with ten minutes to spare, I decide to try and talk to Millie now, as we make our way through the school.

'Listen, I understand why you called that boy what you called him, but you have to play by the rules here,' I tell her. 'Just knuckle down, try your best, get out of here and then you can try and change the world.'

'Mum, he called me a slag,' she protests.

'Yeah, and that's awful,' I tell her. 'And he deserved to be called what you called him, but calling him that won't help him to change, it will only hurt you. He's a stupid boy who's going to need to change his attitude if he ever wants a girlfriend. You're a smart young woman who can make a difference, in the right setting, so pass your exams and get out into the world where you can make changes, with the strongest possible hand.'

Millie has a bemused smile on her face.

'Erm... OK, Mum,' she says with a laugh. 'That makes sense.'

Wow, it does, doesn't it? When I'm totally myself, or totally Emma, I never seem to get things quite right, but when I dig into both our traits, I find balance. Emma would probably tell Millie to cut it out, I'd probably tell her to call him worse next time but, with the balance, my advice seems pretty spot on. That really is exactly what she should do.

'Thanks for not shouting at me,' she says.

'Well, shouting never achieves anything,' I reply. 'It certainly never got through to your Auntie Ella.'

'Was she really that bad?' she asks curiously. 'I know sometimes when you tell me off, you warn me I'll end up just like her, but—'

'Your auntie was misunderstood,' I tell her, biting my tongue before I say much else. I cannot believe Emma says that to her! 'Listen, while I've got you...'

Now feels like a good time to bring up the pill packet, because this is the softest and most talkative I've seen Millie so far.

'I found your pill packet on the floor the other day.'

'Shit,' she whispers under her breath.

I hesitate, wondering what to say next, but Millie speaks first.

'I'll be more careful,' she says. 'Thanks for not telling Dad. He'd never understand that they're for my period.'

When we were younger, I remember Emma taking the pill as a teenager, because she had quite difficult periods, so Mum took her to the doctor and that's what they thought was best. Suddenly it makes sense. That's why she's on it – and Emma knows about it. It's only Rich who doesn't know and, to be fair, you wouldn't want your dad knowing stuff like that, would you? Men can be so weird about periods.

'Yeah, no worries,' I tell her, right as the lunch bell goes off. 'OK, go have a good day, and just do your best, OK?'

'OK, sure,' she says. 'See you later.'

'Hug?' I suggest.

'Be cool, Mum,' she insists awkwardly as she walks away.

As I head back to the car, where I left Marco happily on his heated seat, listening to music through the car stereo, I feel really happy with myself.

'You're smiling,' he tells me. 'Was she not in trouble?'

'She was, but it's fine,' I tell him. 'I really feel like I got through to her. She listened to me. I honestly think she paid attention and she'll be better now. And Emma already knew she was on the pill – it's a period thing, not a sex thing – so there's no crisis there.'

'Well, that's good,' he says. 'Great, in fact. So, how did you find going back into your old school?'

'I certainly made a lasting impression on the head teacher, that's for sure,' I say with a laugh. 'She brought my name up.

Cited me as a bad example. In fact... you see that statue over there?'

I point out the statue of an old man – Mr Hammond, who was the head teacher before Mrs Robinson took over. He did a lot for the school, before he retired, so they had a statue of him erected out in the car park.

'Someone removed a hand from the statue,' I tell Marco. 'And Mrs Robinson has always been so convinced it was me. She brought it up today.'

Marco gasps theatrically.

'Ella, are you telling me that you vandalised a statue?'

'I am absolutely not telling you that,' I insist. 'We'd better get going to work, we've got so much to be getting on with... but can you work in my office with me today, please? Just in case John comes in.'

'Of course,' he replies. 'He's probably still icing his balls under his desk. I still can't believe you did that.'

I feel bad, but only for a second.

'He literally *forced himself* on me,' I stress. 'Even if I were Emma, he never gave her a chance to object. I don't think it was ill intended, just completely misjudged.'

'Just because I can't believe it, doesn't mean I don't agree with what you did,' he says. 'Now, come on, let's get to work so you can dish out more advice while you're on fire.'

I really am on fire, aren't I? I feel like I've found a sweet spot, between mine and Emma's lives, and somehow, I'm just happy here. Suddenly, I feel as though I have a purpose, a reason to get up on a morning – I'm making a difference. I've gone from ticking along to being excited about what's coming up, and I absolutely love it.

27

I think one of the most fun things about being Emma is that things crop up that I have absolutely no idea about.

Someone will say something that, if I were the real Emma, I would know exactly what they were talking about, so I have to improvise.

Take this morning, for example. A woman I have never laid eyes on in my life knocked on the door, while I was chilling at home with Marco, and handed me a sealed jar.

'Hello, darling, sorry I can't stop,' she said, leaning forward to air kiss me on each side. 'But here's Herman, as promised, see you later.'

And with that she dashed off.

I looked down at the jar containing Herman with absolutely no idea what was going on and wandered back into the kitchen with it.

'I think I've just been given the remains of someone or something called Herman...' I said, my face scrunched up with disgust.

I placed the jar down on the worktop and washed my hands.

'Oh, God, not Herman,' Marco replied. 'That thing is a curse. I'm sick to death of mine.'

It turns out Herman is a sort of baked version of a chain letter. It's a whole long and complicated thing, where you tend this mixture that just sits on the worktop and it bubbles up to the surface until you stir it, and you do it for ten days, and then something like you give nine blobs of it to other people before baking the last blob, which apparently makes a cake. A Herman the German Friendship Cake. Honestly, I can't think of anything else more ridiculously suited to the locals here.

Another example is when people say things to me like 'see you at the spelling bee', as Christian did. The spelling bee? Is that an actual spelling bee? Is it a trendy new nightclub? It's so exciting, having no idea.

It was less exciting learning that, yes, it is just a spelling competition that some kids from Henry's school were taking part in, and Emma agreed to chaperone.

I couldn't think of anything more boring to do with my Friday evening than travel to a hotel in Manchester and watch a bunch of kids successfully spelling words I probably couldn't spell myself. Hanging out with Marco and Josh – who are looking after Henry – is more my scene. At least Christian was there too, so I've mostly just been having fun hanging out with him, getting to know each other better, talking about the upcoming fundraiser.

We're at The Prestige Hotel in Manchester city centre. It's a gorgeous place, in an old Victorian listed building, with impossibly high ceilings and big windows. They're currently renovating the place, a bit at a time, but you can definitely see where they've been. It's going to be one hell of a place when it's finished.

The spelling bee, which went ahead without a H-I-T-C-H, was fine, even if our team didn't win.

We're currently all assembled in the large lobby, doing a headcount, getting our ducklings in a row before we all get back onboard the minibus.

There's a woman – a teacher – whose name I haven't managed to catch, because presumably I should know it already, taking the lead. Once she has the kids lined up, she gestures for me and Christian to pop over to one side with her.

'So, because Ms Bird and Mr Maxwell brought the late child along in a taxi, we're a couple of seats short on the bus,' she explains. 'So, two lucky chaperones get to take a taxi home – so if you fancy a break from the kids? You've been with them all day.'

This seems like it's mostly for Christian's benefit, and it's just another example of women seemingly giving him special treatment, because he's handsome and charming. I don't mind though, I'm happy to lap up the perks.

'Sure,' I say, perhaps a little too quickly. To be honest, I hated being on the bus with the kids; it was like being trapped inside a headache.

'I'm happy to do that too,' Christian replies.

'Great, the school will reimburse you, in the usual way,' she tells him. 'I suppose I'll see you Monday.'

'OK, Laura, see you then,' he replies.

Laura. I'll try to remember that name, with all the other names. It would just be nice to be better with names, that's all, because at the moment the second I hear them, I forget them. I'm sure that makes me sound self-involved, but I think it's a pressure thing: I know I'm meeting someone, and that I need to absorb their name, and so it makes me balls it up.

'Thank God for that,' Christian says when we're alone. 'I thought I was going to have to listen to a bunch of tone-deaf kids singing shit songs from TikTok all the way home.'

I smile. Teachers swearing, man. It does it every time.

'Me too,' I reply. 'Shall I find us a taxi?'

'Yes... unless you want to pop upstairs for a drink?' Christian suggests. 'I'm sure we shouldn't but we're off the clock now, and they've got a rooftop bar...'

I shouldn't say yes, should I? It's just a drink, but still.

'Unless you think it's a bad idea,' he backtracks. 'Sorry, I shouldn't have said anything.'

'No, no.' I feel bad now. 'That would be lovely, let's do it.'

'Yeah?' he asks with a smile.

'Yeah, sure,' I reply.

I'm not sure though, but it's just a drink, right? Sometimes I wish things like horoscopes and that were real, because I could really do with the universe giving me a sign right now.

'I'm really looking forward to the fundraiser,' he tells me as we head for one of the lifts. 'And I think I've decided who I'm going to dress up as.'

'Ooh, so have I,' I reply excitedly. 'I'm going to be bad girl Sandy – finally!'

'I would have thought you were more of a good girl Sandy,' he points out. 'But that's great. I think I'm going to be Danny – I bought a leather jacket years ago that I've always thought I was too old for. This might be my one chance to wear it.'

I laugh as we step into the lift.

'That makes perfect sense,' I tell him. 'I'm going to have to shop for my outfit.'

Even with the sexy designer clothes Emma never wears, I definitely didn't see a pair of leather pants in her wardrobe and, believe me, I've been through it a bunch of times now.

'Well, I'll get the drinks in, then maybe we can—'

The lift grinds to a halt, flinging me into Christian's arms a split second before everything goes still and we're plunged into darkness.

Thank you, universe. But could you not have done this before I got in the lift?

28

I take off my sheer jumper to reveal my silk cream camisole before unzipping my boots. I brush the sweat from my brow with the back of my hand. I had no idea things were going to get quite so steamy.

They're steamy because, it turns out, when you get stuck in a lift, inside the lift gets absolutely roasting – well, this one has at least. Perhaps it's being in a small metal box in the heart of the hotel, with a double dose of claustrophobia thrown in for good measure, but we're both boiling. The emergency lights are on, so we're no longer in total darkness, but they're more like candle-light than light-light. It would be kind of romantic if we were a couple and if we were, y'know, *not trapped in a lift*.

Christian undoes the top two buttons of his shirt.

'I don't really rate the sauna at this hotel, do you?' he jokes.

'It's bit small for my liking,' I reply, forcing a smile. 'Did the person on the phone not say how long they thought it would take?'

'No, sorry,' he says. 'All they said was the lift was out of order, there should have been a sign, someone will be here to get it moving again asap.'

'Oh, boy,' I say in a voice that sounds a little as if someone is standing on my throat.

'You OK?' Christian asks.

'I was today years old when I realised I'm claustrophobic,' I joke. 'I'm not liking this at all.'

'Hey, come on, don't worry, it's going to be fine,' he tells me, scooting over to my side of the lift, to sit on the floor next to me.

Christian wraps a reassuring arm around me.

'Let's talk about the fundraiser,' he says. 'Let's talk decorations. I have endless schoolchildren and an army of crafty mums desperate to get started.'

'OK, OK,' I say, getting my head in the game. 'We should have replica props from different musicals,' I suggest. 'Like the toilet-paper sculpture from the school dance in *Grease*.'

'Giant cans of hairspray from *Hairspray*,' he adds.

'The radio tower from *Rocky Horror* – that would look cool,' I say, relaxing a little. 'You know, if this wasn't a school event, I'd definitely be dressing up as someone from *Rocky Horror*. Magenta or Columbia.'

'Emma, seriously?' Christian replies with a laugh. 'Where have you been hiding this side of yourself? I like it!'

It's on the tip of my tongue to say: 'I kicked her out when my mum died' but it wouldn't make much sense to him anyway.

'I'm really enjoying getting to know you too,' I tell him.

The lift makes some sort of mechanical noise, only for a few seconds, but the drama queen in me thinks I'm about to plunge to my death, so I grab a tight hold of Christian's arm.

'Shh, shh, it's OK,' he tells me, stroking my cheek with the hand I'm not currently cutting off his blood supply to.

'I think my life just flashed before my eyes,' I tell him breathlessly.

'And were you happy with it?' he asks.

'No,' I admit.

Me breaking character is enough to make Christian pause exactly where he is, his hand still on my face as he looks into my eyes. Is he... is he leaning in? If he is, it's ever so slightly, just enough to give me an opening, for me to take the lead.

Right on cue, before I have time to worry about what I should do, the lift lights come back on and we're moving.

We let go of each other and quickly scramble for our discarded clothes and shoes as we descend, but the lift doors open in Reception before we've had chance to put them back on. Of course, the fact that we're putting them on only makes us look shady, even though nothing happened.

Oh, for fuck's sake, the actual fire brigade is here, and I swear these ones are even younger than the ones from my flat fire.

'Everything OK?' one of them asks with a cheeky smile.

'It was very hot in there,' I reply, pushing past him to head outside and get some air.

'Changed your mind about that drink, then?' Christian jokes.

'Yeah, I reckon it's probably time for us to go home, don't you?' I say, suddenly feeling a little awkward.

'OK, I'll book our taxi.'

Christian wanders off to a quieter spot to call us a taxi.

I feel even more rattled now than I did when we were trapped in the lift because, is it me, or were we having a moment then? Because I am absolutely not allowed to have moments and now, I don't know what I'm supposed to do.

29

Tonight is my first night off from being Emma and it could not have come at a better time.

While Rich's suggestion that I 'go for a drink with my girlfriends' might have sounded great in theory, I have to admit, I really, *really* don't like Emma's friends, and I don't feel as if she has all that much to do with them anyway. I never hear from them, and there's never anything in the diary. It certainly wouldn't have felt like a night off.

The only friend I have here (unless you count Christian, which I'm not, because I'm avoiding him) is Marco, and he jumped at the chance to do something fun.

I suggested we go to one of the cute little wine bars in the heart of the village, because I've been eyeing them up every time I've driven past them, but Marco had two thoughts about this. One was that it might look suspicious, just the two of us going for a drink together on a Saturday night, and the other was that going to a wine bar isn't how you let your hair down. Sure, it's how the Yummy Mummy Mafia do it – a few cheeky gins while him indoors minds the kids – but he says that's not very 'us' at all, and what I need right now is to be myself.

He's right, I do need to be myself, even if it's just for one night, because I'm in serious danger of getting lost in Emma's life.

Take Christian, for example. He's this great guy, we've hit it off, he's exactly the kind of guy I should be with. And, best of all, he seems as if he likes me – *really* likes me – but he doesn't really, does he? He thinks I'm Emma, so he likes Emma, but the version of Emma I've created, so what the hell does that all mean?

When I was younger – and not quite old enough to go out drinking – there was only one place to go: Gloria's.

Gloria's was a nightclub on the outskirts of the nearest town – and our only nightclub for miles, without trekking into Manchester, but as the quality of the club goes up, so does their adherence to the law.

So, Gloria's was the only option for a good night out, but it was kind of a shit hole. It was also a seventies-themed place, so it was fresh out of a scene from *Saturday Night Fever*. It sort of worked though, if you liked disco music, and if you could get into the spirit of dressing up it would be all the more fun. I might not have had many friends at school but in that last year before I moved away, Gloria's was my escape. I made friends with a couple of girls, who I would share taxis back and forth with, but when I was there I didn't even mind spending time on my own. I would drink and dance and try and forget about everything going on at home. Especially when things got bad with Mum.

Well, would you believe it? It turns out Gloria's is still there, still the same, still clearly serving the same purpose. Being such a niche place, it's still mostly used by young people looking for somewhere to drink, illicit meetings (you can spot the shifty-looking couples wearing weddings rings that were probably given to them by someone else, from a mile away), and somewhere to just completely let loose.

Because the playlist hasn't changed since the place opened (I sometimes wonder if it opened in the seventies and just decided to stay the way it was) it's the same songs playing, many of which have dance routines, so by the time I was a regular I knew my Hustle from my Night Fever and both were perfect. Being here now, after all these years, seeing people doing the same old dance routines, is like being wrapped up in a warm blanket where nothing bad can happen.

The main room is large, with an old-school illuminated dance floor at its heart, and a huge disco ball hanging above it. The walls that surround the dancefloor, and all around the bar, are covered in sparkly stuff, and the ceiling is a mess of those multicoloured disco lights that twirl around, so light bounces off pretty much every available surface. The biggest nostalgia hit of all is the smell of the smoke machine – it smells exactly how I remember it smelling, even though I haven't thought about this place in years.

I was so excited when I was getting ready. I rummaged through Emma's wardrobe to find the perfect outfit – a short red Bardot dress, that I can't believe my sister owns, and a pair of black heels. I even took the time to learn how to curl my hair with that Dyson curling thing she has, that basically sucks your hair around it. That was a learning curve. Finally, I caked on some make-up and covered myself up in a big coat, ready to sneak out, just like I used to when I was a kid. Well, I wasn't sure Rich would sign off on me going to a club with Marco, and it's always easier to get forgiveness than permission, right?

Marco looks amazing. He's wearing a pair of tight-fitting jeans – well, I assume they're tight-fitting, they might just be stretching themselves a little thin over his muscular legs – and a shirt that, upon his arrival, he decided should probably be unfastened another button or two. He looks incredible, and I'm not the only one who thinks so; pretty much every girl, woman and a few of the men in here are drooling over him.

'This might actually be my favourite place on the planet,' I tell him as I sip my cocktail. Some passionfruit and vodka combo served in a disco ball glass – it's amazing. It's also my first drink in a little while. Well, technically it's my fourth tonight, but tonight is my first... oh, never mind.

'Well, that's just sad,' Marco teases.

He swigs his beer with such an easy confidence, as though he doesn't have a care in the world. Marco is another reason I feel so peaceful; it's hard not to be when you're around him, he's so chilled out and so in control. I would say his life is as chaotic as mine – if not more so – but he just keeps on keeping on.

'It's not sad, we've got a history,' I insist. 'I used to come here all the time when I was a teen – it was the only place I could get in.'

'Same,' he says with a laugh.

'What, really?'

'Yeah,' he replies. There's a little chuckle in his voice that makes it seem almost like an admission. 'I grew up here – not at Gloria's. In town. I'm "town trash" – isn't that what they call us back in the village?'

I scrunch up my face.

'They do,' I reply.

I take a big swig of my drink to wash the nasty taste of those words away.

'But so is my brother,' Marco says. 'Ant married into that village, and look at him now, just as snobby as the rest.'

'It's shit growing up there,' I tell him. 'Unless you want to play the game – which I didn't. If you're happy to compete, earn the most money, have the best stuff and so on, then the place is your playground. It just feels like no one ever grew up. They're all trying to be the kid who got the best bike for Christmas – which, incidentally, is a competition none of their kids can win, because everyone gets whatever they want basically thrown at them.'

'Kids who get everything that they want are the worst,' Marco says. 'Some of Josh's friends are so entitled already – at nine or ten.'

'When I was in secondary school there was this kid called Simon Wright – his dad owns the swanky car showroom on Elm Street. He was an entitled little shit. He used to try and scare me, when I was walking to school, by pretending to ride his bike into me.'

'What a wanker,' Marco says. 'I've no time for bullies at all.'

He looks as if he means it.

'One day he didn't pull away quick enough and he hit me, in the school car park, where a teacher saw, so they confiscated his bike… His dad had bought him a new one by the next day, and do you know what? He just kept doing what he did before.' I sigh. 'I'm sure he doesn't have a care in the world. People like that never get what they deserve.'

'Well, screw him, because look at us, sitting here in the seventies, living our best lives in other people's houses – in other people's lives, in your case,' he jokes. 'Cheers to that.'

'Cheers,' I say, clinking my drink with his.

'And at least you're doing a great job with your own fake kids,' he says with a smile. 'Henry is a sweet kid, and it sounds like you got through to Millie.'

'Yeah, and if that's all I've done while I'm here, then it was all worth it,' I say with a smile. 'I feel really good about our chat. Hopefully she realises the most important thing to do is just crack on with her school work.'

'Are you excited for Henry's birthday tomorrow?' Marco asks. 'I know I am.'

'Weirdly... yes. I think you're going to be disappointed when they don't let you in the ball pool, but I think Henry is going to love it, and his friends will too.'

My mind wanders for a second as I think about Emma. Obviously, she knew she was going to be away for Henry's birthday – which she must be absolutely devastated about – so she planned everything out in great detail and put all the plans into action before she left. She even bought and wrapped his present and hid it in her dressing room. Emma didn't leave anything to chance but I'm going to do everything I can to make sure it's even better. I've even been out and bought him a present from me – not that he'll know it's from real me, his auntie – with my own money. I have a lot of birthdays to catch up on.

'I didn't know whether to invite Christian's son,' I wonder out loud.

'Even after the crazy spider saga?' Marco replies in disbelief.

Marco has become my BFF – the person I tell everything to. I feel as if I can trust him, and he does give pretty good advice for a hot mess... a bit like me, I suppose.

'Is this just so you can try and kiss his dad again?' he adds with a grin.

As supportive as Marco is, he does love to tease me... but if I'm being honest, I quite like his teasing.

'I did not try to kiss him,' I insist with an awkward giggle. 'I don't even know what that was, but it was not that. I'm just thinking, it's like every other kid in his class is going... he'll be the only one not invited.'

'Would Henry want him there?'

'I doubt it,' I admit. 'He'd probably lose his spider in the ball pool and close the place down.'

'So, unless you do just want an excuse to spend time with his dad...'

Every now and then his teasing gets under my skin.

'OK, fine, fine, I won't invite him,' I insist.

I think Marco thinks he's upset me because he jumps to his feet and pulls me towards the busy dance floor.

'OK, no more of this,' he insists. 'We're supposed to be having the night off from your double life, remember? And if you came here as often as I did back in the day, you will absolutely remember the dance to this one.'

I notice 'Night Fever' by the Bee Gees has just started playing, and I absolutely do remember the dance.

'You remember the dance to this?' I laugh.

'It's not exactly hard, is it? It's just walking, pointing, twirling – easy.'

'Well, I can't turn down the chance to see this, so OK,' I reply excitedly.

We slink into position on the dance floor with everyone else who has been coming here long enough to know the moves too.

It's a bit like the dances you learn at school discos, like the Macarena or Agadoo – such simple, repetitive moves that stay with you forever.

Marco is doing his best John Travolta impression – taking the dance so seriously, with a straight back and an even straighter face – doing everything he can to make me laugh.

I'm a bit drunk, and it's been a while since I did this, so I'm sure I'm messing up, and I must look hilarious, but so does everyone else. We're not dancers, we're just a mishmashed crowd looking for a good time in the least reputable joint in all of Cheshire.

'Do you think we were ever here at the same time, when we were younger?' I ask him over the music.

'Who knows?' Marco replies. 'No one looked twice at me back then. I was a fat teenager – and I was shy. I got the crap bullied out of me at school, really knocked my confidence.'

My smile drops. Why are kids so horrible? I'd think twice before having them, only because I couldn't stand the thought of sending them to school to be miserable.

'That's horrible,' I reply. 'But what a revenge body!'

He shrugs modestly.

The DJ blends the end of the track seamlessly into 'September' by Earth, Wind & Fire and for some reason this feels like my track, my time to let loose – a chance for the real Ella (emboldened by all the cheap cocktails) to rear her head.

I get lost in the song. I'm singing along, I'm dancing with Marco – and I mean with him. On him, practically. I twirl around and back myself up into him, wiggling my hips, which he must have put his hands on at some point. I fling my arms in the air and I drop it like it's hot, but as I'm on my way back up, time slows down, the music goes quiet in my ears, everyone seems to be suspended in time. Is that...?

As reality hits me I panic.

'Shit! Shit, shit, shit,' I say as I grab Marco by the hand. 'We need to get out of here.'

'What? Why?' he says. 'You were just starting to enjoy yourself.'

'Millie is here!' I say, nodding over towards her.

She's just across the dancefloor, dirty dancing with that older boyfriend of hers. She's wearing a tiny outfit and holding a massive drink – I doubt it's a soft one.

I pull Marco outside into the cold car park before he stops me.

'You're not going to leave her here, are you?' he says.

'What choice do I have?' I reply. 'She's not supposed to be here, but neither am I. She thinks I'm her mum. What's her mum doing here, all dressed up, grinding on men that aren't her dad?'

'Point taken,' he says. 'So much for thinking you'd got through to her.'

'The lying little cow – she told me she was sleeping over at Fay's,' I say. I can hear the disappointment in my own voice. I know what you're thinking – that I'm a hypocrite, but I was seventeen when I started coming here, not fifteen, and I definitely wasn't here with an older boyfriend. It's not just that he's older. I mean, he drives like an idiot, takes her to clubs, buys her drinks, dances with her with his hand tucked into the top of her micro mini.

'What are you going to do?' Marco asks.

'Nothing, I guess... not yet anyway,' I reply. 'Let's just go home. We've got Henry's birthday party early tomorrow. That won't be fun with a hangover. I'll have to find another way to try and get through to her, but she can't go on like this...'

Suddenly I feel like a mum. I feel as though I am responsible for this person and my blood is boiling that she lied to me, that she's in there, drinking... but I can't blow my cover. I'll have to think of something else.

'OK,' Marco replies. 'But it's a shame we're leaving. Things were just starting to get good.'

30

When you haven't had a hangover for a little while you forget how bad they are.

I always underestimate mine. As I've got older, my hangovers have got worse, and it's only once I've got one that I do the whole 'that's it – I'm never drinking again' thing, and no one really means it when they say that, do they? Except I can honestly say, with my hand on my heart, that I will never drink again the night before a kids' party, because the combination of a barrage of their joyous squeals and that godawful 'Baby Shark' song on repeat is making me want to see if I can't just suffocate myself in the ball pool.

We're at Captain Crazy, one of those children's play centres that looks like a giant death trap – but one that's covered with foam so it's actually safe. You know the type of thing – I don't know what they call them – but the whole place is basically a massive climbing frame with a series of slides and ball pools. There are climbing walls, ropes, ladders, bumpy slides, near-vertical slides – all things I would have absolutely hated as a kid because they kind of seem like exercise to me.

Marco plonks himself down on the beanbag next to me. I'm glad he's here because Rich is at work right now, but he's joining us later to eat. I wouldn't be surprised if he just wanted to avoid the noisy part of the party, but you'd think he'd be here anyway.

'You're putting on a very brave face,' he tells me. 'Turtles or starfish?'

'Turtles, please,' I reply.

Marco hands me a pair of turtle-shaped sunglasses before putting on the starfish ones himself.

'Best I could do at short notice,' he says. 'But it's fine, we look like we're getting into the spirit of things.'

'Even if they just hide my tired eyes,' I say. 'Especially now the Yummy Mummy Mafia have arrived.'

Jessica walks through the door flanked by her stooges, Abbey and Cleo. The kids charged in way ahead of them, obviously, and jumped into the ball pool to rough up the birthday boy.

'Good luck,' he says as I pull myself up.

'Hello, ladies,' I say brightly as I approach them.

'Jessica wants me to tell you that she is not speaking to you,' Cleo informs me as Jessica watches on. 'She's still upset about you stealing the fundraiser from her.'

'Oh my God, Jessica, I'm sorry,' I say. 'I wasn't trying to steal it from you, I was just making suggestions. I'd wish I'd known you were upset – I would have apologised sooner.'

'Come off it, Emma,' Abbey chimes in. 'You must have known something was wrong when we unshared the squad calendar with you.'

Well, that explains why I didn't get summoned to any more boring mummy stuff.

'We're just here for the kids,' Jessica – who is not speaking to me – says.

The three of them walk past me – practically through me –

and head for the café.

Well, that's me told.

I plonk myself back down next to Marco.

'That was fast,' he says.

'Apparently they're not friends with me right now,' I tell him. 'Honestly, they're pathetic. They're like bitchy school girls.'

'You could try hitting one of them with a foam bat?' he suggests jokily. 'If school tactics are on the table.'

'I don't know if the chairs in the café might be a better shout – WWE style,' I reply.

Marco laughs.

'I should go try and smooth things over, shouldn't I? Not because I want to – I really, *really* don't want to,' I insist. 'But this is Emma's life I'm living and these are her friends.'

'Yeah, I guess... don't hit them with anything, then,' he says with a faux seriousness. 'Not if you're trying to patch things up.'

'Noted,' I reply. 'Wish me luck again.'

I scour the room for them, spotting them tucked away in a leafy corner of the café. They're plastic leaves, of course, but they give the parents some kind of shield from their kids.

I'm just approaching their table slowly – because I'm not sure what I'm going to say – when I overhear something that stops me in my tracks. I hang back, behind a plastic tree.

'Are you going to lift your ban on speaking to her to ask her about John?' Cleo asks Jessica.

Oh my God, does she know? Because if she does, that's not fair at all. I'm not getting punched in the face for getting off with someone's husband when I haven't actually done anything wrong.

'Yeah, if anyone will know if John is having an affair, it's Emma,' Abbey adds. 'She sees him at work. She'll know how long he's there, if he's ever there alone...'

'That's true,' Jessica replies. She thinks for a minute. 'You know, I wouldn't be surprised if Emma was having an affair...'

'With John?' Cleo squeaks.

'No, of course not with John,' Jessica insists. 'Gosh, he wouldn't look twice at her. No – with Christian. I've seen the way she is with him, hanging around him like a bad smell, pushing her way into the fundraiser. Jane Roberts told me she saw Christian and his son leaving Emma's house, and Laura Wood, who was on the spelling bee trip, said she left the two of them at the hotel, and that they were getting a taxi back together instead.'

'Well, maybe it's Christian,' Abbey joins in, leaning forward, lowering her voice, smiling widely as if she's got something juicy. 'Or maybe it's Lisa's deadbeat brother-in-law – she's spending an awful lot of time with him.'

'The convict?' Jessica replies, horrified. 'Are they really spending a lot of time together?'

'Yes, but can you blame her?' Abbey says. 'Convict or not, he's so hot. I'd certainly try and get my claws into him, if I wasn't married.'

'Wouldn't we all?' Cleo replies.

Jessica smirks and bobs her head from side to side, as though to say she probably would too.

* * *

'They said *what*?' Marco says after I sneak back to tell him everything I just heard.

'I know, right?' I reply. 'Convict! If I hadn't been earwigging, I would have told them you were never convicted – you were never even charged—'

'Not that,' Marco says. 'They all want to shag me?'

'Wow, that's really all you took from that?' I reply.

'I'm kidding, I'm kidding,' he insists. 'It's just nice to know I have options.'

I don't blame them at all, for lusting after Marco; he is gorgeous. The problem with them lusting after him is the way they view him. They think he's a bit of rough, a criminal, a 'deadbeat', just because his life isn't quite on track. But he isn't any of those things; he's a kind, caring man with an amazing sense of humour. Exactly my type – if I were myself these days, but I'm not, I'm Emma, so I'm keeping thoughts like that out of my head. I need a friend far more than I need a roll in the ball pool, shall we say.

'We'll just need to be more careful,' he says, making it sound as if we are actually having an affair. 'And... I don't know, with Christian, they're probably just jealous you're teacher's pet now.'

'Yeah, maybe,' I reply. I think for a second. At least I try to, but they're taking 'Baby Shark' from the top again.

'I don't know, romantically linked with four men,' Marco teases. 'You've certainly caused some excitement since you came to town.'

'Erm, my sister is responsible for two of them, thanks,' I say. 'But that's a good point. I just need to keep my head down, get back on track. Perhaps we need to make sure we always have the kids around us, when we hang out.'

'Worried you're going to try jump on me now you know every woman in the village wants me?' he jokes.

'That'll be it,' I reply with a smile.

'Here's my darling wife,' Rich announces as he approaches the table.

He extends an arm, and beckons for me to come close with his hand.

'Hey, I thought you had work,' I say as I get up to accept the kiss he's waiting to plant on my cheek. I'm actually really pleased to see him. It felt like he was missing.

'I thought I'd finish early, make the tail end of the party,' he says as he keeps me held close. 'Just in case the kids were running you ragged.'

'It's not the kids who are the problem, it's the mums,' I reply.

'Ignore them, they're just jealous,' he says, squeezing me again. This must be for the benefit of everyone else in the room. Everyone but me, the person he's hugging, and Marco too, I guess, because Rich knows that he knows the truth.

Still, it doesn't stop Marco staring at us with an inquisitive look on his face.

'OK, I'm going to go find Henry, see if he's having fun,' Rich says. He kisses me on the cheek again. 'Back in a moment.'

'Are you sure he knows you're faking it?' Marco asks me as I sit back down next to him.

'Yeah.' I laugh awkwardly. 'Why?'

'You're looking pretty close,' he points out.

'It's all for show,' I assure him, not that he needs me to.

'You wanna make sure he knows it,' Marco warns. 'You look just like his missus, remember? What if he's starting to get confused? Or maybe he has Stockholm syndrome after a few too many cheese and pineapple sandwiches.'

'You leave my sandwiches out of it,' I joke back in faux anger.

As much as I love Marco's teasing, there's something about the idea of Rich falling in love with me that's too terrifying to consider. I've already sort of ruined Emma's relationship with her friends, imagine if I ruined things with her husband too? Thankfully I know that could never ever happen, but the concept alone freaks me out. I'm supposed to be making her life easier, not destroying it, and I know that if Emma lost Rich, she really would think her life was over.

31

Emma always has everything all figured out. Everything is planned in advance, everything is booked into the diary, the entire house is organised from top to bottom. I had been wondering if there were any flaws in her system at all, but I didn't consider one variable: the rest of her family.

So, while Emma might be Housewife of the Year, she has no control over the things Rich and the kids throw at her, and it turns out sometimes they throw big stuff.

Take this evening, for example. With little more than six hours' notice I received a call from Rich saying that he had forgotten to mention that he had invited two of his bosses and their wives over for dinner. He was pretty stressed out about it, to be fair; he was panicking about what to do. As he babbled out potential – but highly implausible – fake emergencies to get him out of it I decided that I just needed to do what Emma would do.

'Don't worry, I can handle it,' I told him.

'Ella... are you sure?' he replied.

His voice didn't exactly show a great deal of confidence in my offer but that only made me more determined to prove him wrong.

I do have a secret weapon, of course... Marco!

We've been sticking to our new rule of only hanging out when the boys are around, or when we're at work, and I've been keeping my ear to the ground for any more rumours but they seem to have died down. The same goes for Christian, who I've been totally avoiding since the last time I saw him, and with event planning mostly being done by email, now that we're just down to the finishing touches, it's pretty easy. Well, it's easy in that it's not technically difficult to execute, but I am finding it a little hard just because I was enjoying spending time with him, seeing where things were going. Of course, they weren't going anywhere, because he thinks I'm Emma, and he's a good guy; I'm sure he'd never actually make a move on someone he thought was married, which is exactly what makes him so attractive – argh. It's messy, to say the least. The only thing messier right now is this kitchen.

The weather isn't quite as bad as it has been, and the kitchen is roasting because we've been cooking for what feels like hours, so we've got the door open. Marco encouraged Henry and Josh to go in the garden and practise their football, because they're at full volume today, but every time I look out at them, they're gleefully hitting each other with sticks.

Marco is sitting on the worktop next to me, overseeing the three-course Italian meal I'm cooking for the dinner party tonight.

We decided on three dishes that Marco assured me were mostly quick and very easy to make, and he promised to help me every step of the way, which makes me feel a bit better. Still, I'm feeling pretty frazzled, because Rich is relying on me and I really want to get this right.

To start, we're making a Caprese salad, which might just be

the easiest salad to make in the world. The main course is tagliatelle bolognese, followed by a tiramisu for dessert and, yes, I do feel kind of like I'm on *Come Dine With Me* right now – but not one of the earlier episodes, where it was all people who thought they were excellent chefs, one of the newer ones with people who can't cook but just want to be on TV.

We made the tiramisu first, so that's just chilling in the fridge, and everything is ready to make the salad when people arrive. So, the only real heavy lifting to do is for the bolognese.

It's been interesting, cooking with Marco, I feel like I've learned a lot. We're making a traditional bolognese, which, it turns out, is nothing like the way most people prepare it in this country. For starters it's made with tagliatelle (not spaghetti), it only requires a tiny amount of tomato sauce (just enough to bind the ingredients together), and there's much debate about whether or not the dish should contain any garlic at all, so we're not using any.

I think it's going well, and Marco keeps telling me I'm doing all the right things – the thing stressing me out the most is probably Marty who, at the first smell of mince, just barks and barks and barks.

'It's smelling...'

Marco says something but Marty barks right over the second part.

I open up the cupboard where all of the doggy supplies are and grab Marty's favourite frisbee. This usually makes him bark too, because he will demand you throw it for him repeatedly, and he would probably keep chasing after it until he died, if you didn't eventually hide it from him so he would have a drink of water and a rest. At least if I throw it outside, he might pester the boys to throw it for him.

'Marty, play frisbee,' I shout as I launch the frisbee through the open door.

'Playing "Kiss Me" by Sixpence None The Richer,' the Smarty announces, in that irritating robotic voice of hers, before she starts pumping it out at quite a high volume.

'Arrrgh!' I moan, my stress levels rising. 'Whatever they're paying you to hack that thing – I will double it if you just kneecap the thing instead, make it so that none of them ever work again.'

Marco laughs.

'OK, you need to relax,' he insists. 'Your food will taste bad if you were stressed when you made it.'

'Will it?' I squeak, suddenly feeling even more stressed.

'Of course it won't, that was a joke,' he points out, as though it should have been obvious. 'Come on, we need to get you to loosen up.'

Marco takes me by the hand and pulls me close.

'Dance with me,' he insists.

'What? No, come on,' I say, laughing it off. 'The bolognese...'

'...is simmering,' he says. 'Come on, it made you feel better the other night. Just let loose.'

I can't help but smile as Marco twirls me around before pulling me close again.

'Mum, why are you being so weird?' I hear Millie's voice call out over the music.

'Smarty, stop,' I say quickly as I wiggle out of Marco's arms. 'Honey, hello.'

'Honey? Right,' she replies with a roll of her eyes. 'Listen, I need a favour.'

I feel my eyebrows shoot up curiously. I can tell by the quick shift in her attitude that she wants something. That flip from mocking me to staring at her feet, every word that leaves her lips suddenly and clearly so begrudgingly blank – she doesn't go as far as sucking up. Well, that wouldn't be cool, would it?

'What's that?' I reply, getting back to my bolognese.

'There's a party on Friday night,' she starts.

'Where?' I reply. 'What kind of party? Whose party is it?'

'Oh my God, I knew you'd be like that,' she snaps. 'It's just a party, Mum. Just a party-party, and everyone else is going.'

'I'm not going,' I say, with a little attitude of my own. I turn to Marco. 'Are you going?'

'My invitation has not come through yet, no,' he replies in a similar tone.

'Oh my God, why are you being such losers? It's just a house party,' she says. 'I'm sixteen soon anyway, then I can do whatever I want, so you might as well let me go.'

'That's eighteen, kiddo,' I point out. 'So, you might as well do what I told you to do and focus on your school work. After you pass your exams, you'll have all the time in the world to party.'

'It's like you're trying to ruin my life, just because yours is so bleak,' she replies.

This is the first time since I've been here that Millie has gone full teenager on me. I can't say I'm a fan.

'If you don't let me go, I'll tell people about the two of you dancing together – I'll tell Dad,' she threatens.

'Tell Dad what?' Rich asks as he walks in the room, dumping down his briefcase, shrugging off his coat.

'I just caught Mum dancing with Josh's weird uncle,' Millie tells him smugly, as if she's got me bang to rights.

I look over at Marco, who looks incredibly amused by the identifier she used for him.

'Millie, it's 2021, your mum is a grown woman, she can dance with who she likes,' he tells her. 'Even Josh's uncle.'

'I am so glad I'm having dinner at Fay's tonight,' she says stroppily, turning on her heel. 'I might never come back.'

'OK, well, make sure you keep flossing,' I call after her.

'Oh, wow, look at this,' Rich says as he admires our handiwork. 'And the smell! Amazing! You've really pulled out all the stops – I can't thank you enough.'

I shrug.

'All in a day's work,' I tell him. 'Josh's weird uncle deserves some credit too. He made the tiramisu, and he says he'll babysit Henry this evening.'

'Oi,' Marco says with a laugh.

'Mate, I can't thank you enough,' Rich says, slapping him on the back. 'I'll go get ready, then I'll come down and do my bit while you get ready.'

'OK, sure,' I say with a smile. Ever the dutiful wife.

Rich seems to have U-turned on Marco – he doesn't seem worried by his presence at all now, although that might just be because he's helped me save the day.

'Do you think Millie really is going to Fay's? 'Marco asks me quietly once we're alone.

'God knows,' I reply. 'I guess I'll just have to try talking to her again – unless you're allowed to return kids to the hospital or something. Can you return the ones that turn out horrible?'

'I don't think so.' Marco laughs. 'But... wow, did you sound like a mum before! What a performance.'

I smile to myself.

'I did sound like a mum, didn't I?'

'And look at you here, wife-ing, doing an amazing job,' he continues.

'I've had a lot of help from you, but I will take that compliment, thank you,' I reply.

I really do feel I'm getting better and better at this every day. I might be having problems with Millie still, but so was Emma, so I'm not going to be too hard on myself about it. I am going to try and talk to her again but I'm not going to worry about it tonight. Tonight, I'm going to worry about whether or not this food is good enough for Rich's bosses, and whether or not I can pass for the perfect wife in front of them.

32

The tiramisu is the only course I actually enjoy, not because the others were bad – the food was a roaring success – but because I was so nervous about the others.

Once everything was ready and the table was set, I headed upstairs to get ready. I didn't have to look through Emma's wardrobe for long before I found an appropriate cocktail dress. I imagine this is one of the ones she always wears to stuff like this – a long black one that I can tell was expensive by the way it skims my hips, rather than clinging to them and making me look on the chunky side. Having said that, I think I might have lost a few pounds while I've been trying to keep up with Emma's hectic life... at least people have stopped thinking I'm pregnant, anyway.

'Well, Emma, I have to say,' Piers starts, pausing to shovel in his last mouthful of dessert. 'I knew you were a bloody good cook, but I don't remember you being *this* good.'

Ahh, 1-0 to Ella!

Piers is one of Rich's bosses. Martin is the other, and their wives are... Helen and Judy. I actually chanted their names to myself, in my head, while I prepped our starters, to make sure they stuck.

'Absolutely delicious, dear,' Judy adds. 'And I've just realised you've changed your hair – that's what looks different about you. You're looking positively radiant.'

If only you could see the smile on my face right now. That's 2-0 to me – probably 3-0, if you count the whole prison thing, which we won't, because if we're scoring points based on our wider lives (rather than just how well we do dinner parties) then taking into account things like my finances and living situation probably gives Emma like a twelve-point lead.

'That's lovely of you to say, thank you,' I reply. 'Can I interest anyone in a coffee or something a little stronger? A shot of grappa perhaps?'

'Oh, Helen, we haven't had grappa since we visited Lago di Como – what do you say, shall we?' Piers asks excitedly.

'Why not?' Helen practically laughs.

Everyone apart from me and Rich must be in their late fifties/early sixties. I can feel how rich they are, just by being around them, hearing how they speak. They could not be lovelier people though. Not like the snobs that live in this village. I'm actually having a really nice time.

Martin and Judy look at each other with mischievous smiles.

'Go on then, count us in too,' Martin says.

'Coming right up,' I reply.

Rich smiles at me as I stand up to head to the kitchen. He looks bemused, as if he can't believe this is going as well as it is, but he looks pleasantly surprised so I'll take it.

Now that I'm getting to grips with all the weird and wonderful contraptions in the kitchen, I'm starting to utilise them a lot more. Take, for example, what I thought was just a fancy bottle holder built into the worktop. I thought maybe you could drop ice in it or something, like a built-in ice bucket, but it seemed way too skinny for that. Turns out it's a hi-tech built-in electric wine cooler, so you just place your bottle in and tell it what temperature you want it to be and boom – done.

I grab some glasses before removing the grappa from the cooler, now that it's reached the perfect temperature – which is somewhere between 16-18 °C.

You weren't expecting me to be a grappa expert, were you? First of all, how dare you... OK, no, on a serious note, of course I'm not a grappa expert. No prizes for guessing that Marco gave me this bottle to offer to my guests tonight, and it was he who told me what temperature to serve it at.

'Here we are,' I say as I carry the tray over to the dining table.

I pour a little glass for everyone and hand them out.

'OK, well... *salute!*' Piers announces.

We all join him in raising a glass.

I take a cautious sip of my drink, because I've never tried it before and it smells pretty strong and – good God, my tongue feels as if I just licked the Aga!

'Whoo! You could remove paint with that stuff,' Martin announces.

'Bloody good though,' Piers joins in. 'Emma, when did you get so fun?'

And there's the 3-0 I was hoping for.

I shrug modestly.

'I love this song,' Judy announces as Neil Young's 'Harvest Moon' starts playing.

'I danced to this song at my wedding,' Rich tells them, smiling to himself as he looks down into his glass.

'I imagine Emma did too,' Judy says with a chuckle.

'Oh, yeah, of course,' Rich quickly adds, smiling over at me.

'Let's have a dance,' Helen suggests. 'All of us. To celebrate what a fantastic couple you are.'

'Oh, no, we don't have to do that,' Rich insists.

'Come on, you've got the floor space for it,' Piers insists.

I smile at Rich, to let him know I'm happy to do it.

'OK, then,' he says. He springs to his feet with a smile I've not seen on his face the whole time I've been here. 'May I have this dance?'

Oh, man, Rich is being fun! Who knew Rich could be fun?

'Thanks for doing this,' he whispers into my ear as we slow-dance to the music.

'Ah, it was nothing,' I reply.

'No, it wasn't,' he insists quietly. 'You've really pulled out all the stops. In fact, you've been doing such an amazing job of everything.'

I just smile.

There's something about Rich today... I don't know... he seems so different. He seems far less stressed, he seems happier – he literally seems lighter as he dances, slowly and gracefully moving me around the room.

I'm going to call it – that's 4-0 to me; I am officially the winner. I am the best wife at throwing dinner parties and it feels so good to be able to tell myself that I am fully capable of doing something that Emma probably thinks I could never do, and I've maybe even done it a little better.

'Aww, don't they make a gorgeous couple?' Judy calls out.

Rich leans forward and plants a kiss on my cheek.

'You'll never know what you've done for me,' he whispers in my ear.

Uh-oh!

'It's no big deal,' I say quickly, because suddenly he seems different. I swear, he's holding me closer, he's looking at me differently... is he? There's a happiness in his eyes that's been missing until tonight.

'It is a big deal,' he replies. 'I might actually be the most relaxed I've felt in a long time. So, thank you.'

Marco's words about Rich falling for me echo around my head.

Suddenly I feel weird... I wanted tonight to go well, I wanted to be good at it, I wanted to beat my sister's efforts. I so wanted to win at something... I just didn't bargain on the prize being her husband.

33

I feel as though I'm doing a great job at being a wife, a mum, a homemaker – by regular standards and by Emma's standards – and I'm so proud of myself... but...

I turn on the hot tap and flood the bowl containing Herman the German friendship cake mix with water. I watch as the water makes the mixture thinner and thinner until eventually, I say '*auf wiedersehen*' to Herman as I pour him down the drain.

'Hi Mum me and Josh are going to play Animal Crossing,' Henry says quickly, as though the whole sentence were made up of one word – as he and Josh charge towards the TV.

'No worries,' I call back. 'Has Marco left?'

He agreed to pick Henry up from school today, which I really appreciate.

'Nope, I'm right behind you,' he says. 'Watching you euthanise poor Herman.'

'Honestly, I just can't be arsed,' I reply under my breath. 'Friendship cake, my arse. It requires more attention than the bloody kids.'

'I chucked ours in the bin after a day,' he admits with a cheeky smile. 'So, how are you?'

'Yeah, I'm good – thanks for picking Henry up,' I reply.

'It's all good,' he replies. 'You OK?'

'Yeah, I... I kind of got distracted reading my mum's book,' I confess, as though it's something to be ashamed of.

'How's that going?' he asks.

'It's so weird,' I admit. 'I hear her voice in my head when I read her words, because I can imagine every single one coming out of her mouth. It's all such Auntie Angela advice. I've just been reading the chapter about relationships and it got me thinking: either my mum had relationships that she kept from me and Emma, or... after my dad died, she genuinely never loved again. And while I might not agree with her advice about how to keep your husband happy – not like that,' I quickly add, before Marco makes a Marco joke. 'But parts about how important it is to have good relationships in your life – that spoke to me,' I continue. 'Of course, what it said to me was that I had no one.'

'That's not what it says on the Village Echo forum,' Marco replies. 'I thought that might be why you were in hiding.'

'Oh God, go on...' I say, bracing myself.

'Well, the bad news is that someone on the message board has started a rumour that a teacher is having an affair with a parent, and you only need to know a few details to start putting the pieces of the puzzle together, to figure out who it is,' he explains.

'What's the good news?' I ask.

'The good news is that everything we are doing for the site is working. All the new content is a hit – all those local guides you've been writing and stuff like that – and the ad revenue is up... It's really up.'

'So, the good news is that lots of people are reading the bad news,' I point out.

'That's a terrible spin to put on it,' Marco replies with a laugh. 'Don't worry, I can delete that stuff as and when it pops up – it's potentially libellous. It won't stay up long.'

'Thanks,' I reply. 'I'm glad you've got my back.'

'I do – and not just with this,' he insists. 'You might think you don't have any real relationships, but you do. It might not seem like it, but you're getting to know your niece and nephew, and Emma isn't going to just send you packing when she gets back. This is your chance to be in their lives.'

'I'm not sure about that,' I reply. 'She wanted me as a stand-in, so that people didn't know she was in prison. She can't exactly come back and keep me around without people asking questions, can she? As soon as people see us together, they would know it had been me all this time. Me filling in for her only works because people either don't know that I exist, or they never think of me any more, which means they just accept that I am Emma.'

'Well, say all that's true, and she tells you to hit the road the day before she comes back to reality... You'll always have me. And life might seem a bit shit for us now, but it's really just a race to see which one of us can get rich first,' he jokes. 'Either you'll finally get your inheritance or I'll finally hack the digital assistant we can't say the name of...'

I laugh.

'Thanks,' I tell him. 'You'll always have me too.'

'So, day in the office tomorrow?' Marco says. 'Still down for it?'

'So long as I have you there to protect me from John, then yes, absolutely,' I reply. 'It's so satisfying, seeing all our hard work pay off.'

'It's a shame we can't do this full-time,' Marco replies. 'It's weirdly quite a lot of fun. Although that might just be because we have so much fun together.'

He smiles.

'Probably,' I reply. 'Sounds like the set-up was pretty odd until we took over.'

'Sounds like it was a den of iniquity,' he jokes.

Millie saunters into the room, shooting us a look as she heads to the fridge.

I resist pointing out that she decided not to run away forever in the end because I don't think she'll find it funny.

'Are you two always together?' she asks us as she grabs a drink.

'I brought your brother home,' Marco tells her. 'I was just going, actually.'

'OK, well, thanks again,' I tell him. 'I'll see you at work.'

'Yeah. Joshy boy, home time,' he calls out.

'He's a good guy, you know,' I tell Millie once Marco and Josh have gone. 'You don't have to put on such a hostile front.'

'I'm not hostile towards him, I'm hostile towards you,' she tells me. 'You're ruining my life – why can't you just be cool?'

'Is this because I told you that you can't go to that stupid party?' I reply. 'Teenage house parties are rubbish anyway.'

'OK, one – like you'd know, you didn't do anything cool when you were my age,' she claps back. 'And two – I know it was you who got the party cancelled.'

'What? Millie, that had nothing to do with me,' I insist. Of course, I didn't, but she doesn't look as if she believes me.

'Whatever,' she says.

'Everything OK in here?' Rich asks as he joins us.

'Yeah – you're home early,' I point out.

'I squeezed in a gym session,' he says. 'I need to go back to work but I always prefer to shower here.'

'I'm going to my room and I don't want disturbing,' Millie announces as she leaves the room.

'OK, darling – don't forget to do your homework,' Rich calls after her.

He's in such a good mood and it's kind of freaking me out a little bit. He's been so moody and so distant. This... this is new. This is for a reason.

Rich dumps his gym bag on the floor.

'The mood at work today was great,' he tells me. 'Last night scored me some major brownie points.'

'It was fun,' I admit.

'And they were all quite taken with you,' he continues. 'I really can't say thank you enough. Right, shower time. Back in a bit.'

Is that why he's in such a good mood – because work is going so well? Surely there's only so much money you can make before it makes absolutely no difference? My mum used to joke that Rich's parents called him Rich because that's what he was the second he was born.

I'm quite house-proud now, which is odd because, not only is this a big departure from the usual me, but also this is not my house.

I pick up Rich's gym bag and start sorting through his sweaty things – with that unflinching level of indifference you usually only get from being actually married to someone – to sort out what needs washing.

I'm not snooping, I swear I'm not, but the receipt for the flowers practically jumps into my hand as I sort through the bag. He spent £52.80 on flowers today – who spends £52.80 on flowers? – but who is *he* buying expensive flowers for?

My suspicions that Rich might be having an affair rush back to the forefront of my mind... Is that why he's in such a good mood?

As I stare at the receipt and go over all the evidence in my brain, I completely lose track of time – or maybe not all that much time goes by – but soon enough Rich is standing in front of me. He's all smiles until he sees the receipt in my hand.

'Can I have a quick word with you in the hall, please?' I ask, because I honestly have no idea how to tell if Henry is or isn't listening.

'Erm, yeah, sure,' he says. 'After you.'

'I was just getting your dirty washing out of your bag and I found this receipt. I wasn't snooping,' I insist – why am I being defensive?

'Just... wait there,' he says as he hurries his shoes on.

Rich is only outside a matter of seconds – he doesn't even close the front door behind him, he's so fast – before he re-emerges with a huge bunch of flowers.

'These are for you,' he tells me. 'To say thank you for last night.'

I narrow my eyes at him. He should know better than to think I was born yesterday – I have the same birthday as his wife, after all...

'Really?'

'Really, read the card,' he says.

Sure enough, there's an envelope on one of those little plastic sticks they shove into the bouquet. I open it and there's a cute little card, covered with love hearts, that reads:

'Emmylou. Beautiful flowers for my beautiful wife. Rich x'

'Emmylou?' I say out loud.

'In case the kids see the card,' he tells me. 'Writing "thank you for last night" felt really weird, so I just wrote something generic.'

'Aw, Rich, they're beautiful,' I reply. 'God, I actually thought you were having an affair.'

'Well, congratulations, then, you've got the wife thing down to a fine art,' he jokes.

'Sorry,' I say. 'This really is very sweet of you.'

'You deserve them,' he insists. 'Right, I really am going back to work now. I'll see you when I get in.'

'OK,' I reply. 'Sorry again.'

'Don't worry about it.' He laughs.

As I stand at the door and wave Rich off, with my gorgeous flowers in my arms, I can't help but laugh to myself. Rich, writing mushy cards to me, and me, getting personally offended at the idea of him having an affair. It's hilarious really, I suppose, because I've been working so hard at being his wife, it just seems like a slap in the face, if he were to be going elsewhere. Although I am just cooking his tea and washing his dirty pants, and I doubt that's what he would be going elsewhere for.

As for Rich's card, I'm sure he is just trying to keep our secret, and not blow our cover by addressing something to me with my real name. Unless of course he meant what he said... but that wouldn't be funny at all.

34

'Can we talk?' John asks me under his breath.

I dared to venture to the kitchen at work, alone, to make myself a cup of tea and he's pounced on me – well, so to speak. He hasn't literally pounced on me, not again.

'There's nothing to talk about,' I tell him. 'Let's just forget it.'

'But you told me you love your husband, but everyone is talking about you, and I'm starting to think you were just using me,' he says, sounding a little hurt.

'John, they're just rumours, started by horrible, jealous women,' I tell him. 'What we did was wrong, and it was a mistake, and you should just focus on making things work with your wife – for your family's sake.'

Ergh, this is horrible. I'm more than used to putting out my own fires – sometimes literally – but I begrudge taking the flak for other people's mistakes.

More than anything, I can't understand what Emma was thinking, kissing this guy. Her life seems perfect, and not just from the outside looking in – I am literally living her life and I'm really starting to love it.

'Here she is,' Marco says, physically pushing himself between us. 'I thought you'd gone to China for that tea. Come on, back to work.'

I grab our drinks and head back to my office, with Marco close behind me, hurrying me along.

'Well, you were right,' I tell him, the second we're back behind closed doors. 'He was over before the kettle boiled.'

'He'll get bored if you just ignore him,' Marco says.

'Don't they say absence makes the heart grow fonder?' I reply.

'Speaking of that...' Marco pauses to sip his tea, which has to be way too hot to drink; It seems as if he's stalling. 'I got a call from Zoe today.'

'Zoe?'

'My ex,' he says. 'The one who gave me the boot when I lost my job.'

'Ah,' I reply.

'She wants me to go for a drink with her tonight... apparently she wants to talk now.'

For some reason just hearing the words leaving Marco's lips gives me this strange feeling in my stomach, as if my breakfast is trying to come back up, and now that I'm thinking about how I feel, my breathing doesn't feel quite as it should. Oh my God, I'm jealous. I'm actually jealous.

'So, er, are you going to go?' I ask him.

'I thought I might "Ask Alison",' he says with a laugh. 'See what she says...'

Oh, God, no, please don't ask me. How am I supposed to answer that? If Marco were just anyone, knowing what I know about their break-up, I would tell him to run a mile, because when the going gets tough, you need a partner who isn't going to tell you to get going. She kicked him out on his arse when he was down, and I know what that feels like...

However, given how inexplicably jealous I'm feeling right now, am I just telling myself that I would tell him to do that, to stop him going?

I've always fancied Marco, from the second I embarrassed myself in front of him, but several factors – me pretending to be my sister, needing a friend, him having recently had his heart broken, the fact he's so totally completely out of my league but also way too much like me and so on – made me realise that a crush was all it was ever going to be. But I'd already considered this and just shoved it to the back of my mind, happy to have him as a friend when I really needed one. Plus, I was so distracted by Christian, who seems perfect on paper, but now that Marco is talking about seeing his ex, it's all coming back to the forefront...

'Do you want to go?' I ask him.

'Kind of,' he says. 'I'd be interested to hear her out... she sounded like she thought she'd made a mistake.'

'Well, you should go, then,' I tell him. 'Go and hear her out and then see how you feel.'

'Do you really think so?' he asks. He seems surprised by my reply, as if he was expecting me to say something different. This just makes me double down.

'Yeah, absolutely,' I say confidently. 'We all make mistakes.'

'*We* definitely do,' he replies. 'Me and you, that is.'

I laugh.

'We certainly do,' I say with a smile.

I think that might be why I've ruled out the idea of anything happening between us, because we really are so alike – too alike, probably. Whenever you have someone who is a natural disaster in a relationship, it needs to be with someone who can neutralise them. I'm a fire and Marco is petrol – what I need is water, or it will be absolute carnage.

'Take the rest of the afternoon off, if you need to get ready,' I tell him, trying to sound as OK with this as possible, and probably sounding the opposite.

'Ella, she dumped me. She'll be lucky if I brush my teeth,' he jokes. 'It's fine, we've got work to do. You got any big plans for this evening?'

'Hmm, let's see,' I wonder out loud. 'Loads of washing – in both senses of the word – making dinner – and half the battle with dinner is thinking of what to have, day after day, figuring out what to cook, and making sure it's something everyone will eat.'

Marco laughs.

'Family life, eh?'

'You can't beat it,' I reply. 'You'll just have to have enough fun for the both of us.'

Of course, I didn't think that through before I said it, and it sounds completely weird, out loud. As if I just gave him the verbal equivalent of a packet of condoms, a Barry White CD and an encouraging pat on the back.

I'm not going to sit here and feel down about it, I'm going to get on with my day and make the most of my situation. I might try and initiate some family time for the four of us tonight – perhaps we could get a takeaway and watch a movie? Yes, that's what I'll do. I'll focus on my family... while they're still my family, at least.

I wonder what my niece, who is convinced she is fat, will be more likely to eat: Chinese or fish and chips. I imagine she'll make a case for both being too unhealthy – but that's if she'll even speak to me, because it's been radio silence since the last time. It's funny – as much as I had my issues with my mum and her parenting techniques, I wouldn't have dared ignore her if she spoke to me.

I call Rich, to see what he fancies, but he doesn't pick up, which means he must be still working.

Henry is so engrossed in his game that his eyes have glazed over and his tongue is poking out of the side of his mouth, he's concentrating so hard. With Millie not even home from school yet I allow myself to lie down on my bed, just for a few minutes.

I close my eyes and puff air from my cheeks as I wonder what Marco is doing right now. He might be getting ready – he might even be on his way there. I wonder if he's nervous or excited and it irritates me that I care.

When I hear my phone ringing I jolt upright and snatch it up from the bed – it's probably Rich returning my call but the idea it could be Marco...

Oh God, it's Christian!

'Hello,' I say brightly, as though I've not been avoiding him – probably too brightly; I need to dial it back a little.

'Hello, Emma, how are you?' he asks me.

'Yeah, doing great, thank you,' I reply. 'You?'

'All good at this end,' he replies. 'Just a quick call about the fundraiser... the band have pulled out. They've been booked for a wedding the day before and they don't think they'll be able to make it back in time.'

'Someone has booked The Sound of Musicals for a *wedding*?' I reply with a laugh.

'Apparently so, and it must be paying way better, if they're cancelling on us,' he replies.

'Well, I can kind of sing, if you can play any instruments?' I joke.

'I have some experience playing the recorder – I hit it pretty hard, around the time I was six,' he replies. I can hear him smiling down the phone and it makes me smile too.

'There is a plan B though,' he says. 'There's another band who do music covers – Anything Goes – who have said they can do it.'

'That's good,' I reply.

'Yeah, and they're actually playing a gig at a pub in town tonight... I wondered if you wanted to go along, and check them out?' he suggests.

'Erm, yeah, I can do that, if we need someone to do that,' I reply.

Well, it's not like my fake family want to spend time with me, is it?

'I thought we could go together,' he says. 'Just to make sure they're the right band, and it feels like ages since I saw you last, so it would be good to catch up... and I never did get to buy you that drink.'

I smile to myself. I think Christian misses me. And it sounds to me as if he's extending an olive branch, to get our friendship back on track. You know what? I'm going to take it. I'm not going to sit here pining after Marco. Christian is the kind of man I should be spending my time with, and I know it's messy, but maybe I could figure all this out? Maybe I could come clean to him and admit who I really am? But will he be upset that I've lied to him all this time?

I think I should just go along tonight and see how I feel. And I should absolutely stop thinking about Marco. Easier said than done though, right?

* * *

It's Friday night, I'm all dressed up, and I actually have somewhere to go.

I haven't just made an effort to look good, I've made an effort to look like me, the real me, for the first time since I got here. A short black skirt and a shimmery silver vest top, topped off with an army of accessories, a leather jacket and pair of high-heeled black boots. Well, I'm going to a gig, so the rock-chick look feels appropriate. I'm also wearing way more make-up than Emma ever would, with smoky black eyes, and bright red lips.

As I look myself up and down in the full-length dressing-room mirror I genuinely feel like myself and it feels good.

I hear my phone ringing in my clutch bag so I scramble to get it out.

'Hi, Rich, where are you?' I ask.

'I'm just in the office,' he tells me. 'I popped up to see you, when I got in, but I heard the shower running.'

That's the problem with big houses – I had no idea he was in here too.

'No worries,' I tell him. 'I was calling to see what you wanted for dinner, but Christian just called to say the band has pulled out of the fundraiser, but he's found another one and he's asked me to go see them live tonight to make sure they're OK.'

'Oh, lucky you,' he replies. 'Getting to go out and have fun and file it under charitable work for the school. Well, I might see if Henry wants to go bowling and for a pizza, perhaps, seeing as though Millie is sleeping at Fay's again.'

'Aww, he'll love that,' I tell him. 'Well, if you're definitely in the house, I'll get going.'

'OK, see you later,' he replies.

I gather my things and head downstairs. I call out goodbye as I pass Rich's office door, as well as ducking my head into the kitchen to say goodbye to Henry, who is so engrossed in his pond-building efforts that he doesn't even form a proper 'goodbye', he just makes a nondescript sound.

I climb into the car, start the engine, and I'm just about to turn it off when something occurs to me. I switch the engine off again.

When Millie knows she's going to be sleeping at Fay's she takes an extra bag to school with her. When it's more of a last-minute thing she comes home after school to grab her things before going back out. Perhaps she popped in while I was getting ready, but knowing that it's the night that the party was supposed to be has me suspicious... I know she's lied to me before, and snuck out to clubs, but she wouldn't just lie to my face, about something so big, which I specifically told her not to do, would she?

I search through my phone until I find Fay's mum's number. I know that I should be trusting Millie to make the right choices, but I just need to check, so I can relax.

'Hello, Emma,' she says, answering after pretty much no time at all.

'Hello, Julia, how are you?' I ask.

'I'm OK – is everything OK there?' she asks quickly.

'Yes,' I reply. 'All fine.'

'Thank goodness,' she replies. I hear her exhale with relief. 'When I saw you calling, I was worried something might be wrong with Fay. Are you sure it's OK, her staying the night again?'

Oh, that lying little bitch. No more Ms Nice Auntie, that's it, I am going full Ella on her when I get my hands on her.

'Yeah, of course,' I reply.

'It must feel like you have three kids, the amount of nights she's there,' she replies with a laugh.

'Honestly, I don't even notice she's here,' I insist. 'OK, well, I'll let you get back to your evening.'

'What did you call for?' Julia asks.

'Oh, right, yeah... I just called to make sure you knew Fay was staying here tonight,' I lie.

'OK, thanks, Emma,' she replies. 'Thanks again, take care.'

I can't believe Millie has gone to the party – all that 'oh, thanks, Mum, it's cancelled' bullshit was to throw me off the scent, and it worked! No one likes having the wool pulled over their eyes, but I'm definitely not taking it from a fifteen-year-old.

Someone needs to teach her a lesson, and the best way I can think of to do that is to ruin her life with the strongest weapon I have: embarrassment. Nothing means more to a teen than their reputation, so if her mum turns up at the party and kicks up a fuss, drags her out of there... ha! She won't be invited to another party again until she's at uni.

The only problem is, I don't actually know where this party is, but I do know someone who can probably work it out.

'Marco, I am so sorry to bother you on your date,' I blurt the second he answers the phone.

'So much to take issue with there,' he says. 'But you sound upset. What's wrong?'

'It's Millie – she's gone to that bloody party!' I reply. 'I need to work out where it is so I can go there and drag her out.'

'Uh-oh,' he replies. 'I wouldn't like to be in her shoes tonight. Tell you what, I was only just heading out – come and pick me up. I've got time to help you.'

'Are you sure?' I reply.

'Of course,' he insists. 'See you in a minute.'

'OK, I'm on my way.'

I feel terrible, calling on Marco, and I promise this isn't just a way to sabotage his date with his ex, but if he can hack into Millie's social media or something, I'm sure it will be easy to work out where she is.

I connect my phone to the car's Bluetooth and tap the screen a few times before I set off.

'Hello?' Christian answers.

'Hi, Christian, I'm really sorry, but I'm not going to be able to make it tonight,' I say. 'Are you OK to go without me?'

'Of course,' he replies, although he sounds disappointed. 'Is everything all right?'

'Family emergency,' I tell him. 'You're lucky you don't have a daughter.'

'I hope she's OK,' Christian replies.

Oh, I'm sure she's fine. I'll bet she's having a lovely time. But she won't be when I turn up...

36

'Why have you dressed so sexy to crash a party full of teenagers?' Marco asks me the second he gets in the car, before he even says hello.

'I'm not dressing sexy to crash a party full of teenagers,' I quickly insist. 'I had plans to go to a gig, actually, but then my bloody fake daughter had to pull a stunt like this.'

'Ooh, get you,' he replies. 'Date night with the hubby?'

Suddenly the truth sounds so bad, when I think about saying it out loud.

'No, we lost the band for the fundraiser,' I reply. 'So, we were going to check out the only other one available.'

'You and Christian?' he says.

'Yeah.'

Marco thinks to himself for a moment before he snaps back to his usual jokey self.

'Well, if they're the only other band available, you'll have to book them anyway, won't you?' he points out with a smile. 'At least you've got a party to go to now – you look amazing.'

'You're not looking so bad yourself,' I point out.

Marco is wearing a pair of jeans and a black shirt, which is his version of making an effort, and he smells incredible, from his aftershave right down to his shampoo.

'Thanks,' he replies. 'Right, you drive, I'm going to give you directions to where she is.'

I glance at Marco, who is staring down at his phone screen.

'Oh my God, is that how fast you can hack into someone's social media account?' I ask, a little alarmed, suddenly concerned about everything from my Instagram account to the MySpace page I had as a teenager, that I never actually shut down.

He just laughs.

'No, my nephew is going,' he replies.

'Josh?' I squeak.

'No, my other nephew.' He laughs. 'Tom. He's in Millie's year.'

'Shit, I didn't know you had a teenager on your plate too,' I reply.

'He's all right, bit of a nerd too. We mostly just play COD together,' he says. 'He said he was going out with his friends tonight – I figured he'd be going to the party.'

'And you think he's just going to tell his nerdy uncle where it is?' I ask in disbelief.

'Ouch!' he replies. 'Of course, I don't think he'll tell me, but I do have him added on Snapchat, and the youth of today are very stupid. They share their real-time location with their friends. Tom is currently showing up as at his friend's house – I know it because I've dropped him there before. So, let's head there and either follow them to the party, if we can, or wait for his location to update once he gets there.'

'God, you're amazing,' I tell him. 'It's kind of scary.'

'Thanks,' he replies. 'Now, come on, let's go – this is weirdly exciting.'

'This is definitely the fun part,' I reply. 'It's not going to be pretty when I find Millie.'

'What are you going to do?' Marco asks.

'I'm going to embarrass her so hard she'll spend the next year in her room trying to work out how to change her identity,' I reply. 'Millie has been walking all over Emma for too long. I'm going to go in there and – maybe I'll grab a drink? Maybe I'll get up on a table and dance?'

'That poor girl,' Marco replies with a chuckle. 'As much as I'd love to see you dance on a table, she's going to be traumatised.'

I smile to myself.

We're not far from Tom's friend's house when Marco tells me that his location has updated again.

'We're really close,' Marco says. 'Just a left here, up this road...'

As we drive uphill the houses become more spaced out, until we're driving up a road completely surrounded by trees. Eventually we start passing parked cars that have 'rich teenager' written all over them leading to the mansion at the top of the road. It's a Victorian gothic-looking building that would be dark and gloomy were it not for the party going on indoors. The music is so loud we can hear it from inside the car and every window seems to be glowing a different colour.

'This isn't a teenagers' house party,' Marco says. 'This is a Playboy Mansion house party.'

'Exactly the kind of place you want your underage niece to be,' I say sarcastically. 'Oh, shit, that's her boyfriend's car.'

I recognise it – how could I not? It's lime green after all.

'You know what the best thing about having a massive car is?' I say as I park up. 'Blocking people in.'

'Nice,' Marco says. 'He's not going anywhere until you do.'

We get out of the car and walk up the drive, through the large front garden and into the house.

The place is in full-on party mode, with people absolutely everywhere, and I mean everywhere. In the hallway, sitting on the stairs – any room we walk into is just full of party-goers, drinking, dancing, kissing…

It's mostly young people, and by that I suppose I mean twenties and teens, which makes me feel incredibly old all of a sudden.

We make our way to the kitchen and just spend a minute or two taking it all in.

'This is actually kind of bleak,' Marco says.

'For them or for us?' I reply.

'Both,' he says. 'Have you recognised a single song that has played since we got here?'

'No,' I admit. 'And I feel like we stand out a mile – do you think we do?'

'*You* don't,' he says. 'Not dressed like that.'

'Thanks,' I reply. I'm sure he's just being nice. 'I have no idea how to figure this one out…'

I sigh.

'Hey,' Marco says, flagging down the nearest party-goer.

It's a girl – in her late teens, maybe her early twenties – who is basically wearing fishnet everything.

'Oh, hi,' she says. She plays with a piece of her hair with one hand and walks the other up Marco's chest. 'Do you wanna dance with me?'

'Do you know Millie Cooper?' Marco asks her, ignoring her question.

The girl just shakes her head.

'OK, thanks,' he says. 'Ella, let's go.'

'Rushing off?' I tease as I follow Marco back into the hallway. 'You were in, there.'

'Yeah, well, if I ever want to end up on a list, I know where to go,' he replies.

'Hey, girl,' a random boy says to me.

'You were in, there,' Marco teases me as I quickly shuffle away, mocking my voice.

The atmosphere here really is depressing. Considering it's a party, I just feel kind of sorry for everyone, which I suppose says more about me. I swear, at the start of the year, I would have said that this was my scene, but all I want to do is grab Millie and go home.

'What do we do? Do we split up?' I suggest. 'Try to cover more ground?'

'Look, there's Tom,' Marco says. 'Let's go ruin his night.'

''Sup?' Marco says as he approaches his nephew with a fist bump.

'What the fuck?' his nephew replies. 'What are you doing here?'

He looks past Marco and spots me. It takes him a few seconds to recognise me as Emma. When he does his jaw drops.

'Here's what's going to happen,' Marco tells Tom as he drapes an arm around him.

The two friends he was standing chatting with are already giving him a wide berth, now that they've realised we're basically parents.

'I'm going to pretend I didn't see you here,' Marco starts. He notices the beer in Tom's hand. 'Can I have some of that? Thanks. So, I pretend I didn't see you here and in return for my silence you're going to tell us where we can find Millie Cooper, and then you're going to go home. Sound good?'

Tom sighs.

'I thought you were cool,' Tom tells him.

'You were way off the mark with that one, pal,' Marco replies. 'So, Millie, you seen her?'

'She went upstairs with Eddie,' he says.

'Eddie?' I chime in.

'Yeah, I guess he's her boyfriend,' Tom replies. 'Can I go before someone sees me talking to you?'

'OK, go on,' Marco says. He only lets Tom get a few steps away from him before he calls after him. 'Love you.'

'Love you,' everyone in the room joins in, roaring with laughter.

'That's how you embarrass them,' Marco tells me, swigging his beer.

'Noted,' I reply with a smile, but it quickly drops. 'She's upstairs with him...'

'Come on, let's go,' Marco says. 'It's going to be fine.'

We have to step over a couple practically shagging on the stairs, which makes me worry even more about what we're going to find upstairs. We begin searching the hallway before looking inside the rooms with doors open.

'Jesus, some of them don't even close the doors,' Marco says, quickly closing the door in front of him with a horrified look on his face.

'How are we going to do this?' I ask. 'We can't just barge in the closed rooms.'

'Don't worry, I've got an idea,' Marco tells me.

He walks up to one of the closed doors and gives it a knock.

'Yo, Eddie,' he says, in his best cool guy voice.

'Wrong room, man,' a voice calls back.

'Smart,' I tell him.

'Thanks,' he replies with a smile.

He repeats the procedure at a couple of other rooms with no luck.

'Yo, Eddie,' he calls through the door of another.

'Occupied,' a girl calls back.

'That's not Millie's voice,' I say. 'And there's only one door left.'

'OK, here we go... Yo, Eddie,' Marco shouts.

'What? Can you come back later, man? I'm busy,' he replies.

'Cover up, we're coming in,' Marco calls back.

He gives them a second before he opens the door.

'What the hell do you think you're playing at?' I say, as the two of them scramble to pull the covers up over themselves.

'What the fuck?' Eddie says, clearly very annoyed at us for interrupting.

That's when I realise the girl in bed with him isn't Millie. She's older than Millie – probably more like Eddie's age – and she doesn't look happy.

'Who the fuck are you?' she asks.

'Who the fuck am I?' I reply as I wonder what to say.

What *do* I say?

'I'm Edward's mum,' I lie. 'He forgot his anti-diarrhoea medication. I thought I'd better bring it.'

'You're not my mum,' he says angrily before turning to his lady friend. 'She's *not* my mum.'

The girl looks Eddie up and down.

'We'll give you guys some space and leave your medication outside the door,' Marco tells him as he ushers me out of the room.

'If he's in there with her, then where has Millie gone?' I say.

'There's still places we haven't checked. Come on, maybe Tom was mistaken – he definitely seemed a bit drunk.'

'Will you tell his parents?' I ask.

'Nah,' Marco replies. 'But he'll be so scared that I'm going to, it'll make sure he behaves, at least for a while.'

At the top of the large staircase there are two sets of double doors that open out onto a terrace where people are smoking.

'Come on, it's worth a look,' Marco says.

The smokers are huddled together, gathered under heat lamps to keep warm. It only takes us a couple of minutes to realise she isn't there, but as I glance down into the back garden, I notice a girl sitting on the side of the fountain.

I narrow my eyes.

'Is that...? That's her,' I say. 'Oh, thank God.'

I recognise her blonde hair and the hot-pink coat she always wears – which I'll bet Emma absolutely didn't want her to have.

'Perhaps this is a job for just her mum,' Marco says. 'I'll get going.'

'It's not too late, you still have plenty of time for your date,' I point out.

'Yeah, I'll grab a taxi,' he replies. 'Good luck with your girl.'

Marco gives me a reassuring hug and, I swear, if I didn't need to go and talk to Millie, I wouldn't ever want him to let me go. I feel so safe in his arms, and I feel as if he was telling the truth earlier, when he said he'd always have my back.

We say goodbye at the front door before I venture back through the house, to find a way into the back garden.

As I spot Millie by the fountain, I take a deep breath before heading over there.

I'm just hoping I'll know what to say and do by the time I get there because right now, I have no idea.

37

There is a large circular stone fountain in the centre of the patio. The water feature isn't turned on but the lights are. It's beautiful – and bigger than the living room of the flat I burned down.

Millie is sitting on the edge, facing away from the house, looking down a garden that is so long it genuinely fades to black.

It's obviously too cold for everyone else out here, which I imagine is why she's here. She must be freezing because the first thing I notice is that she's hugging her legs. The second thing I notice is that she's crying.

As she wipes her nose on the back of her hand, she must notice me out of the corner of her eye, which makes her jump. She practically jumps a second time when she realises it's me.

'Mum,' she blurts, hurriedly wiping her eyes.

Her surprise to see me turns into fear, having been caught red-handed.

'What's going on with you, Millie?' I ask sympathetically, sitting down behind her. As I sit down my super-short skirt rides up and the bare skin above my stockings (because my sister is too fancy for full gusset, apparently) touches the cold stone. I quickly stand up again, and sit back down closer to the edge, so my skirt goes some way to shielding me from the chill.

'I'm sorry,' she says softly. 'I shouldn't have come. Can we just go?'

'Sure, we can go,' I tell her. 'I'm not going to say I'm not upset that you lied – not to mention low-key terrified about the ease with which you did it – but I'm worried about you more than anything right now.'

Millie sniffs hard.

'I'm fine,' she insists.

'Right, well, I obviously don't believe that,' I tell her. 'What happened with Eddie?'

As soon as I say his name Millie spins around in one swift movement. She stares at me, freaked out, as if I'm reading her mind.

'Nothing,' she says.

'I know he's your boyfriend,' I tell her. 'I saw the two of you kissing. I know he's here – I know he's upstairs in a bedroom with another girl, and I'm pretty sure you know that too, and that's why you're out here crying.'

Millie nods as she tears up again.

'Come here, babe,' I insist as I wrap my arm around her. 'It's OK, you can talk to me about him – you're not in trouble, I promise.'

'He just dumped me,' she sobs. 'He... he wanted to *do it*...'

Oh, God, I feel terrible for her. She thinks she's having this conversation with her mum and, honestly, I would have rather died than try and talk about sex with my mum when I was her age.

I squeeze her tightly, to let her know it's OK.

'I told him I wasn't ready so he dumped me. He said he could get someone else to in a heartbeat, so I called his bluff,' she explains. 'But he did find someone else, and he took her upstairs with him, and he made sure they walked right by me – Mum, it was so embarrassing.'

Oh, that little shit. That horrible, horrible boy. I mean, the whole statutory rape thing alone is categorically wrong, but, even if she wasn't still underage, the emotional manipulation and general disregard for her feelings has my blood boiling.

'Where's Fay?' I ask.

'She must have left,' she replies. 'I tried to find her before I came out here.'

'Come on, let's talk in the car,' I say, because I can feel her shivering.

'OK,' she says softly. 'You look really nice, by the way.'

I smile.

I might not be a mum, or an especially well-rounded person, but even I know that what I say to Millie right now will have a profound effect on the rest of her life. It will shape the way she sees things – the way she sees herself. I cannot get this wrong.

I give Millie a tissue from my clutch bag before we head back inside. We push our way through the rowdy crowd until we're at the front door, thankfully not coming face to face with Eddie again. I suppose he's still trying to convince that poor girl I wasn't really his mum, and that his bowels are perfectly fine (aside from the fact that he speaks from somewhere in that vicinity, obviously).

'You'll warm up in no time,' I tell her with a smile as I start the engine. I only just about manage the smile because I am seething. I genuinely don't think I've ever been so angry.

I reverse out from where I (rather impressively, in my opinion, given how big the car is) parallel-parked. I'm about to set off home but I just can't take my eye off Eddie's lime-green sporty rich-kid car, and I can't shake the feeling of how angry I am, for the way he's treated Millie, and for the way he clearly thinks he can treat all women.

'Is that his car?' I doublecheck.

'Yep,' she replies. Her face is scrunched up as if she's just sucked a lemon slice. 'I think it might be the only thing he cares about.'

'Huh,' I say thoughtfully.

I think for a few seconds – tops – before I act. I reverse a little more, start driving, and bump the side of Eddie's car with the side of mine. I don't do it hard, but this car is way bigger, and weighs tons, so it doesn't take much to scrape the side of his and take his wing mirror clean off.

'Little prick,' I mutter to myself as I drive back down the road.

I glance into my mirrors to check for witnesses but it's such a dark, quiet, lonely road, and everyone at the party will be hammered – it could have been anyone who pranged him.

See, I told you, when I see an injustice, I can't help but act. My temper gets the better of me. I just hate to see people getting away with things – especially the rich morons in this village.

The realisation of what a very Ella thing to do that was, hits me. I slowly turn my head to look at Millie and she looks stunned.

'Erm...' I start, but she gets there first.

'You're not my mum,' she tells me, as though she's never been more sure of anything in her life.

'Well...'

'You're not my mum – my mum would never do that,' she says, seriously freaked out.

'To be fair, I think she might have, having heard what he did,' I tell her, knowing full well that the jig is up.

'Auntie Ella?' she squeaks as the most logical explanation occurs to her.

We're away from the scene of the crime now, so I pull over again, take off my seat belt and turn to look her in the eye.

'Yep,' I say, kind of casually, given the circumstances.

'Oh my God,' she blurts. 'Oh my God! What are you doing here? Where's Mum?'

'Look, it's all OK, your mum is fine,' I reassure her. This has already been one hell of a day and she seems so freaked out – the last thing she needs to hear is that her mum is in prison.

'Your mum just needed a break,' I tell her. 'So, I said I'd fill in.'

'You look just like her,' she tells me. 'Only much cooler. So, it's been you since Mum supposedly got a haircut?'

'Just before my haircut,' I admit. 'But pretty much around that time.'

I watch as a visible wave of relief washes over her.

'Oh my God, I'm so glad you're not her,' she says. 'She would have killed me for going to that party, and then for what I said after – I was expecting you to drown me in the pond, or, I mean, I was expecting *her* to drown me... This is confusing.'

'Oh, believe me, I know,' I say with a laugh. 'I think your mum would have handled it better than you think, you know.'

'No, she definitely would have flipped,' she replies. 'You're being so cool about it. Mum always talks about you like you're the worst-case scenario.'

I don't know what to say to that. It feels like a huge slap in the face, that Emma would say that about me. Especially given her current circumstances, and the fact that I'm the one here, looking after her kids, taking care of things.

'Maybe I'm misunderstood,' I tell her. 'Or maybe my life went a little off course, and your mum struggles not to compare how I'm doing to how she's doing... You need to make sure you get the best start in life. You're an intelligent young woman – and you're way more like me than you are your mum – but you need to do what I didn't get chance to, which is to harness all of it and put it into something good. I know you think I'm a square, banging on about your exams, but, seriously, just do them. Just boss them, get them out of the way, and then do whatever you want but know that you have them under your belt.'

'I guess I got distracted,' she says. 'I just wanted to have some fun.'

'You have so much time for boys – and they're not all like dip-shit Eddie,' I tell her. 'Some of them are worth it.'

'Like Josh's uncle?' she says with a cheeky smile. 'Suddenly that makes a lot more sense.'

'I was thinking more along the lines of your dad – not for me, obviously, but for your mum. She's so lucky to have him,' I say.

'Josh's uncle is seriously hot though,' she says, chatting to me as though I'm her friend now.

'Oh God, yeah,' I reply, pretending to fan myself with my hand. 'He's on a date with his ex tonight though.'

'Thanks for being so cool,' Millie tells me. 'Mum really never would have trashed his car like that – if only because she loves this car more than anything on the planet.'

Fuck, I really hope I haven't damaged it.

'She probably wouldn't have told the girl he was in bed with that he had a diarrhoea problem either,' I add with a laugh.

'Oh my God, you didn't?' she replies.

'Yep,' I reply. 'You're welcome.'

The satisfied smile on her face makes it all worth it.

'You're not going to tell my mum about any of this, are you?' she asks.

'If you promise to knuckle down at school, and give the shady older boys a miss, then I don't need to tell her,' I say. 'And I can give you my number, so that you always have someone you can talk to about these things. I need you to do me a favour though.

The, erm, relaxation resort that your mum is at – she's there for another couple of weeks, and you know what she's like, she's terrified of looking bad in front of other people, even though I tell her not to give a crap what other people think of her.'

It's fascinating, how easy it is to just be myself in front of Millie now, but I can't help but notice how, even though I'm being me, I'm still curbing my bad language a little.

'I need you to keep pretending that I'm your mum,' I say. 'Only your dad and Marco, Josh's uncle, know the truth. As far as everyone else is concerned, I'm your mum.'

'OK, sure,' Millie replies.

She unfastens her seat belt and leans across the car to hug me, squeezing me tightly.

'Thank you so much,' she says. 'Thanks for everything.'

'It's all good,' I tell her. 'It's just nice to get to spend time with you. Come on, let's go home. Your dad has taken Henry out bowling and he said they were going to get dinner somewhere after. We could grab a takeaway and have a girly night?'

'I would absolutely love that,' she replies.

'Awesome,' I say. 'We can ransack your mum's dressing room, use some of her fancy face creams.'

I think Millie and I are about as excited as each other at the idea of a girls' night. But it's about so much more than whacking on a Hugh Grant movie, ordering a pizza and slathering our skin in something from Yves Saint Laurent. I'm excited to hang out with my niece, to get to know her properly, and for her to get to know me – the real me, not the urban-legend version of me that her mum warns her about.

This is what I'm going to miss, when Emma gets out and things go back to normal. It isn't the heated car seats and the Balenciaga trainers that make me feel as if I'm walking on clouds; it's having a family. Now that I've got one, I don't want to let it go.

38

Weeks ago, when Marco was trying to rumble me and he caught me out with the whole 'rugby away game' line, I assumed the early morning away game was made up. Turns out it isn't made up, it's a football game instead. So, I was up early this morning, convincing a reluctant Henry that he'd have such a fun time at his football match, even though I was fairly sure that couldn't possibly be true, not being up this early on a weekend, in the cold and the dark.

I reminded him how excited his dad was to see him play and, God love him, he reluctantly got up and got ready.

It turns out, because we were going to a football match, Emma's car is the car for stuff like that; Rich's car is a muddy-chil-dren-free zone, so I had to drive. Also, because I genuinely had already offered to give Marco and Josh a lift, they travelled with us. So, it was me and Rich in the front and Marco, Henry and Josh in the back. We all made small talk, all the way here, but what I really wanted to ask about was last night, and how Marco's date went. But I knew I couldn't do that in front of Rich, not without him wondering why I was asking – I really don't want to seem like I care, even though I really do.

Watching kids play football would be like watching paint dry – if paint were really bad at drying, and you were terrified the paint was going to break its neck.

It's so cold out here. Not even the half-time cups of cheap instant coffee are doing anything to help take the chill off. I honestly think that the only way to keep warm would be to see if one of the coaches would sub me in, but I know for a fact these kids could run rings around me. Then again, if I did try my luck running around the pitch in these heeled boots, I suppose the inevitable ambulance might be warm…

Rich is loving spectating, cheering the boys on from the sidelines, and, I have to admit, it's hard not to root for Henry when he gets the ball, not that he does all that often.

The final whistle is blown and, with a score of 7-5, the boys' team is named the winner.

'Is everything OK?' I ask Rich, noticing the look on his face as he stares down at his phone.

'Yes,' he replies. 'I do need to pop into the office though.'

'Oh, OK,' I reply.

'Don't worry, a taxi to Manchester from here isn't far at all. I'll just get a taxi there and then another one home later,' he reasons.

'Are you sure?' I reply. 'I can hurry the boys up?'

'No, no, it's fine,' he insists. 'Let the boys enjoy their victory. See you at home tonight.'

Rich gives me a peck on the cheek, for appearances, before he leaves. Then it's just me and Marco.

'Hi,' I say, kind of awkwardly.

'Hi,' he replies with a smile. 'How did it go last night?'

'It actually went well,' I tell him in hushed tones, just in case any of the other parents are listening. 'It sounds like the little shit was trying to pressure her into having sex and when she said no, he just did it with someone else.'

'Wow, that is brutal,' Marco replies. 'Someone needs to teach the bastard a lesson.'

'They do,' I reply. 'But I hear someone smashed into his car while he was at the party – such a shame.'

'Oh my, what a terrible accident,' Marco replies sarcastically. 'How was—?'

'Mum, we won, we won,' Henry interrupts, grabbing me by the wrist, yanking on my arm like a bell-ringer.

'I saw! I'm so proud of you,' I tell him as I ruffle his hair. 'You too, Josh.'

I really am proud of Henry. He might not be my kid, but I've got such a lump in my throat, seeing him so happy and so proud of himself. It's nice.

'Why don't we all go for some lunch?' Marco suggests. 'To celebrate.'

'Yes, let's do it,' I reply. 'I'm starving.'

The boys charge off towards the car. Marco and I follow closely behind.

'What were you saying before?' he asks me.

'What?'

I play dumb, because I don't really care, do I? (Spoiler alert: I really do.)

'You said "how was" and then the boys interrupted,' he says, refreshing my memory.

'Oh...' I pause, as though this information isn't at the forefront of my brain. 'Oh, yeah, I was just asking how your date went last night.'

'My *non*-date,' he corrects me. 'I didn't go in the end.'

'Is that my fault? I'm so sorry, I really didn't mean to ruin your night with my dramatic family.'

'No, it's fine,' he insists. 'I just thought about it and, well, someone who would kick me out on the street for losing my job isn't someone I want to go for a drink with.'

I can't help but smile.

'That's pretty good advice you gave yourself,' I tell him.

'Yeah, it sounded like the no-nonsense advice the new and improved Ask Alison would give,' he replies.

Finally, at the car, we strap the boys in before getting into the front seats.

'I'm so hungry I'll eat anything, anywhere,' Marco tells the boys. 'What do you fancy?'

'Can we go to McDonalds?' Josh asks.

'Ooh, yeah, I could murder some Maccies chips,' I reply, with an enthusiasm I only seem to reserve for food.

'Can we *really*?' Henry replies.

Oh, God, is that another thing Emma isn't a fan of? I'd feel terrible saying no now, and they have just been running around all morning, and it is just once…

'Yeah, why not?' I reply. 'Let's go!'

I can't believe Marco didn't meet his ex last night. He was all dressed up and ready to go, and I know he helped me find Millie, but the night was still young. He must have just genuinely decided that he didn't want to, which sounds to me as if he's definitely over her.

Oh, if only I weren't a married woman. But I don't suppose I will be for much longer.

39

'Mum, dinner is amazing,' Millie announces, all smiles.

Rich practically chokes on his ratatouille.

'Are you feeling OK?' he asks her. 'You're being nice.'

Henry sniggers.

'I just really appreciate everything Mum is doing for us,' Millie insists, potentially laying it on a bit too thick to be true.

'It really is good,' Rich says. 'You're not eating much.'

'I'm worried I'm not going to be able to fit into my outfit for the fundraiser,' I confess. 'Not that I'm losing weight for an outfit – I would never do that – I'm just so bloated. I've had a few days of eating rubbish.'

'What are you wearing?' Millie asks curiously.

'You know the scene in *Grease* where Sandy finally decides to be a bad girl?' I say. 'That.'

'Oh my God, what's Dad wearing?' she asks with a playful look of worry.

'You won't believe what your mum's got me wearing,' he says – but he sounds pretty excited about it. 'A black suit with a bright pink shirt, and a ridiculous black wig.'

'No!' she shrieks, but she's smiling. 'I cannot imagine you in that.'

'I did ask him which Danny Zuko he wanted to be, and gave him all the options, and you know your dad, obviously he chose the one in the suit,' I say with a laugh. 'Always business.'

After dinner the kids head up to their rooms and Rich helps me clear the table.

'I don't know what you've done to Millie, but thank you,' he says. 'Thank you for everything, across the board, you're doing such an incredible job.'

'She's such a brilliantly intelligent young woman,' I tell him. 'And she had that going on long before I got here.'

'It's just so nice to see everyone so happy,' he says – he's obviously not including the whole 'wife in prison' thing, which he never seems to want to talk about, even when we're alone, and I'm not going to make him. 'I'm so relaxed, I might even chill out down here, watch a bit of sport.'

'Well, have fun,' I tell him. 'I'm going to go upstairs, read some more of my mum's book. I'm flying through it now.'

'Are you enjoying it?' he asks me.

'Enjoying isn't the word,' I reply with a laugh. 'I'll let you know when I finish it.'

I had to break off for dinner, but I was reading one of Mum's later chapters, which was all about making amends. Auntie Angela is firmly of the opinion that you cannot live a peaceful life if you have anything hanging over you. Covering everything from never going to bed on an argument to forgiving and forgetting before you pass away (Mum sure knew how to poke people in the emotions), the chapter could not be clearer: clear your conscience.

I know I haven't been the world's best *anything* during my

thirty-four years on this earth but I don't think I've ever done anything I truly regret... except maybe one thing.

I shove on some warm clothes and head back downstairs.

'I'm just going to get some air,' I call to Rich.

'OK, no worries,' he calls back.

As I head for the front door Marty comes bounding over, hoping it's time for a walk, even though Rich only took him for one, before dinner.

I open the door just enough to squeeze my body through, so that Marty can't run out with me. As I do, I hear a notification come through on my phone.

It's from Marco:

What are you up to?

I reply:

Digging up the garden – want to join me?

I'll be there in 10.

* * *

'I have to admit, when you asked me if I wanted to dig up the garden with you, my brain went somewhere else completely,' Marco jokes.

I smile as I hand him a trowel.

'You actually want to dig up the garden?' he says with a laugh. 'Why?'

'Do you remember me telling you about Simon Wright, the kid who hit me with his bike?' I say, keeping my voice low because we're in the garden, at the side of the house.

'Yeah, he got his bike confiscated for it, so his dad bought him a new one,' Marco recalls.

'Well, I didn't exactly leave it at that,' I admit. 'He turned up to school with this new bike, even better than the last, and again, he did his usual swerve into me as he rode past me. I was so, so annoyed. It just felt like such a huge slap in the face, I wanted him to pay.'

'He's buried in this garden, isn't he?' Marco jokes with a faux-serious look of horror.

'Nothing quite so sinister, although it was a body part I buried,' I admit.

Now Marco looks worried for real, which only makes it funnier.

'He parked his bike at the front of the school and – remember what I told you about the school statue? He parked it next to that. And that day in particular, we were playing hockey in PE, and I wasn't enjoying it at all, so I pretended I needed the loo, to kill some time. And as I walked past that new bike, with the hockey stick in my hand...'

'You hit his bike?' Marco replies.

'No, I missed his bike. I hit the statue,' I confess. 'Took its hand clean off.'

'Oh, shit, so that was you?' Marco laughs, quickly lowering his voice again. 'So, it's the hand that's here?'

'Yep,' I reply. 'After years of pretending it wasn't me, it's a hard habit to break. But it was me. I shoved it up the back of my polo shirt, and tucked the shirt into my PE skirt, until I could get it inside to hide in my locker. I'd brought it home and buried it in the back garden before anyone even noticed it was missing. It was a CCTV blind spot, but they just about pinned down a shortlist of suspects, and I was one of them. I really wanted to return it, maybe try and fix it back on myself, but I didn't know how and then suddenly, you know, it's today, and a million years have gone by.'

'So, what? You want to dig it up?' he asks.

'Yeah, and return it,' I reply. 'I'm sure they could fix it.'

'You never cease to amaze me, Ella,' he replies. 'Not just with your stories, but with your criminal damage rap sheet.'

'I guess that's my go-to,' I reply. 'But that's how you hit rich people where it hurts.'

'And potentially how you end up in the cell next to your sister,' he adds.

'I know, I know,' I reply. 'But that's why I'm trying to make amends.'

'Well, OK, let's get digging,' he says.

It's cold out, and quite dark without the bigger outside lights on. We're at the side of the house, so not in Rich's eyeline, if he's still downstairs watching TV, but I don't want to take any chances. We're looking pretty dodgy right now.

We both search through the flower beds, careful not to disturb any of the plants, but we don't find anything.

'My hands are seizing up, it's so cold,' I say, dropping the trowel for a second to rub my hands together. 'There was nothing here but mud when I buried it.'

'If they've had it all landscaped, it might be gone,' Marco points out.

He stabs his trowel into the soil, dusting off his hands before he rubs my arms to keep me warm.

'You don't understand. I have to make amends,' I tell him. 'I can't have this hanging over me, I really can't.'

'Why do I get the feeling this is about so much more than the hand of a statue?' he says softly.

'Sorry, I was reading my mum's book earlier, and now I'm thinking about what's going to happen to me, if I don't put this right, and if perhaps my negative behaviour is the reason for my, shall we say, negative life.'

I sigh.

'This coming from the woman who wanted to report the Blackpool fortune teller to the fraud squad,' Marco reminds me.

'I didn't like the way she said my pink aura made me highly sensitive,' I tell him.

'Yeah, because you're not highly sensitive at all.' He laughs. 'She told me I didn't even have an aura.'

'That checks out,' I joke.

Marco stops rubbing my arms and instead wraps his arms around me to keep me warm.

'It's not that I think something magical is at play,' I insist. 'I meant it quite literally. Am I a negative person who seeks out negative things?'

'Of course, you're not,' Marco replies with a reassuring smile. 'Ella, I don't think you realise just how amazing you are.'

'I'm not amazing, I'm ridiculous,' I insist. 'This isn't me having a pity party, this is just me stating the facts, and the facts are—'

Marco plants his lips on mine. He kisses me, lightly, just for a few seconds, before he releases me again.

'Was that just to shut me up?' I ask, a little taken aback, and with no idea what else to say. Thinking about it, that probably wasn't my finest line.

'It was only partly to shut you up,' he tells me. 'It was mostly because I've wanted to do it for a really long time, but I figured your fake husband might frown upon it.'

I bite my bottom lip gently as I wonder what to do next.

This time I kiss him, with a little more passion, for just a few seconds longer.

'Do you want to come inside?' I ask him.

'I don't think that's such a good idea,' he replies. 'Your fake husband really wouldn't appreciate that.'

'Come with me,' I insist. 'Quickly – and quietly.'

We sneak around into the back garden, only just stepping around the corner, so we're not in view of the bi-folding doors.

'Follow my lead, OK?'

I place my hands on the side of the pergola and test one of the lower pieces with my foot.

'What are you doing?' Marco whispers in disbelief. 'Are you climbing up the wall?'

'I used to do it all the time, it's fine,' I insist as I finally make my first move. Thankfully it holds my weight.

'When you were a kid,' he reminds me. 'I'm a grown man, it'll never hold my weight.'

'Chicken,' I tease – which is very much something a kid would say – before I clamber up on top of the pergola and then over the little wall to the terrace.

'I can't believe I'm doing this.' Marco laughs to himself as he follows my lead. He makes it to the top and, right as he swings his body over the little wall, the pergola makes a snapping sound.

We both peer back over the terrace wall, and it looks absolutely fine, but I don't think it would have taken Marco's weight for another second, and I'm not sure it's going to be safe for anyone to do it again – if it ever was. My last act of teenage rebellion.

I find the key and let us into Rich's office, which is in total darkness, apart from the light coming in from the moon outside.

'I can't believe you're sneaking me into your room,' Marco whispers, pulling me close for a moment as he runs his hands up and down my back. 'That's kind of hot.'

'I'm technically sneaking you into someone else's room,' I reply.

'Well, that's even hotter,' he says, leaning in for another kiss. This time I quickly pull away.

'Wait,' I tell him. 'Wait until we're upstairs.'

This sounds like me being sexy, making him wait, but it isn't. I'm just worried if I start kissing him again here, I won't be able to stop.

I lock the terrace door behind us before we sneak towards the hallway. I check the landing for things like husbands, children or dogs. Once I'm sure the coast is clear I grab Marco by the hand and drag him towards the door that leads up to the third floor. Once we're through it, and it's closed behind us, we start kissing again. Marco picks me up so I lock my legs around his waist. He carries me up the stairs, eventually dropping me down on the bed, once he works out where it is with some impressive peripheral vision.

I watch as he takes off his jacket and peels off his T-shirt to reveal his muscular torso. Marco's body tells me that he's no stranger to the gym. My body tells people that the only working out I do is what my pizza is going to cost me with my '20 per cent off' code. But do you know what? I genuinely don't think Marco cares about where I'm squashy, or the parts of my legs I haven't shaved, and while I'm sure he'll tease me for the tramp-stamp tattoo I regret having done as an act of rebellion on my eighteenth birthday, I just know he's not going to kick me out of bed for it. And because of that, I don't really care either.

'Smarty, play romance music,' I command, just loud enough for it to hear, as I wrestle my top over my head.

I don't need to worry about anyone hearing the music – they certainly don't hear The Beach Boys every morning.

'All right, playing music by My Chemical Romance,' she replies.

I launch my top across the room before leaning over the bed to unplug the Smarty from under the bedside table.

'Why do people even have these things? They're useless,' I say with a breathless laugh.

'It's the thought that counts,' Marco replies as he climbs back onto the bed. 'They listen to everything all the time anyway.'

'Oh, well, I definitely don't want them listening to this,' I tell him, pulling him down on top of me so that we can pick up where we left off.

Call it a bit of a delayed reaction but a voice in my head has just pointed out what I'm doing. I'm kissing Marco – I'm in bed with him, my sister's bed, no less. How very, truly Ella of me. I couldn't think of anything more on-brand. And I'm doing exactly what I said I shouldn't do, the very thing I worried about, the thing I've told myself all along was a bad idea. It doesn't feel wrong though, being in bed with Marco (apart from feeling wrong in the sexiest of ways, obviously) it feels right.

I just need to make sure I find a way to sneak him out of here in the morning. Because wouldn't it be terrible if my husband caught us...?

40

What are you wearing?

I blush as I read Marco's message. There's something about getting sexy messages when you're in a public place that makes you blush something fierce. I know that I'm the only person that can see my phone screen but it still feels like something hot in my hand.

Behave yourself. I'm working.

I'm currently at Henry's school, getting things ready for tonight. School is still in session, for another fifteen minutes at least, and then it's officially half-term. This means that, not only have I successfully got the kids through to their break under my watch, but tonight is the big fundraiser we've all been looking forward to.

I do find it amusing that people pay so much for their kids to come here, but then essentially have a whip-round as soon as something needs paying for. That said, this fundraiser is worth every penny, because it's going to be epic.

Rather than the school just essentially extending an open hand and seeing what people give them, the fundraisers are more like fancy parties for the parents, with the proceeds just happening to go back into the school, which is good. It's going to be one hell of an event, and it had quite the budget behind it, so everything is amazing.

For some of the decorations they've actually had the students creating things in their art lessons. So we have our massive toilet-paper sculpture from the school dance scene in *Grease*, and we've got this beautiful dark blue material that we're going to hang on the wall, covered in twinkling stars and the iconic face of the man in the moon from *Moulin Rouge!*, which is my absolutely favourite musical, and I wish so much that I were dressing as Satine tonight, but I really didn't think that would go down well with the Parents' Association.

I'm currently dragging a life-sized papier-mâché Audrey II from *Little Shop of Horrors* across the room, which is absolutely incredible; I can't believe kids made this.

So far, it's just me and a couple of other volunteers, setting things up for this evening, but once the school day is over and the kids go home Christian and a few other teachers will be in to help too.

I haven't spoken to Christian since I cancelled our plans, and he hasn't even tried to contact me, but it's probably for the best. He's a lovely man, and I enjoyed hanging out with him, but I don't imagine Emma wants to continue a friendship with him when she gets her life back in just over a week.

I can't believe my time here is nearly done. It feels as if it's flown by, but I'm not all that worried about what comes next any more, not now I've found Marco. We're kind of a thing – not that we've labelled it or anything, but we've been sneaking around like a couple of lovesick teenagers all week.

I check my phone the second I feel it buzz again, because every message from him is like a drug to me; I just can't get enough of them. Two messages from him this time.

I meant what are you wearing tonight. I wish you'd tell me.

I can see that you're working – look out of the window.

I glance around the room until I spot him standing outside. As soon as I have eyes on him, Marco presses his face up against the glass and pretends to kiss it.

I reply...

Careful, someone might see you... Thanks for picking Henry up for me. Just want to make sure everything is perfect for tonight.

I see him typing on his phone, as well as the little dots on my screen that tell me he's replying. A man who texts back straight away – did you know such a man existed?

No problem. Have you seen this?

An image comes through. It's a selfie that Millie took of the two of us the other night, in our facemasks, watching *Pretty Woman*.

My brother found out Tom was at the party and had me block his social media access on his computer. It was the first thing on his newsfeed so it caught my eye.

You can tell how much she loves you. But how many teenagers have an auntie who will commit criminal damage to get back at a boy for them?

I smile to myself as I reply.

I'm so glad she knows the truth. I'm really happy with the way things are working out. And I'm really looking forward to tonight.

I make an attempt to continue shifting Audrey II while I wait for his reply to come through.

I can't wait to get my hands on you later. Whatever you're wearing, it won't be on for long.

I glance back towards the window, only to see that Marco has vanished. I look at my watch and see that it's home time, so I'd better get a move on.

Just when I didn't think I could possibly be looking forward to tonight any more, suddenly, I'm even more excited. I just need to finish up here, get home, squeeze into my outfit, curl my hair, and hope that the fake cigarettes I ordered through the Smarty have arrived, because I'm really going all out to look the part.

I can't wait for Marco to see my outfit, and I really can't wait to see what he's wearing. Even if it does sound like we won't be keeping them on for too long...

41

I'm going to say it: I look awesome. I may not be as thin as Olivia Newton John (I read somewhere that they had to sew her into the leather pants she wore in *Grease*), and I sound more like a character from *Hollyoaks* than an Australian babe, but I am really feeling this look.

Disclaimer: my pants are not leather, they're like super-shiny Lycra, so there wasn't much squeeze into them to do at all, instead they stretched to fit me. I'm wearing a black form-fitting Bardot top, with a sweetheart neck, almost exactly like the one bad girl Sandy wears, and I've given myself big curls and sexy make-up to truly look the part. And then there's the sky-high heeled sandals.

My fake cigarettes arrived in time, and they're just like the ones I bought from a joke shop when I was a kid. They appear partially smoked, with a fake burned end, and they're packed with some kind of powder so that when you 'smoke' it looks as if smoke comes out; you just have to remember to blow, not suck.

Rich looks wonderful in his 'Danny at the dance' costume. I reckon he chose the suit because it was the least out of his comfort zone, but the bright pink shirt and the black wig are not the type of look I've ever seen him sporting. Still, I think he feels cool in his outfit, and he's clearly so excited for the evening, because he has the biggest smile on his face, genuinely, like he doesn't have a care in the world.

'Hello,' the host greets us cheerily – I think his name is Andrew, but I wouldn't put money on it. It's hard when people think you already know their names, because they don't often have cause to say it to you again randomly.

'Aren't you both looking fantastic?' he says. 'That's you both ticked off my list, you can head inside, but just before you do, we have a number of karaoke slots so that parents can show off their own musical skills, up on stage with our band. What do you say?'

'Not a chance, pal,' Rich tells him, making a move to head inside.

'Erm, yeah, let me think about that,' I say politely. 'I'll just check my coat for now, please.'

'OK, well, slots are filling up fast, so don't wait too long,' he replies.

I don't think I fancy taking to this stage in front of this judgemental lot, and I don't reckon Emma would be too happy with me hamming it up in front of all of her friends either.

Now that it's dark outside and the fundraiser is in full swing the place really does look amazing. We're in the large school hall that opens up into an outdoor quad, which is usually surrounded by classrooms, but today the walls and windows have twinkling stars projected onto them.

Inside the hall, up on the stage, the band are already doing their thing, currently performing a rather funky rendition of 'Time Warp'. They're doing such a fabulous job, I'm actually glad the original band pulled out.

'I'm going to see if I can find Marco,' I tell Rich. 'And do the rounds, saying hello to everyone.'

'I'm going to go find Alan Rodgers, see if he went through with the Edna from *Hairspray* costume he's been threatening,' he replies.

God, I really hope he has.

I admire my own work – and the work of everyone else involved – as I walk around the room looking for Marco.

Eventually I spot him, on the dance floor, doing the Time Warp. I almost don't recognise him, in his costume, given how committed he is to looking the part.

'Marco, look at you,' I squeak as I approach him.

He's dressed as Danny from *Grease*, from the final scene in the fun house, where he's wearing his usual black trousers and a tight black sleeveless vest, except he's wearing a white and red replica Rydell High cardigan over it, just as the character does when he's trying to be good. Most notably, he's shaved away his stubble, and he's managed to slick his own hair into that iconic greased-back style.

'Oh, Emma, darling, look at you,' one of the mums slurs at me.

I recognise her as the woman who gave me Herman – I really hope she doesn't ask about him, RIP – but I still don't know her name. She's dressed as Tracy from *Hairspray* and she's absolutely nailing it. Just imagine a forty-something version of Tracy with a glass of wine in her hand and about six or seven under her belt.

'Thanks. You look amazing too,' I tell her.

'Thanks, lovely,' she replies. 'Link was the only costume I could talk Peter into– it's not much different from his usual look, is it? I told him I wanted to be characters from *Frozen* and do you know what he said?'

I shake my head.

'He said "Erica, piss off" – can you imagine?'

As Erica gestures with her hands wildly she sloshes a little wine out of her glass, which makes her cackle like the Wicked Witch of the West.

'Oh, "You're The One That I Want", this is your song,' she tells me, pointing to the band, just in case I wasn't sure what she was referring to.

'Well, I'd better go dance to it,' I tell her. 'Lovely to see you again.'

'You too,' she calls after me. 'I'm going to grab another drink. I'll see you around.'

I make my way through the small crowd that just formed, blocking my view of where Marco was, but he's still right where I last had eyes on him, still dancing.

I think one of my favourite things about him, and it's one of my few favourite qualities about myself (second, of course, to my dedication to revenge) is that he's happy to dance at clubs and parties. Lots of men just won't dance, full stop, no negotiations, but Marco doesn't dance like no one is watching, he dances like everyone is watching and it doesn't affect his confidence for a second.

The moment he claps eyes on me he widens his eyes (genuinely, I think) but then he discards his cardigan just like Danny does in the movie.

'Look at you,' he says.

'Look at *you*,' I reply. 'You shaved.'

'We chose the same movie in the end,' he points out.

'We chose the same scene,' I tell him.

It's hard, when you're here, in the outfit, with the music playing, not to dance along.

We dance together, but as we find our bodies pulling towards each other we quickly move apart again.

'Hey, come with me,' Marco insists. 'I really want you to meet my brother and sister-in-law.'

'OK, sure,' I reply nervously.

Eek, no one has ever wanted to introduce me to their family; why am I so nervous?

I follow him over to a couple who are dressed as Maria and Captain von Trapp from *The Sound of Music*. I know it's Marco's brother before he says a word because there's a strong family resemblance.

'This is my brother, Ant, and my sister-in-law, Lisa,' Marco tells me excitedly.

'Yeah, she knows that,' Ant tells him with a laugh. 'Our kids have been best friends since nursery.'

'Right, yeah,' Marco says awkwardly.

Shit, I was so nervous about meeting them, I genuinely forgot for a few seconds I'm here as Emma. I think the same goes for Marco, who just really wanted me to meet his brother.

'Hey, Emma,' Ant says with a bemused laugh. 'Is my brother bothering you?'

'No, no,' I insist. 'Just an in-joke.'

I'm pretty sure you can get yourself out of almost any situation by simply citing: in-joke.

'You've got a look of a young John Travolta,' Lisa tells Marco.

'He really does,' I say. 'You should have seen him at... ah...'

Shit! I was going to tell them about when we were dancing at Gloria's but I can't say that, can I?

'Forgotten what I was going to say,' I say with a chuckle.

Well, the in-joke thing works a charm, but I'm pretty sure you need to let at least a minute or two pass before you say it again.

Ant laughs.

'Don't worry, lots of people are smashed already,' he says. 'Have you seen the state of John Cunningham? I can't believe what a state he's in.'

Ah well, at least they think I'm just drunk.

I glance around the room nosily, looking out for people who are worse for wear, and taking in all the different costumes.

I'm seeing lots of costumes from *Grease*, and I'm seeing plenty that I can't quite figure out, but when I clap eyes on the Yummy Mummy Mafia, I instantly know who everyone is. Jessica, the leader of the pack, is dressed as Audrey from *Little Shop of Horrors*, even though I would describe her personality type as more Audrey II.

As always, she is flanked by Cleo and Abbey, but they've both got their fellas in tow today. Cleo is dressed as Gabriella from *High School Musical*, with the oldest Troy Bolton I have ever seen in my life by her side. Abbey and her husband (who, jokes aside, I think I might actually kind of recognise as a Premier League footballer – I'm no expert though) have come as Mia and Sebastian from *La La Land*, which I like; that's a bit cool and a bit different.

'Next up for the karaoke we have John Cunningham,' I hear a member of the band announce.

Ah, the aforementioned, absolutely hammered John Cunningham; this ought to be good.

Now that I'm looking at him up there on stage, dressed as Orin, the dentist from *Little Shop of Horrors*, I realise that it's Jessica's husband, John, aka Emma's lovesick, fleeting bit on the side, and oh, boy, does he look drunk. He's absolutely hammered and he's even drinking now, during the intro to his song, which is obviously 'Dentist!' from *Little Shop of Horrors*.

It's absolutely hilarious, the way the band are singing the backing vocals, but that's about all that is funny about it. John is tragic, screaming out the lyrics, slurring some of the words.

All I can think to do is keep out of his way this evening, because he really seems as if he's going through it right now, and with the amount he's had to drink, he's a ticking time bomb. I don't think it would take much for him to start blabbing.

A tap on my shoulder snaps me from my thoughts. I turn around, expecting to see Marco taking the piss out of John, but it's Christian.

'Oh, hello,' I say.

Christian is yet another Danny Zuko. This time just a classic Danny in his T-Birds jacket, which is what he told me he was going to wear.

'Hi,' he replies with a smile. 'Your outfit looks great.'

'Yours too,' I tell him. 'You finally got to put that leather jacket to good use.'

'First and last time.' He laughs. But his face quickly falls.

We fall silent for a second or two. John's vocals are absolutely deafening in the background.

'Everything looks amazing,' I say, filling the silence.

'Could I have a word with you?' Christian asks, raising his voice a little to cancel out John's. 'My office.'

'OK,' I reply.

Ooh, 'my office', what a very teachery thing to say.

'Back in a minute,' I tell Marco before I jokily bite my bottom lip with pretend nerves at being called into the deputy head's office. I suppose I am a little nervous though, following him along the lonely corridor towards his office. I can't help but wonder what he wants that he has to tell me right now, in private, with a serious look like that on his face.

This can't be good...

42

'It's such an amazing event,' I tell him, just in case he didn't hear me before. 'Everything looks amazing. Everyone is having so much fun.'

'Shit, the cleaner must have locked it,' Christian says to himself as he tries his office door.

'It's OK, we can talk out here,' I say. 'I'll feel less like I'm in trouble... I'm not in trouble, am I?'

I'm smiling, but I am worried.

'Of course, you're not in trouble,' he says with a smile. 'I don't *think* I have the power to give parents detention.'

'Oh, but wouldn't it be amazing if you did?' I reply. 'If someone could send John to isolation that would be great. *That* singing.'

'Are you going to sing something?' he asks me. 'Finally live out your dream of playing Sandy on a school stage?'

'I'm happy to blend into the background tonight,' I admit. 'I'm just so pleased to see it all going so well. Who knew it felt so good, to see your hard work paying off? Well, you do, I suppose – you are a teacher.'

'Did you get your family emergency sorted last week?' he asks, changing the subject.

'I did – don't ever have a teenager,' I tell him. 'Well, probably let Calvin grow up.'

Oh God, I'm being so awkward. I guess I feel kind of awkward, standing here in the corridor with him, the noise of the party muffled in the background, even though we haven't come far.

'I thought maybe you were avoiding me,' he says softly.

'No, of course not,' I reply. 'You know what it's like when you've got a partner and kids.'

Annnd I've put my foot in it again.

I know that, at the start, I thought that Christian was the kind of guy for me, but I think I liked the idea of him more than anything. He seemed like a good man, with a good job, a family, strong principles. And all of that is still true but – even if I pretend he doesn't think I'm Emma – it's Marco who I want to be with.

It's funny because, while I was so focused on how good Christian would be for me, I had myself convinced that Marco would be bad for me, and that I would be bad for him. But he's been there for me, all this time, he's always had my back. And the fact that he doesn't think I'm Emma is a double positive, not only for the obvious reason – that it's not true – but because he knows me, the real me. He knows I'm skint, unemployed, that I've tanked every opportunity that I've ever been given, and he doesn't care. He just sees me, he sees me through all the mess, and he always has. He's seen me since day one, and that's as terrifying as it is amazing. I can't hide from him, but I don't want to.

I have enjoyed hanging out with Christian, planning the fundraiser (hilariously, I still have no idea what we're actually raising money for), but this friendship just can't continue, not while I'm Emma, because there's no way she's going to resume it once she's back. Now that the fundraiser is nearly over, we won't have to be around each other at all, and that will help things go back to normal. If I were me, of course, I'd want to stay friends, but I'm still Emma for another week, so I've got to do what's right.

'We've done so much planning in such a short space of time,' I remind him. 'It's no wonder it feels like suddenly something is missing.'

'That's exactly what it feels like though, Emma, like you're missing all of a sudden,' he explains. 'I've really enjoyed spending time with you, and I thought we were getting closer...'

'We've done such a good job with the fundraiser—' I start.

'Screw the fundraiser,' Christian interrupts. He sounds a little flustered. 'We both know this is about more than the fundraiser.'

He doesn't give me a second to even think before he pulls me close and plants his lips on mine.

I quickly push him away.

'Oh, boy,' I hear a voice say from behind me.

In a cruel and unusual twist, and a fine example of life imitating art, my life appears to have musical-worthy timing at the moment.

'Marco,' I blurt.

'I'll talk to you when you're done,' he replies as he heads back around the corner.

'Dude, what are you doing?' I ask Christian, allowing myself to be, well, myself for a moment. 'What is it with the men in this fucking village just going for it with women? It's 2021. Don't they make you watch DVDs that tell you no means no?'

Christian seems a little taken aback, as if all of a sudden, he doesn't recognise me any more – well, as if he doesn't see Emma in me any more, I suppose.

'We've been getting on really well,' he says.

'I'm married,' I tell him.

'We've been getting closer...'

'Still married,' I point out.

'Oh, screw your marriage,' he replies. 'You've been after me for weeks, making up excuses to be around me, and now, what? You're too scared to go through with it because *you're married*?'

He says the last two words in such a horrible, mocking tone. I get it, he's pissed off at me, and he's frustrated because he thought we had something, but at no point have I told him that I was interested in him, at no point have I made a move on him, so what the hell is he thinking? I thought he was such a good guy, but the kind of guy I thought he was is not the kind of guy who puts the move on married women. I certainly wasn't expecting him to act this way. He just didn't seem the type.

'I'm going back to the party,' I tell him.

Well, that's only where I'm going if that's where Marco is, because I need to find him and explain.

I hurry past the toilets, back towards the party, but as I pass a door that leads to a stairwell, I spot Marco sitting there out of the corner of my eye.

'Shit, there you are,' I say breathlessly. 'Listen, we weren't kissing, he kissed me, I didn't ask him to, I stopped him.'

'Ella, calm down,' Marco insists. 'Sit down for a second.'

Sit down? Sitting down is for bad news. Fantastic. He's easily the best thing that's ever happened to me and I haven't even been able to keep hold of him for a week.

I sit down on the stairs next to him and puff air from my cheeks.

'Marco, Christian kissed me,' I insist again. 'I would never.'

'I told you, it's fine,' he says with a smile. 'I heard everything he said. I saw what happened. You really need to be more careful having private conversations – anyone could be listening around the corner. Where's your phone? I tried to call you.'

'It's in my coat. I checked it at the door – where am I going to put a phone in this outfit?' I reply. '*Don't* answer that.'

'I've got good news. I didn't want to tell you earlier, until I was sure, but I cracked the Smarty,' he explains. 'I just got the email confirmation. I was first. I'm getting the bounty.'

'The £50k?' I reply, in possibly the highest pitch my voice has ever reached. 'Marco, that's amazing. Who knew being a geek paid so well?'

'The geeks shall inherit the earth,' he jokes.

'Just think what you can do with all that money, Marco! You can turn your life around.'

'*Our* life around,' he corrects me. 'I told you, if I got back on my feet first, I'd make sure we were both OK. I know £50k isn't much around these parts but it's enough for me to stop crashing at my brother's, it's enough to live on while I sort my next job. And while you figure out what you want to do next.'

'You are amazing,' I tell him. 'So amazing. So talented and caring and wonderful and I'm so lucky to have you in my life.'

I jump to my feet and grab Marco by the hand. I'll let go of it again before anyone sees.

'Come on, this deserves a drink,' I tell him.

Marco stands up but instead of following my lead he lifts me up and pushes me back against the wall.

'Uh-oh,' I say quietly.

'Just a few more minutes,' he whispers before he kisses me.

For a second, I get lost in the moment but then I stop him.

'Oi, come on, we can't do this here,' I say through a playful giggle. 'As much as I'd like to.'

'OK, fine, we'll do it your way,' he says with a smile. 'We'll go back to the party. But can we get together later and celebrate properly?'

'Of course, we can,' I reply. 'I'm sure we can sneak you in again.'

'OK, I'll go back out there first, so it doesn't look suspicious,' he says.

Marco kisses me again before he disappears.

Wow, this is like having an affair. It's like all the sexy danger of an affair without anyone's feelings getting hurt. I'm sure there's almost no other way to replicate this feeling without ruining people's lives so I'm going to make the most of it.

I casually make my way back into the main hall, as though I've just popped to the loo or something, and slink up to one of the open bars to grab myself a drink.

I just need to blend back in, as if I never ducked out, and I should probably find Rich and spend some time with him, for appearances. This is our most public event so we need to make it count, otherwise all this was for nothing.

I'm avoiding John as though he's an actual dentist, and the Christian thing is officially nipped in the bud. I just need to get through the rest of the event, get over this final hurdle, and then soon enough I'll be able to stop living my sister's life and start living my own again.

Game face on, Ella. You've almost done it.

43

'Emma, darling,' Erica slurs, far drunker than she was earlier.

She grabs two drinks from the open bar and hands one to me.

'Cheers,' she says.

'Cheers,' I reply, clinking my glass of white wine with hers.

'You are just something else,' she tells me. 'With your fabulous costumes. Frenchy was always my favourite.'

Oh, boy, it must have been wine o'clock for hours for Erica. She's barely coherent.

'Yeah, she's great,' I reply. 'I chose Sandy in the end.'

'Huh?'

'I'm Sandy,' I tell her, loudly and slowly.

'Yeah, I can see,' she replies. 'Really impressive. Really fast.'

'I just need to go find Rich,' I tell her, because, honestly, she's at a level of drunk that's kind of freaking me out.

'Next up for the karaoke we've got Emma Cooper,' a voice announces over the sound system. 'Emma Cooper, where are you?'

What? I didn't put my name down to sing.

Erica screams like a madwoman.

'She's here, she's here,' she cries out.

'Come on, Emma, come on up here,' the frontman of the band calls out.

With all eyes on me I have no choice but to make my way to the stage.

When I get there, I walk straight to the front, rather than to the stairs.

'I didn't put my name down to sing,' I tell him.

'I've got you right here,' he tells me. 'Emma Cooper – "If I Only Had a Brain".'

'Ah,' I reply. 'I think that might be a prank – I don't even know the words.'

'Oh, OK,' he replies, suddenly getting the joke at my expense. 'Don't worry.'

'OK, apparently there's been a mix-up,' he announces. 'So, I'm going to sing it instead. Take it away, boys.'

Mortified, I shuffle away from the stage, keeping my eyes peeled for Rich. I eventually spot him outside, in the quad, so I make my way towards him. I'm just passing through the large open doors when I cross paths with Christian.

'Hilarious,' I say. 'Really fucking mature.'

'What?' he calls after me.

'The song,' I snap back.

Well, he's obviously put me down as singing *that* song to have a dig at me. I can't believe a grown man could be so pathetic.

I slow down for a few seconds when I notice Jessica talking to Rich. He doesn't look happy, but she looks delighted. That can't be a good sign.

'Hello,' I say as I approach them. 'Apparently someone put me down to sing "If I Only Had a Brain" as a joke. Rude.'

'I think "If I Only Had a Heart" might have been more appropriate,' Jessica says. She clicks her tongue.

'Erm, what?' I reply.

I notice Abbey and Cleo standing behind her. I can't help but feel as if they're here for back-up.

'I'm just filling your husband in on your antics,' Jessica informs me.

'Emma, I didn't pick that song,' Christian interrupts. He must have followed me. 'I'm not having that.'

'Sorry, I jumped to the wrong conclusion,' I reply. 'I'm suddenly getting the feeling it was Jessica...'

'Oh, it wasn't me,' she insists with a laugh. 'I'm not about the petty digs. I'm here to tell the truth.'

'Incoming drunk,' Marco announces as he joins us. He's practically carrying John. 'This yours?'

'Oh, for God's sake,' Jessica says. 'I'm in the middle of something, just prop him against a wall or something.'

Marco shrugs and does as he's told. Jessica clearly has no time for her husband right now. John leans back against the wall but he can't hold himself up so he quickly slides down to the floor.

'Right, I'm glad everyone is here,' Jessica announces. 'It's about time the truth came out.'

Oh, God. I don't know what she thinks the truth is, but it's not going to be the actual truth, is it? Because only me, Rich and Marco know the actual truth.

'Rich, I hate to be the one to tell you this,' Jessica starts, but she doesn't sound as if she hates it; she looks and sounds as if she's loving it. 'I just caught your wife, red-handed, kissing this one down the corridor.'

'It wasn't what it seemed,' Christian insists. 'We were just talking.'

'Not you,' Jessica says. 'Him. They were practically doing it against the wall. *In a school.*'

She points Marco out to everyone.

First of all, there are no kids here tonight. Second of all, the hypocrisy of the woman; she's got a gin and tonic in her hand.

'Wait, you just kissed *him*?' Christian says. 'Because you just kissed me and you gave it all that "oh, I love my husband" bullshit – but then you go and kiss *him*?'

'Do you see the kind of woman you're married to?' Jessica tells Rich. 'Do you see?'

I don't know what to say so I say nothing. Marco doesn't know what to say so he says nothing.

'Look, don't worry, it's fine, I know,' Rich tells her quietly. Perhaps he should have said nothing too.

'What? You know?' she shrieks. 'You know about her just running around the village, having multiple affairs? You poor, poor man. I feel so sorry for you. Emma Cooper, you're nothing but a hussy.'

'Enough,' a voice shouts over us. 'Enough.'

We all turn to face the person calling time on our little Jerry Springer pop-up show. I expect it's some school employee whose job it is to ask unruly parents to quit with the floorshow or leave. It isn't though, and when I see who it is, all I can manage to do is blurt her name.

'Emma!'

44

The first thing I notice is Emma's face. It's the most familiar face in the world to me – well, of course it is, it's basically my face – but she's the last person I expected to see here.

The second thing I notice is the headscarf on her head.

'Emma, what are you doing here?' Rich asks her as he hurries over to her. He wraps his arms around her and holds her tight. 'You're not supposed to be here.'

'A few weeks in the clink and you're dressing like a jailbird?' I blurt, but it's obvious something else is going on here.

'OK, I have two questions: who or what the hell are you?' Jessica asks me, then she turns to Emma. 'And you were in prison?'

'Oh, for God's sake, I obviously haven't been in prison,' Emma says with a roll of her eyes, and then she pulls her headscarf off.

My breath catches in my throat. I quickly place my hand over my mouth. I don't think anyone knows what to say.

'Emma...' I say softly, my voice almost failing me. 'Emma...'

'I've got cancer,' she blurts. 'Breast cancer.'

My ears start ringing loudly, like my own personal alarm

bells. I feel as if I've been punched in the face *and* the stomach. No, not again. This can't be happening again.

'Emma, you're not supposed to be here,' Rich says again.

'What choice did I have, Rich?' she replies. 'This one is running amok. Have you seen the state of the village website? It's completely different. I've lost track of the rumours doing the rounds about me. And all of my messages still come through to my laptop, so I've been following it all. Well, no more, I can't sit by and watch her tank my life any more.'

'Emma...'

All I can say is her name.

'I want you gone,' she snaps at me. 'I ask you for one little favour, I trust you with my world, and suddenly I'm the star attraction at... at this freak show.'

'Let's just get you home,' Rich insists, ushering her away. 'This isn't good for you.'

'Wait, which one of you did I kiss?' a drunken John pipes up from the floor.

And just when you think things can't get any worse...

'What?' Jessica says angrily.

Emma isn't looking a great colour right now, obviously, but I see what little colour she has left drain from her cheeks as panic takes over.

'I kissed one of them,' John says. I don't think he'd be saying this if he wasn't drunk, and luckily, he's being quite vague with the details.

I think Rich must notice the look on Emma's face – well, he knows his wife – so he lets go of her for a second and takes a step back while he waits for her to say something.

'That was me,' I quickly insist, just about finding my voice again. I cough to clear my throat. 'I kissed him. I did it at work. I didn't know who anyone was, I didn't know he was married, and I didn't give him much choice. It was a mistake on my part. I'm really sorry, I just... I didn't know who anyone was. No one is to blame but me.'

'Let's go,' Rich tells Emma as he ushers her away from the group.

'Who are you?' Jessica asks me.

'I'm Ella,' I reply. 'Emma's twin.'

I finally look over at Christian, who looks as if he's just been hit by a bus. I think everyone is shaken up. But no one more than me.

'Come on, let's go,' Marco insists, taking me by the hand. 'Let's get out of here.'

45

I wake up in the exact same position I eventually fell asleep in: confused and wrapped up tightly in Marco's arms.

The first thing I did, after we left the school, was message Rich and ask him if he wanted me to find somewhere else to spend the night and he said yes. He told me that he was going to sneak Emma inside without the kids seeing. Thankfully Marco was willing to take me in and, given the circumstances, Ant and Lisa were fine with it.

So, it might not have been the night we planned together, but it couldn't have meant more to me. Marco held me all night long. He talked when I wanted to talk, he didn't when I just wanted to be in silence. I don't know what I'd be doing now without him.

I haven't really slept all that much, or all that well. I'm wide awake now but my phone still makes me jump when it vibrates against the bedside table.

I wiggle free from Marco's arms to grab it. Obviously, I still have Emma's phone.

It's Rich.

'Hello,' I say, answering as fast as humanly possible.

'Hi,' a voice replies. It's not Rich, it's Emma.

My own voice vanishes again.

'Rich has just taken the kids out for a few hours so that I can move around the house without them seeing me,' she says. 'We're going to have to figure that one out... Do you want to come over and talk?'

'Yes,' I reply, my voice cracking a little. 'Sure, I'll be right over.'

'Is everything OK?' Marco asks once I've hung up.

I jump out of bed and start putting on my outfit from last night.

'Yeah, Emma wants to talk,' I tell him. 'And I have to go over there looking like Sandra-fucking-D.'

Marco is out of bed in a second.

'Here, wear this,' he says, handing me a plain black T-shirt to wear instead of my Bardot top. 'Come here.'

He wraps his arms around me for a few seconds and squeezes me tightly.

'Listen to me – Emma is not your mum,' he insists. 'You have no idea what she's going to say. Just keep calm and hear her out – and remember, however shitty this feels for you, she's feeling worse.'

'That's pretty good advice,' I tell him. 'And exactly what I need to hear, thank you.'

'I'm learning from the best,' he says. 'I'll shove some clothes on and give you a lift.'

* * *

Marco drives me over to Emma's. He kisses me on the cheek before I get out of the car.

'I've got your back,' he says.

'I know,' I reply.

I take a deep breath before letting myself in with my keys. I wander into the kitchen, where I find Emma sitting on the sofa with Marty cuddled up next to her, his head on her lap.

'Hi,' I say.

'Hi,' she replies. 'Come in, sit down. Can I get you a cup of tea?'

'I should be offering you the tea,' I tell her.

'Why, because it's your house?' she replies with a raised eyebrow.

'No, Emma, because you're ill,' I point out. 'Why didn't you tell me? Why did you tell me you were going to prison? Did you really think people would judge you for being ill?'

'Ella, the people in the village will judge anyone for absolutely anything,' she reminds me. I knew that. 'But that's not the main reason. You know what it was like growing up with a mum who had cancer. I didn't want that for my kids.'

'I don't understand what you were thinking,' I say. 'What was the plan? I thought you were supposed to be coming home next week. Were you just going to use me as a placeholder until...?'

'Until I died?' she says.

'That's not what I was going to say,' I reply. 'Is it that bad?'

'The outlook is positive,' she tells me. 'They caught it early. They thought all I would need was an op, which was when I figured I could have you fill in for me, but afterwards, because the tumour was right on the threshold, size-wise, they said it was best I had chemo, to be on the safe side. To be honest, I'm sick of talking about it, and I know that, with Mum, you didn't like to hear about it.'

'Emma, it wasn't that I didn't *like* to hear about it. I was a teenager and my mum was dying,' I remind her.

'Yeah, and so was mine,' she says. 'I'm not sure you ever

thought about that. And the main reason I didn't tell you about me is because you couldn't handle it before, with Mum.'

'I'm thirty-four and I'm your sister – you should have told me,' I insist. 'Instead of turning up at the school and just blurting it out.'

'That was never the plan,' she admits. 'I knew I was going to have to come up with an excuse to stay away longer because, look at me, I look nothing like me. *You* look like me. You've got my hair, my make-up, you wear my clothes, you have my family. But then I made the mistake of looking at the website, on Facebook, in my messages. And what do I see? You've taken over the website and completely changed it – and the forum is abuzz with rumours about me. You're besties with my daughter, who apparently knows you're actually her auntie, based on your messages to each other, and you're having some sort of fling with Josh's uncle. I just totally freaked out. But now I'm here, and I'm trying to look at things from the inside, with a clearer head.'

'It's not a fling,' I tell her softly. 'And we worked on the website together, and the ad revenue is pouring in now, the traffic is way up. And I did everything I could to keep Millie in the dark, but she needed me, so I stepped up. I really got through to her though. She's so much better now, so much softer.'

'You think you're doing a better job at being me than I am?' she says.

'Oh, not at all,' I insist. 'I can see why you came back when you did.'

'I think perhaps I was worried you were doing a better job at being me than I was,' she admits.

'May I remind you of the amateur dramatics at the fundraiser?' I point out with a smile.

'I *was* terrified the fundraiser was going to be a disaster,' she replies. 'It's nothing like the event I would have thrown, not *at all*... but, dramatics aside, it turned out great. To be honest, people probably quite enjoyed the floorshow.'

Emma ruffles Marty's ears for a few seconds as she gathers her thoughts.

'Thanks, for covering me, about John,' she says. 'It was a few months ago, before my diagnosis, and Rich was working all the time, I felt so alone. It was just a kiss and I've regretted it ever since. You don't know how many times I've wondered if I'm being punished.'

I reach out and take her hand.

'That's not how this works,' I tell her. 'And you know it.'

'Not just for the kiss,' she says. 'I made a mistake, all those years ago. You needed me, after Mum died, and I let you down. She worried about you so much. She worried you wouldn't be able to stand on your own two feet, she said you just needed the chance to shine, the opportunity to take care of yourself... but I shouldn't have listened.'

'It worked, didn't it?' I reply. 'It hasn't been easy, but I've done it, I've taken care of myself. I find it so easy to paint Mum as this villain when I think about her. I focus on how hard she was, all the embarrassing things she did, how often she wasn't there. I've been reading her final book – I found the copy she gave me, in Rich's office – and while I might not always agree with her advice, I know now that I shouldn't let that distract me. Everything Mum did was for us. She worked all the hours she could because she was a single mum. She provided for us, she put us through school. My God, even when she was dying, she kept working, just to make sure she left us with something.'

It's only now that I'm saying it that I'm realising it. Mum worked and worked and worked and it was all for us.

'I always thought she was favouring you and punishing me, for not having a family, as though she could have known I'd still be single at thirty-four. But she knew what she was doing. She didn't want us to end up like most of the other rich brats around here.'

'Mum loved you,' Emma tells me. 'She loved us both. She didn't want to leave us.'

'I know you're not going to end up like Mum,' I insist. 'But you shouldn't be keeping away from your kids right now, you should be spending even more time with them. They're good, smart kids. They can handle it.'

'You haven't been doing a totally terrible job of being me,' Emma admits, almost reluctantly. 'You seem like you've come a long way since you were younger – I'm really proud of you and the work you've done here. And it doesn't sound to me like you're still single.'

'Well, now that I'm no longer being you, I guess I have all that to figure out,' I reply with a half-smile. 'I need to work out how to be me again.'

'Let's go upstairs and pack your things,' she suggests, carefully moving the dog before pulling herself to her feet.

'Oh, OK,' I reply. 'I can do that.'

'It's OK, I can help,' she says. 'We're only moving you to the spare room.'

'Oh... Are you sure?'

'I know you're keen to get on with your own life, but I could really do with you sticking around for a while,' she says. 'I'll need help with the kids, and the house, and if you and Marco could keep up the good work at the website, because it sounds like you are actually doing a really good job... I've been trying to get the ad revenue up for years, with no luck.'

I grab Emma, carefully because I have no idea how she's feeling, and hug her.

'I love you,' I tell her. 'Please don't ever keep anything like this from me again.'

I do understand why Emma did what she did, but it hurts my heart that she didn't tell me. Everything makes so much sense now. Rich wasn't having an affair, he was texting, calling and visiting Emma. That's who the flowers were for. And when he seemed less stressed, it wasn't because I was doing such a good job; it was probably because Emma had just found out the outlook was positive. I'm so, so relieved that it is.

'I love you too,' she replies. 'If I call Rich and tell him to come back, will you help me tell the kids?'

'Of course, I will,' I reply. 'We can figure this out together.'

46

Here I am, back where it all began, putting away my things in my old bedroom.

I moved everything from Emma's room down here, but I barely had time to sort through it before Rich was back with the kids and it was time to sit them down and explain everything. I think, having been through it, Emma and I knew exactly what we should and shouldn't say.

Millie knew that I'd been filling in for her mum but she had no idea why.

'Are you going to be OK?' she asked her mum. All at once she looked like a kid again, and all that anger and faux rebellion she aimed at Emma before, just vanished.

'I am doing everything I am supposed to do to get better,' Emma reassured her. 'You're not getting rid of me that easy.'

Henry just kept staring at me.

'You OK, kid?' I asked him. 'You're looking at me like I'm a freak.'

'Do I have two mums now?' he asked.

'Not at all,' I quickly insisted.

'Josie Martin has two mums,' he said. 'Is it like that?'

'Ella is your auntie,' Emma told him. 'I'm your only mum. Auntie Ella was just looking after you while I was away getting better. I didn't want to worry you, but I should have trusted you all to understand.'

It was tough, but the most important thing of all was reassuring them that their mum was getting the help she needed, and that I was going to stick around to take care of them all, so they didn't need to worry about anything. I think one of the hardest things for me, when I found out about Mum, was feeling as though I didn't have any back-up. All I had was Emma, and I was terrified of what would happen to me if something happened to her too.

Now that I'm alone again, I remove Mum's book from one of my bags. The first things that pop into my head are her words about making amends, and how important it is. I feel as if I've come such a long way, but I can't get Christian out of my head.

I still have Emma's phone in my bag, so I take it out and call him.

'Hello?' he answers.

'Hello,' I reply. 'It's me.'

'Which one?' he replies sarcastically. 'Now I know that there's two of you.'

'It's Ella,' I reply. 'The one you've spent the last few weeks with. I just wanted to apologise. I was thrown in at the deep end, and you were one of only a few people who were nice to me, and any mixed messages you might have picked up on came from the confusion I was feeling. So, I'm sorry.'

'I'm sorry too,' he says. 'My feelings were hurt. I was a dick.'

'It was a very unique situation,' I reply. 'I think we should both cut ourselves some slack.'

'Is Emma going to be OK?' he asks.

'She says the outlook is good,' I tell him. 'And I'm going to look after her and the kids, but as myself this time.'

'So, you're sticking around indefinitely, then?' he says.

'I guess I am,' I reply.

'Well, I'll see you around the school gates,' he says. 'I imagine you'll be blocking them.'

'See you then,' I reply with a smile. You really do feel lighter when you make amends.

I pick up Mum's book and flick through the pages, happy to have taken something positive from it, but as I hit the blank pages at the back, I notice something written on them.

It's a bonus chapter, just for me – a handwritten letter from my mum.

Dear Ella,

I hope you've enjoyed reading this book, and that you've been able to take lots of helpful advice from it... or not, to be honest, I'm not sure that it matters all that much any more. I've spent years dishing out advice but I've never stopped to take any myself. Really, I've just never stopped at all. I wanted to keep smiling, keep helping people, keep moving – but we all have to stop eventually. I don't worry about you, you're the strong one, you've always been able to take care of yourself, but I do worry about your sister so please take care of her. She's going to need it. Take my advice – don't take my advice. Do whatever you want, marry whoever you want, quit your job to go travelling or just curl up on your sofa every night. If you have kids, let them eat chips. If you don't have kids, that's OK too. I used to think a life without kids was an empty one but now I'm not so sure. Just do what makes you happy, Ella. I know that you always do and that's a quality I admire about you. Whether it's from the chocolate wrappers I always used to

find stuffed down your bed or the tattoo I don't think you know
that I know you have... Just be happy. All my love, always...
　　Not Auntie Angela – Mum.

I smile to myself as I snap the book closed and place it inside
one of the bedside cabinets.

I always wish I'd spoken to Mum more, during her last few
months, but talk was always about what she needed to feel better,
or much-needed distractions when she needed those. That letter
is the chat that I was in desperate need of, to know that she loved
me, that she believed in me, that all she wanted was for me to be
happy, and I feel so, so lucky to have it. I'm sure she must have
known that there was no way I would read her book straight away
– perhaps that's what she wanted?

Things might have been tough, and they might be about to
get tougher, but my mum is right. Whatever happens I can get
through it, and I'll be there for my sister all the way.

47

'I'd buy a Maserati,' Millie says.

'You're not even old enough to drive one, and you wouldn't know a Maserati if it ran you over,' Rich reminds her.

'Well, I'm seventeen next, and that's what I want for my birthday,' she insists.

'Ha! Sure,' her dad replies.

'Auntie Ella will buy me one, won't you?' Millie jokes.

'Oh, don't drag me into this,' I say with a laugh as I place plates down on the dining table. 'Dinner is nearly ready, by the way.'

'Oh, I can't wait, I'm starving,' Rich says. 'Come on, Henry.'

'I'm just harvesting the money tree Auntie Ella planted,' he calls back.

'That might be the first thing I buy, you know,' I say. 'My own Switch, and my own copy of Animal Crossing, so I can have my own island rather than living on Henry's.'

I might be slightly addicted to that game now, having spent the last few months playing on Henry's. I know, it sounds sad, but it's so therapeutic. It's like a much-needed escape from the real world.

'It's hard to believe you're a bigger geek than me now,' Marco says with a laugh as he places a large dish of lasagne down on the table.

'A wise man once told me the geeks shall inherit the earth,' I remind him. 'I'm starting small with my island.'

'I'm not complaining,' he says, kissing me on the cheek. 'That's why I love you.'

'I want to say this is gross to witness at the dinner table, but you two are too cute together,' Millie says. 'You should use the money to throw a massive wedding.'

'We'll see about that,' I say with a laugh. I look over at Marco, expecting him to be freaked out, but he's just smiling over at us while he cuts the bread.

Tomorrow is my thirty-fifth birthday, which means that tomorrow is the day I finally get my inheritance.

'What would you spend it on, Henry?' I ask him.

'I'd go on a Disney cruise,' he replies. Something I don't think any of us are expecting him to say. 'Iron Man goes on them.'

OK, now that makes sense.

'What do you think Mum would do with it?' Millie asks.

'She'd put it in her savings,' I say, in a purposefully low, slow, boring tone.

'She'd pay a scientist to keep Henry young and cute forever, so he doesn't grow into a little monster like his sister,' Rich jokes, tickling Henry as he passes him to take his seat at the table.

'Erm, actually, you're all wrong,' Emma announces as she walks in with Marty on his lead. 'I'd finally book a honeymoon – the honeymoon I never got to have. My dream trip, travelling around all the best cities in Europe.'

Rich kisses Emma on the cheek before pulling her chair out for her.

'You feeling OK?' he asks her.

'Honestly, I'm feeling the best I've felt in a long time,' she says with a smile. 'We had a good jog – it's starting to get chillier out there now though. You know, it's funny you should be talking about what to buy – I've just noticed a for sale sign outside the house next door.'

'I'll go halves with you,' Marco jokes, squeezing my shoulder.

I laugh.

'I suppose the beauty of it all is that you can do whatever you want,' Rich says. 'Whenever *you* want.'

'Right now, all I can think about is taking down this lasagne,' I admit. 'It smells amazing.'

'I kinda thought you'd be more hyped for your money,' Millie says. 'I know I would be.'

'Oh, I am,' I insist. 'I am.'

Of course, I am but – and I know this would only sound lame if I said it out loud –I've basically got everything I could ever want, and it's all money-can't-buy stuff. A happy, healthy family, a job that I love, and genuinely the world's best boyfriend. This year has been one hell of a roller-coaster ride, with some fantastic ups and some difficult downs, and Marco has been there every step of the way.

'I suppose the two of you can live anywhere you want,' Emma says. 'Anywhere in the world.'

'True, but I don't think we'll get too far,' I reply. 'Everyone we love is here in this village.'

If there's one thing this year has taught me, it's just how important family is. Whether it's the family you're born into or the one you make for yourself, you should always keep your people close. I've also realised that it's never too late to fix things, especially relationships, even if they feel irreparable. None of us know when our last day is going to be, or when our loved ones are going to leave us. Don't waste a minute being mad, running away from things you don't want to face. Make things right while you still can because no one on their deathbed is talking about how they wish they'd held more grudges.

In the word of Auntie Angela: take my advice – or don't. Just be happy.

ACKNOWLEDGMENTS

Massive thanks to Nia - the best editor in the world - to Amanda, and to everyone else at Boldwood Books. You are all amazing.

Big thanks to everyone who reads and reviews my books. I really hope you enjoy this one too. Thanks so much for all the lovely reviews, messages and photos you send. It really means so much to me.

I couldn't do any of this without my family - my mum and dad, especially my mum, Kim, who I owe so much to. Thanks to Joey, for all of the super important writer meetings - I hope I help you as much as you help me. Thanks to James, my tech nerd, for knowing everything I don't and patiently making it all happen. Thanks to Aud - you are beyond wonderful and I wouldn't be who I am without you.

Finally, thanks so much to my husband, Joe. I can't believe I finally get to call you that, especially after this year. Sneaky lockdown marrying you is the best thing I ever did. You've kept me going (and writing) through such a strange and difficult time. There's no one I'd rather be stuck indoors with. I love you.

MORE FROM PORTIA MACINTOSH

We hope you enjoyed reading *Faking It*. If you did, please leave a review.

If you'd like to gift a copy, this book is also available as an ebook, digital audio download and audiobook CD.

Sign up to Portia MacIntosh's mailing list for news, competitions and updates on future books.

http://bit.ly/PortiaMacIntoshNewsletter

Discover more laugh-out-loud romantic comedies from Portia Macintosh:

ABOUT THE AUTHOR

Portia MacIntosh is a bestselling romantic comedy author of 15 novels, including *My Great Ex-Scape* and *Honeymoon For One*. Previously a music journalist, Portia writes hilarious stories, drawing on her real life experiences.

Visit Portia's website: https://portiamacintosh.com/

Follow Portia MacIntosh on social media here:

- facebook.com/portia.macintosh.3
- twitter.com/PortiaMacIntosh
- instagram.com/portiamacintoshauthor
- bookbub.com/authors/portia-macintosh

ABOUT THE AUTHOR

Sofia Madison is a bestselling romantic comedy author of [?] novels, including My Great Escape and Honeymoon For One. Previously a music journalist, Sofia writes hilarious stories drawing on her real-life experiences.

Visit Sofia's website: https://sofiamadison.com

Follow Sofia Madison on social media here:

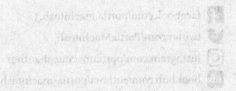

facebook.com/sofiamadison

twitter.com/SofiaMadison

instagram.com/sofiamadisonauthor

bookbub.com/authors/sofia-madison

ABOUT BOLDWOOD BOOKS

Boldwood Books is a fiction publishing company seeking out the best stories from around the world.

Find out more at www.boldwoodbooks.com

Sign up to the Book and Tonic newsletter for news, offers and competitions from Boldwood Books!

http://www.bit.ly/bookandtonic

We'd love to hear from you, follow us on social media:

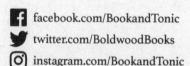

facebook.com/BookandTonic
twitter.com/BoldwoodBooks
instagram.com/BookandTonic